THE SINS OF THE
FATHER

THE SINS OF THE
FATHER

COLIN WADE

The Book Guild Ltd

First published in Great Britain in 2022 by
The Book Guild Ltd
Unit E2 Airfield Business Park
Harrison Road, Market Harborough
Leicestershire, LE16 7UL
Freephone: 0800 999 2982
www.bookguild.co.uk
Email: info@bookguild.co.uk
Twitter: @bookguild

Web: www.colinwade.co.uk
Twitter: @CPWADE1
Also by Colin Wade: *The Lost Years*
Also by Colin Wade: *Plutus*
Also by Colin Wade: *Deadly Connection*

Typeset in 11pt Sabon MT

Printed and bound in the UK by TJ Books LTD, Padstow, Cornwall

ISBN 978 1915352 002

British Library Cataloguing in Publication Data.
A catalogue record for this book is available from the British Library.

For all my lovely readers.
Thank you for enjoying my books

Prologue

Edward Allcock sat at the head of the dining table waiting for his dinner, his mood worsening as the minutes ticked by and no food was anywhere to be seen. He looked at his five sons; Edward Jnr, age fourteen; Andrew, twelve; Peter, eleven; Philip, nine and Stephen, seven, who sat along the sides of the table, bolt upright and ready to speak if spoken to. He shook his head as they stared at him wide-eyed, his short-cropped hair and greying temples making him look more like an East End gangster every day.

A few more minutes passed and still no sign of the food. Edward slammed his fist on the table, sending the neatly laid-out cutlery jumping across the linen tablecloth, making the boys jump.

"Oi, woman. Where's my dinner? We are wasting away in here. You may be able to survive on rabbit food but there are six men in here that need feeding. *Now!*"

A few seconds later, there was movement from the kitchen as his wife, Victoria, rushed out with two plates

1

of food. She placed the first one in front of Edward and the second in front of Edward Jnr. As she hurried away to get the other plates, her progress was broken by Edward's raised voice.

"What the hell is this, woman?"

Victoria looked round. "It's roast beef, veg and potatoes, like you asked for."

"I can bloody well see that, woman, but do you really think a man can survive on three potatoes?"

She turned back towards the kitchen. "I'll get you some more in a minute."

The other boys were served quickly and Victoria brought out a bowl of extra potatoes, placing it in front of Edward and serving up three more onto his plate. She left the bowl and a large gravy boat. As she turned away, Edward spoke again. "Have yours in the kitchen. I need to spend some time with my boys without your simpering face at the other end of the table."

They all started to eat in complete silence. The boys knew their father did not abide idle chit-chat at the dinner table and dutifully got on with the lovely meal their mother had made, which made Peter's decision to say something all the more surprising, as the others almost spurted their food out in shock.

"Why do you treat Mother so badly, Father?"

The other boys held their breath, waiting for the explosion, but it never came. Edward sat chewing a piece of meat, stuffed another potato in his mouth and just stared at Peter. A few uncomfortable minutes passed as the other boys started eating frantically, trying to avoid all eye contact. Peter sat, unmoving, waiting for a reply.

Edward eventually spoke, calmly and authoritatively, wagging his knife at Peter as he did so. "You see, Peter, that's your first mistake. Worrying about other people's feelings, especially a bloody woman. We are the dominant species, the dominant gender. Men. You show any sign of weakness and these bloody women's libbers will be all over you. They need to know their place and it's your responsibility to remind 'em of that. They cook, they clean and produce your offspring. That's it."

The other boys kept shovelling food in their mouths, hoping that the kind of insolence that Peter had shown, which would have normally been met with the back of their father's hand, would somehow be forgotten. Peter hadn't said anything more but was not eating his dinner. He was processing what his father had said, his head cocked to one side as though the information in his brain was too heavy. Peter caught Edward Jnr's eye. He was wide-eyed, trying to impress through his facial expression that Peter should shut up and get on with his food. Peter seemed to have a death wish and asked another question.

"Is that how you run your business, Father? By not worrying about anyone's feelings."

The other boys gasped at Peter's bravado and braced themselves for the physical violence that was sure to follow. Again, it didn't come. Their father seemed to be considering the question without any anger. He looked at his other sons, sensing their nervousness.

"It's okay, boys. Peter has asked a very sensible question. You are all getting to the age where you need to understand how business works because I expect you all to be running the family business when I cark it."

All five boys relaxed and fixed their gaze on their father.

"Business is twenty times worse than dealing with bloody women and, yes, the key to a profitable business is to be your own man and not give two shits about anyone's feelings. If you show any sign of weakness, someone will exploit it and cost you money. Also, don't forget that the bloody immigration policies in this country make it worse. Letting all those foreign bastards into our country, nicking our jobs and livelihoods, threatens our British heritage. I won't employ any of those bastards unless it's to clean the bogs. I want you to protect British workers when you take over the business. It's the only way to keep our business running for another fifty years."

Peter didn't say anything else and the room returned to the silent, compliant space that it normally was. Edward smiled to himself, confident that his boys would make him proud.

*

Victoria finished off her food at the table in the kitchen and quickly served up the suet pudding and custard to Edward and the boys. As she began to wash up, the glint of the steak knife in the light made her stop. She had fantasised so many times about what it would be like to plunge it into Edward's chest, over and over, to release herself from this hell.

Her stomach turned as she thought about the evening to come. He would want his conjugal rights. Pumping away like some amorous elephant seal, every thrust

4

causing her pain as she tensed up against his unwanted advances. People didn't call it rape in a marriage. It was a wife's duty. That's what they said. The men that would legislate on these types of things.

She finished cleaning up and as she dried the last steak knife, she wrapped it in a cloth and put it in her pocket.

1

Present Day

Halle looked in the mirror, checking that the make-up she had touched up was looking okay. She didn't need much. People had always given her compliments about the way she looked, and her healthy skin. She was always uncomfortable with this type of personal scrutiny, but there was no doubt that it helped to garner a good first impression with most people she met. She let out a deep breath. Today was the day. Her big break.

She had been working as a researcher and runner at Goldwin Production Company for six years. The company had just hit the big time, as Channel 4 had agreed to broadcast their new investigative series, which exposed major scumbags that were involved in all sorts of illegal business practices. The first two shows had been met with critical acclaim, and the big boss desperately wanted to recruit more investigative reporters to keep the content flowing and gorge on the gravy train.

Halle leapt at the chance to get a promotion to the job

she had always dreamed of. She loved reading about all the conspiracy theories, real or otherwise, and desperately wanted to get her teeth into her own case. As she stood in the executive washroom, she steeled herself for the most important moment of her life.

Ten minutes later, she was being led into the office of John Grayson, the Head of Production. He introduced himself and his colleague Jane Belmarsh, from HR.

They started with some idle chat as they poured the coffees, and Halle felt reasonably composed until he floored her with his first interview question.

"Right, Miss Jacobs, you are on your first investigative assignment, stuck in the arse end of some London suburb, and a man comes up to you shouting abuse, suggesting you drop to your knees and suck his dick. What do you do?"

Halle tried not to show her shock at the question, looking at the woman from HR to see if she seemed uncomfortable with his questioning, but all she got back was a steely, unflinching expression. She composed herself. "I would ignore him and walk away."

"What if he didn't let it lie and became aggressive?"

"I would call the police."

"What if he became physical?"

"I can hold my own in that respect, but I would also expect some form of support or protection on these assignments, much as you have done with all the other reporters working out in the field."

Halle saw a subtle smile on John's face. He was clearly impressed with her response.

"I apologise for the nature of the question, but I'm

afraid that our type of work will expose you to the worst type of scumbags and pondlife that you would ever care to meet. I'm sorry to say that you will be exposed to that sort of abuse frequently if you become an investigative reporter."

"I understand. I'm ready for the challenge. I worked closely with Jemma Brownley on the benefits scam case and watched everything she did. She was a great teacher and I'm ready to spread my wings."

John nodded. "Yes, Jemma is one of our best. You have done well to learn from her."

The rest of the interview was more routine and Halle felt it had gone well. She answered their questions calmly and confidently. Forty minutes later, she was led out of the office with the usual 'we'll be in touch' message ringing in her ears.

She went straight to the coffee shop next door to the offices and waited for their call.

2

As the CEO of Allcock Land Management Services (ALMS), Edward Allcock Jnr sat at the head of the boardroom table and called the monthly board meeting to order, his four brothers in attendance. The only other person present was his uncle, James Allcock, sat opposite Edward in his role as Chairman of the Board. Their offices took up the whole of the forty-fourth floor of the Docklands Plaza, in the middle of London's financial district. The venue and the sharp, expensive Savile Row suits that they all wore told anyone who was looking what they were all about. Wealth, and lots of it.

Any stranger walking into the boardroom on that day would be forgiven for thinking they had walked into an office of clones. All the boys had such a strong resemblance to their father. Edward started the meeting.

"Okay, everyone, let's get to it. A reminder that as usual this meeting is being recorded and can only be accessed on the secure server by those present at this meeting."

There were collective nods of acknowledgement from all in attendance.

"Let's start with the current projects. Andrew?"

Andrew Allcock took the lead on identifying and

delivering new land projects for the firm and revelled in his role. "It's looking good, Edward. We have five new projects on the books: four brownfield sites across London and one potential greenfield site in Surrey. I should have the contracts in place within the week."

"Cost?"

"Around £25 million for the lot, and I fully expect us to at least double that when we sell on to the developers."

"Excellent. What's the environmental assessment on the brownfield sites?"

"Oh, the usual. Chemical and metal contamination. They were all industrial sites so we expected it."

Edward turned to Peter. "I assume you can line up PEMS (Parkers Environmental Management Services) to do the usual environmental report and complete the remediation actions."

"Yeah, I'm on it but you need to know that old man Parker is stepping down from running the company and is handing over to his son, Ross, and his daughter, Sophie."

"Daughter! I'm not happy doing business with a bloody woman. Dad started working with Parker all those years ago because he held the same values. Business is run by men. What the hell is old man Parker thinking of, letting his daughter get involved?"

Peter attempted to appease his brother. "Parkers have never let us down yet, Edward. Dad always trusted them with his life, and I see no reason for this to change."

"No reason! How do you know you can trust her? You know nothing about her. She's bound to be one of these so-called modern women with equal opportunities oozing from every pore. It could be a complete disaster if old man Parker is not there to steer the ship. You need to get in there and talk to Ross. Find out what influence she has got and make sure they are happy to continue to give us the services we need. Do you agree, Uncle?"

"I do. I knew that Parker would have to stand down at some point, his health has not been good, but we need to manage this situation carefully. I'll go with Peter to meet Ross and make sure our relationships are maintained."

"Thank you. You okay with that, Peter?"

"Yes, boss."

Edward tried to ignore Peter's disrespectful tone and moved on to Philip. "Can we have the financial report?"

"Yes, as you know, we are nearly at the financial year end, and the figures look very healthy. Revenues are up eleven per cent to £757 million and projected profit is £30 million. If we do our usual of reinvesting twenty-five per cent of each year's profit in the business, this should leave us with an annual dividend of £3.75 million each."

There were a few celebratory shouts. Edward and Andrew indulged in a high five. Edward let the noise die down and carried on. "That's great news, Philip. I guess that just leaves you, Stephen, to update on the business operations. I suppose with these good financial figures, the staff will be expecting another bloody pay rise."

Stephen smiled. "Yes, I guess they will, but we must remember that we pay them over the odds to buy their loyalty."

"As well as the non-disclosure agreements."

"Yes, you are right. The NDAs are as tight as a virgin's snatch. They are all very clear that they would suffer financial and reputational ruin if they ever betrayed us."

Edward smiled approvingly. "Okay, Stephen. I suggest we give them all a five per cent rise. What do you all think?"

There was a general sense of agreement from the rest of the room. "Okay, that's agreed. A five per cent rise for all staff from the beginning of the new financial year."

"Anything else?"

"No, retention has been very good and we only have one vacancy for a PA currently out there."

Edward once again nodded his approval. "Just make sure whoever you recruit has a cracking pair of tits."

There were a few schoolboy sniggers from the others before the mirth was broken by Edward suddenly screwing up his face, a mix of anger and confusion evident in his expression. "Oh, I know what I wanted to ask you, Stephen. Who was that foreigner I saw walking around the office the other day? I thought I made it clear that we don't have those types of people in our firm."

"Oh, that was one of the cleaners. We use the building services for that sort of thing and don't have any control over the type of people they employ."

Edward smiled. "Ahh, Father was right. Let them clean our bogs."

As the meeting drew to a close, they all began to make moves to leave when Peter spoke. "Are we all going to ignore the elephant in the room then?"

The rest of the boys and James stopped what they were doing and looked at Peter. As always, Edward took the lead. "What are you on about, Peter?"

Peter stood up. "It's Mother's parole hearing today. Are none of you the slightest bit interested in what happens?"

Edward moved towards Peter and put his face right up to his brother's. "Listen. You are the only one that gives two hoots about that murdering bitch. She killed our father in cold blood and as far as the rest of this family is concerned, she can rot in hell. Please don't bring your personal weaknesses into the boardroom."

Edward immediately turned around and stormed out of the room, closely followed by the others. Peter just stood there, shaking his head.

3

Victoria Allcock sat across the table from the three men and one woman that made up her parole board. She was a little surprised when the woman took the lead.

"Mrs Allcock, my name is Julie Denby and I will be chairing this board today. My colleagues are Jim Nethercott, Daniel Hill and Graham Ashman."

Victoria nodded an acknowledgement with a weariness that reflected her long years in jail.

"This is your first parole hearing, and the purpose of this panel is to determine whether you are suitably rehabilitated to be considered for early release."

Victoria gave a snort of derision, which was met with unapproving faces.

"You have served over thirty years of a life sentence, and it is normal in these cases to give you the opportunity to address this panel with your opinions about your rehabilitation. I would remind you that we are looking for genuine feelings of remorse for your crimes as a key indicator of your suitability to return to normal society. So, Mrs Allcock, the floor is yours."

Victoria took time to take in the faces of each of the panel members, determined not to be intimidated by any of them. She brushed a hand through her greying hair, which had long since lost its lustre. After a few minutes, when the panel members looked at each other wondering whether she would ever speak, she eventually started her pitch.

"The only remorse I feel is that for over thirty years I have been treated as a criminal rather than the victim. I plunged a knife into my husband, Edward Allcock, in self-defence, on one of the numerous occasions he raped me. This was the culmination of years of mental and physical abuse at the hands of that monster. My version of events was ignored by the numerous MALE coppers, solicitors, barristers and jurors who couldn't see past their dicks and couldn't contemplate that a woman might actually be telling the truth about what went on. I have to say I am curious that a woman is chairing this panel. I hope that maybe this is an indication that for once in this torrid period, a female perspective might actually be considered. But, as you can tell, you can forgive me for not feeling overly optimistic about the validity of this panel."

Victoria didn't register much after her little speech. The effort and energy expended to try to demonstrate her passion for what she believed in had tired her out. The panel had continued to probe her with a range of lame, predictable questions. She answered them in a daze, the injustice burning inside her. As she was led back to her cell, she had no expectations that anything good would come of it.

Three hours later, visiting time had arrived. The fortnightly ritual when Victoria was usually disappointed, as the prison officer once again said, *No visitors today, Mrs Allcock*. But today was different. Someone was visiting her. She quickly brushed her hair and washed her face, trying to disguise the degradation that was all too evident after so long in prison. As she walked into the large visitors' room, she was not surprised to see it was Peter. He didn't visit often but he was the only one of her sons that did.

As she sat down, she grasped his hands in hers. "Peter, my darling. It's so nice to see you. I've missed you."

"I know, Mum. I'm sorry. Life just gets in the way. How did the hearing go?"

Victoria leant back, removing her hands from his grip. She turned away, not able to look Peter in the eye. "Oh, a waste of time."

"Why? What happened?"

Victoria finally looked back at Peter, tears in her eyes. "They wanted me to show remorse. REMORSE! For that monster. Everyone I speak to treats me as a murderer. No one sees me as the victim. I even had a bloody woman chairing the panel, but I don't think it made a blind bit of difference. I'm a nobody, Peter. I'll be in here till I die, and all the while, you and your brothers benefit from the legacy of that bastard."

Peter put his head down, the shame evident in his body language. "I'm sorry, Mum, but what were we supposed to do? We were kids. Uncle James kept the business running and Dad's will left it all to us. We had nothing else, and the others were determined to carry on. They have never forgiven you. I'm the only one who thinks you are innocent."

Victoria grabbed Peter's hands again, a pained smile across her face. "I know. I know, and thank you for that.

He certainly made sure that he had poisoned their minds about me, long before I killed him."

They sat holding hands, suddenly nothing more to say.

As visiting time neared the end, Victoria's mind wandered back to the parole hearing. "What am I going to live on, if they let me out?"

"Don't worry, I'll see you right. My brothers can't stop me looking after you."

"How much?"

"What do you mean?"

"How much dirty money have you all made this year?"

"Oh, Mum, stop…"

"How much?"

Peter looked at his mum, her face fixed and determined. She wasn't going to let this go. He sighed. "Philip says we should get about £3.75 million each this year as a dividend."

She shook her head, her expression projecting the obvious distaste for what she was hearing. "How can you do it, Peter? How can you work with them? Their prejudices, their attitudes towards women, their greed. It's unbelievable."

Peter didn't say anything, his head bowed, not wanting to catch his mother's disapproving gaze. She let out a snort. "Of course, why should I expect you to be any different? Even you can't resist the pull of that much money. What a shame."

Peter looked up. "Actually, there is one thing that is causing Edward to 'wet his pants'. Old man Parker is stepping down and is handing the reins over to his son and daughter."

Victoria's eyes suddenly lit up and she sat forward. "What! Edward must be apoplectic at the thought of dealing with a woman."

"Yeah, he's sending me over there with Uncle James to speak to the son. To make sure she doesn't have any influence on our future business relationship."

Victoria leant back, a broad smile across her face. "Thank you for telling me that. It's made my day." A few seconds later, the bell went, signalling the end of visiting time.

As Victoria was escorted back to her cell, her mind was racing. Despite the years of being downtrodden by her abusive husband, she had been savvy enough to keep an eye on what he was up to in his business. She knew where the skeletons were but had never had the means to exploit this knowledge. The news about old man Parker might just give her the opportunity she was looking for. She lay down on her bed and allowed herself to dream.

4

Twenty-four hours had passed and Halle had not heard anything about the outcome of her interview. It was late morning and her stomach was grumbling, reminding her that lunch was not far away. She was trying to finish off the research report on her latest project but the words weren't coming. She decided to go to the loo; anything to distract her from the constant nagging about whether she had blown her big chance.

As she turned the corner, to head towards the toilets, she almost bumped straight into John Grayson. "Oh God, sir, sorry. I didn't see you there."

They both adjusted their positions to remove any uncomfortable personal space issues and John quickly dispelled any awkwardness. "It's fine, Miss Jacobs. I was just on the way to see you. Do you want to come back to my office?"

As Halle followed him along the carpeted corridors, she thought her mind was going to explode. Was he about to let her down gently or was this it? Had she cracked it?

She hurriedly sat down, eager to hear the outcome, the pressure on her bladder suddenly urgent.

John smiled. "I was very impressed with you…"

Halle's inner monologue was threatening to overwhelm her. *Oh no, here comes the but…*

"…so, I have no hesitation in offering you the job."

Halle was wide-eyed with shock. Had she just heard that right? As she refocused, she saw that John had a massive smile on his face. She jumped out of her chair and suddenly didn't know what to do. She wanted to hug him but checked herself, realising that a handshake was probably more appropriate. As she thrust out her hand, she started babbling, "thank you, thank you" over and over again.

He didn't seem put off by her overexuberance and said what she wanted to hear. "Come and see me after lunch and we can discuss your first assignment. I want you to start straight away."

Halle's brain wasn't co-ordinating with her limbs as she almost walked straight into the office chair. She looked around at John, an embarrassed smile on her face, whilst desperately trying to contain the urge to let out a massive roar of relief. She eventually made it out of his office without further incident and headed for the toilet before she peed herself with excitement.

She was back in John's office at 2 pm, having calmed down at a celebratory lunch with her cubicle buddies, Jerry and Rhona. He got straight into it.

"We have an interesting story for you to investigate related to the Pickford housing estate in East London. It was built about thirty years ago, bordering the Thames on its southern side, with about 220 dwellings of various sizes. By all accounts, a very nice place in an area that isn't always the most salubrious. The emerging story relates

21

to an unusually high number of cancer cases in children that have been living on the estate. One of our researchers picked up the story from Facebook, when one of the mothers, whose son has died from leukaemia, was trying to set up a support group for parents. It seems the post generated almost twenty connections from parents on the same estate, all with kids affected by cancer. There was only one other death, but the remaining parents were all at different stages with their children's cancer treatment. Nobody seems to have previously made the connections between these families or can explain why this might be happening. Our researcher made contact with the mother that did the initial post and she has agreed to talk to us."

"Wow, that sounds amazing… God, no, sorry, terrible but…"

"It's okay, you are allowed to be excited at the assignment despite the obvious tragic circumstances. It's what made me appoint you."

Halle grimaced. John carried on.

"We ideally need this story in the can within six months. We have the next three programmes ready to roll with the TV people and two more being recorded as we speak. We need this story to be investigated and the TV production completed within that time period to keep the momentum going with the TV show. I can't afford for us to slow down on this now we have made this breakthrough. If all goes to plan, this will be the first show in the second series."

"I fully understand, sir. I'll get straight on to it."

"Yes, I want you working out of the third floor, where the other production teams are based. The researcher who did the initial work has been assigned to you, as has a camera technician. You have also been given authority to draw from the security team each time you go out on assignment. They will drive you around and give you the personal protection we often need on these things."

Halle smiled, stood up, gave John another overexuberant handshake and, as she began to walk out, said, "I won't let you down, sir."

She practically ran back to her old desk. *The third floor.* It was a simple thing but so symbolic of her changing fortunes. She packed up her stuff and set off to begin the next exciting chapter of her life.

5

Peter sat in the plush office at PEMS with his Uncle James, nursing a steaming espresso as they waited for Ross Parker to arrive.

They hadn't had much to do with Ross, but knew him by sight. A few minutes later, Peter nodded towards James. "He's coming."

They both stood up as Ross entered. His six-foot-five frame towered over them. He greeted them warmly. His sharp pinstripe suit, immaculate dark sculpted hair and well-groomed designer stubble projected a confident young man. Ross launched straight in.

"Gentlemen, it's great to see you both. What can I do for you?"

Peter was about to speak but James cut across him. "We understand your father is stepping down from running the company and we wanted to make sure that you would be continuing to supply the services to ALMS that your father has been providing for the last forty-odd years."

"Er, yes, of course. Dad briefed me on the business and told me to make sure that you were treated as one of our most valuable clients."

"Good, good, and I assume we can expect the same levels of service and discretion that have always been the hallmark of the relationship between our two families."

"Yes, I see no reason for anything to change."

"Will Jeremy Hogan and his team still be handling our projects?"

"Yes, again, Dad was quite clear that I was to keep everything the same with your account. He spoke fondly of your father and I know he valued the ongoing relationship we have had with all of his sons, and of course you, James."

James nodded, seemingly happy with what he was hearing, but he knew he had to deal with the 'elephant in the room'.

"What about your sister?"

"What about her?"

"What influence does she have on the business?"

"Sophie is a joint majority shareholder. Dad has transferred his entire business holdings over to the two of us." James' facial expression told Ross all he needed to know. "Does that present a problem?"

Peter stayed quiet. Despite his annoyance at being side lined by his uncle in the early discussions, he was glad to steer well clear of this bit of the conversation.

"My brother always preferred to do business with men, a philosophy that the boys and I have continued to stick to. We find women are far too emotional to do big business."

"Oh, that seems a rather archaic attitude. I can assure you that my sister is an extremely astute businesswoman. She has been running a very successful advertising agency for nearly ten years. She is an integral part of our leadership team and will be involved in steering the direction of the business as we move forward."

James stood up. "Let me be clear, Ross. Make sure she doesn't interfere with our business relationship. I would hate to have to terminate a forty-year relationship just because you want to play some facile equal opportunities game."

James walked out without another word. Peter stood up and grimaced as Ross tried to process what had just happened. He tried to soften the impact. "Don't worry about him. He's a bit of an old dinosaur. I'm sure it will all be fine."

*

An hour later, James and Peter were sat in Edward's office. "So come on, Uncle. What happened with Ross?"

"It's not good. Ross said his sister is a majority shareholder and will be an integral part of steering the direction of their business moving forward. She runs an advertising agency and has apparently made a great success of it. Old man Parker clearly thinks she has a good head for business."

"Shit, the old codger must be going senile. What a mess. Are they going to change our business relationship?"

"Well, Ross said his father had told him to keep everything the same with our account. Jeremy and his team are still leading all our projects."

"Hmm, I guess that's something, but Jeremy must be over sixty years old now and I don't know how much longer he will be working. If we lose him as well, that stupid woman might interfere. We can't let that happen."

"What do you wanna do?"

"Find out everything you can about her. We might need to take her out if she becomes troublesome, and I want to be ready with something if that time arrives."

"Of course. Leave it with me."

James got up and left the room. Peter remained seated. Edward looked up. "Something I can do for you, little brother?"

"Why don't we embrace this new relationship with PEMS? You never know, she might actually bring something to the party."

Edward stood up and slammed his fist on the table. "Are you for real? Dad taught us that business is a man's world, and I'm not going to let some wannabee business bimbo start playing at it with our account."

"It sounds like she already knows how to run a business."

Edward glared at Peter. "Get out of my office, you spineless wanker."

6

Halle could hardly contain herself as she walked onto the third floor. She had been assigned an office in the west corner of the building. Some people glanced up as she tried to pace with authority and confidence, but all the while, a chronic case of impostor syndrome coursed through her psyche.

As she approached her office, a face suddenly popped up from behind one of the cubicles, like a meerkat looking for danger. Although Halle hadn't worked within the same research team as him, she knew his face. Todd Barkley. He had a reputation for being one of the most dogged and experienced researchers that the firm had, and Halle was both delighted and intimidated to have him on her team. As she got closer, he leapt out to greet her, a massive beaming smile on his face. The Iron Man t-shirt, jeans, unruly hairstyle and Bluetooth earpiece were very much at odds with Halle's designer business suit, but it told you all you needed to know. He was a super nerd, and super nerdiness was what you needed in a good researcher.

Todd thrust out his hand. "Miss Jacobs. It's an honour to meet you."

"Oh Christ, call me Halle, please. I don't know what I'm even doing here. I feel so out of my depth."

"Nonsense. You've done the hard yards as a researcher. From what I hear, you are a rising star and completely deserve this chance."

"Thank you, you're very kind, but I hear the same about you. Why aren't you in this seat?"

"Oh, I'm happy doing what I do. I love being a researcher. Can't be doing with all that people stuff. Give me a computer and the internet any day of the week."

The intenseness of the open exchanges waned and there was a brief, uncomfortable pause. Todd broke the awkwardness. "Right, boss lady. You go and get settled in your office and I'll make you a coffee. What do you have?"

"Oh, Todd, you don't have to do that."

"Don't be silly. The least I can do to get you settled."

Halle smiled. She would have to get used to this. "A latte, please."

Ten minutes later, she was in her office, computer set up and the steaming latte helping to calm her nerves. Todd bounced in. "Shall we get started?"

Halle took a drag of coffee and sat up straight. "Yes, tell me all you know."

*

Victora Allcock sat in the prison governor's office, staring across at the man that would decide her future. She heard what she expected.

"Mrs Allcock, I'm afraid the parole panel were unconvinced about your suitability for release. They cited your complete lack of remorse as a key factor in their decision. Do you have anything to say?"

"Can I go? I'm late for lunch and I don't want to miss the treacle tart."

The governor shook his head. "You really don't do yourself any favours. Despite your flippancy, I have recommended a further review in three months. You are a good prisoner. You never give me any trouble, so I don't understand why you don't tell the parole panel what they want to hear."

She stared back at him, uninterested in anything he had to say. "Can I go?"

*

Todd grabbed his tablet and opened up his notes. "Right, here's the basics."

Halle was wide-eyed with excitement. Her big break was now very real, and a nerd in an Iron Man t-shirt was about to lay the golden egg.

"So, as you know, one of the things we do when researching for new stories is trawl the social media sites. I have been linked into a local East End community forum on Facebook for some time and about three weeks ago, I picked up a load of activity around a woman from the Pickford housing estate, near Beckton in East London. She recently lost her six-year-old son to leukaemia and posted on the forum, seeking other parents to be part of a support group. What piqued my interest was the number of responses she got from people on the same estate."

"Yeah, I remember John saying there was about twenty-odd."

"That's right. It seems there is one father that responded who lost a daughter to cancer a few months ago but another eighteen or so parents whose kids are battling various forms of cancer as we speak. All of them live on the Pickford estate."

"Could it not just be bad luck?"

"Come on, Halle. Don't forget your researcher training. You know as well as I do that we don't deal in luck or coincidences. We are trained to think 'conspiracy' with everything we find, and this ticks all the boxes. Twenty seriously ill kids from a population on that estate of only 500-odd people is a statistical anomaly. There's a story here. I can smell it."

Halle couldn't help but let out a little laugh, energised by Todd's enthusiasm. "Okay, sounds amazing. What are the next steps?"

"You have an appointment with the mother that did the original post at 10 am tomorrow morning, so I need to get the camera tech and security guys lined up to support you."

"Thanks, you sort that out and I'll start thinking about what questions I need to ask."

Todd left her office and she looked out of the window at the fantastic views of the London skyline. The wind was howling but the sun was out, glistening on the Thames in the distance. A sudden shiver went down her spine. She was ready.

7

Andrew Allcock donned his hard hat and walked towards the Portakabin at the edge of the large industrial site, which he had recently acquired for just under £5 million. It was an old metal works just east of Wapping and prime real estate for someone wanting to build a housing development or offices. He had a quote of just under half a million to clear the site to ground level, and with the environmental clean-up and remediation likely to cost the same, the firm was already in to the tune of £6 million. He smiled to himself. To some, that might seem a scary amount of money, but he knew they would probably treble that when it came to selling it on.

He walked up the metal steps and pushed the door open. "Ah, Jeremy, I see you are already here."

"Yes, Andrew, ready to roll."

"So, what do you reckon we have here?"

"Well, we have the lot given the nature of the site. We'll definitely have mercury and lead. Probably lots of nasty chemicals as well, such as benzene. We'll do the usual and have a full report for you by the end of the week."

"That's exce—"

Andrew didn't finish his sentence, as the door to the

Portakabin opened and a woman's face appeared. Andrew shot a confused look at Jeremy, who greeted her warmly.

"Ah, Miss Parker, it's lovely to see you."

"Oh, stop with the formality. Call me Sophie."

Andrew's face turned from confusion to rage, barely containing his distaste as he realised who the unwanted visitor was. "What are you doing here?"

Sophie was taken aback. "I assume you are Andrew Allcock."

"Yes, that's right."

"Well, my father told Ross and I that we must treat you as one of our most valuable customers, so I just wanted to meet with you today to make sure everything is in order."

"It's really not necessary, Miss Parker. We have worked with Jeremy and his team for years. He has never let us down and we don't need interference from the management."

Sophie frowned. "I can assure you that it's not interference. I just want to make sure everything is working to your satisfaction. Is that so hard for you to understand?"

Andrew clenched his fists. He had never let a woman speak to him like that and he wasn't about to start now. He looked away from Sophie, staring out of the window towards the main site, trying to quell his rage. Eventually, he turned, forcing a smile that didn't reach his eyes. "It's fine. Everything is absolutely in order. Now, I'm a busy man, so can we get on with the site inspection?"

Sophie shot a confused look at Jeremy. He picked up on the vibe. "Andrew's right, Miss Parker. Your father did entrust me with the Allcock account. I have been working on it pretty much since the start and we have a well-trodden path when it comes to dealing with these sites. He really didn't want you to have to worry about it."

Sophie looked at the two men in front of her, a microcosm of the archaic male attitudes that were still so evident in many parts of her business life. "Let me be clear to you both. I am now the joint owner and majority shareholder of PEMS and will run this business as I see fit. I don't care about whatever cosy relationship you've had for the past thirty-odd years. I expect full transparency of everything that is going on with this relationship, and if I see things I'm not happy about, I will change them."

Andrew shook his head and walked out of the Portakabin.

*

Later that day, Sophie Parker was in Ross' office, sipping an Earl Grey tea, which was doing nothing to brighten her mood after her morning encounter with Andrew Allcock.

"Have you met any of the Allcocks yet?"

"Yes, I met James, the uncle, and Peter, one of the sons, the other day. They seemed somewhat agitated about your involvement."

"You're telling me. I went to the Wapping site earlier today and met Andrew. He could barely contain his animosity towards me. I don't know what their problem is."

"I understand from Dad that their father, Edward, was a bit of an old-fashioned type. Very much adhered to the idea that a woman's place was in the home. Seems he had a very strong influence on his boys and they have grown up as mirror images of him, which is not surprising given he was murdered by their mother."

"What!"

"Yeah, seems she cracked one night and stabbed him to death. She is serving a life sentence."

"That's unbelievable but it doesn't really excuse their caveman attitudes. Have they not realised that societal norms have moved on since the eighties?"

"Well, I guess when you make as much money as they all do, you probably don't feel you need to change."

"I dunno, Ross. I know Dad wanted us to treat them as some special case, but I'm not sure I can keep on working with them if they don't show me some respect."

"Well, okay, but that account was worth nearly £8 million to us last year, so we need to be careful."

Sophie shook her head and sipped at her tea. There was something more at play here. She was used to misogyny in her working life but never let it get the better of her. The problem was, there were six Allcock men, all with the same bad attitudes, which was going to be a challenge if this business relationship was going to survive. She kept pulling at the metaphorical loose thread.

"What do you know about the Allcock account?"

"Well, as far as I know, we do site surveys on all their brownfield land acquisitions, identifying what they need to do to clean the sites up for selling on. Once they sign off on any remediation plans, we complete the work and liaise with the relevant councils and the Environment Agency to get the final clearances and permits for development. We hand these over to the Allcocks and they sell the land on to a developer for a tidy profit."

"So, we do all the hard work and they pocket the profits."

"Well, not really. Don't forget they put up all the capital to buy the sites in the first place. That costs them millions of pounds a year, before they even know if they can turn the site into something that they can legitimately sell on."

"Really? So, you're telling me that they might buy a piece of land for millions of pounds and get stuck with it if they can't get it cleaned up and signed off for development?"

"Yes, as far as I know."

Sophie looked quizzically at Ross. "That seems like a high-risk strategy."

"I think a lot of these developers do it. Land in this country is so scarce, firms like the Allcocks just land bank as much as they can get their hands on. It clearly works. Dad told me their firm turns over almost £800 million a year."

Sophie grunted at the revelation and walked out of the office. Her ad agency was turning over £3 million annually, and she knew the family firm was clearing nearly £25 million a year, but the types of figures the Allcocks were dealing with just made her queasy. Was she really prepared to keep helping them line their pockets with these obscene amounts of money, especially given their attitudes toward her gender?

She sunk into the plush leather chair that was a dominant feature in her new office at Parkers. She eyed the last dregs of cold tea, wisely deciding not to imbibe, instead buzzing her assistant to get her a refill.

As she waited, she looked around the room. Just what had her father been doing here, selling his soul to work with the corporate devil that was Allcock Land Management Services? Her assistant brought in a fresh tea and in that moment she decided. She was going to take a deep dive into the Allcock account and find out exactly what this business relationship was all about.

8

It was just before 9 am as Halle met Rod, the camera technician that had been assigned to her; and Clayton, her security detail, in the car park outside the Goldwin offices in Kensington. Rod was what most people called 'middle-aged' with a questionable dress sense, but he greeted Halle with a lovely smile that immediately put her at ease. Clayton was a six-foot plus slab of beefcake who looked every inch the bodyguard. She didn't really go for the muscly type, but the moment he smiled and gave her a peck on the cheek, she melted and had an incredible urge to bonk his brains out. She shook the image from her mind and tried to regain some composure.

"It's great to meet you guys. Not sure what you have been told about this assignment but we are meeting a mother on the Pickford housing estate in East London who recently lost her young son to cancer. It seems there are a number of children affected by cancer on the same estate and we think there is a story."

They nodded, alert and on point with what Halle was saying. She still had a sense she was in way over her head, but everyone seemed so nice and supportive of her new role. She cracked on.

"Rod, I'm hoping that the mother will agree to her interview being recorded. I desperately need to start getting some footage in the can. It would be good to get some shots of the estate as we drive around."

Rod smiled. "At your service."

They loaded up their stuff in the SUV and Clayton got in the driver's seat, confirming his role as chauffeur, as well as bodyguard. Halle sat in the passenger's seat, distracted by the pleasant smell of manliness emanating from him, a mix of cologne and testosterone that was causing her to flush with excitement. She tried to shake the unprofessional feelings from her mind, catching Rod's eye as she turned away from gazing at Clayton. Rod smirked, seemingly aware of her turmoil, which just made Halle blush even more.

They began their journey across London, the usual snail's pace at this time of the morning. After half an hour, they were in the depths of East London. Halle hadn't been to this part of London before and was shocked by the signs of deprivation that pervaded the concrete jungle they drove through. Messy shopfronts, offering questionable fast-food options; tattoo parlours; seedy bars with frosted glass and a range of people hanging around, either looking menacing or just pissed. Clayton picked up on her shock.

"Not your sort of place then?"

Halle looked embarrassed. "Oh, er, no, not really, but I guess…"

Clayton roared with laughter. "Don't worry. I'm only jibing ya. This ain't the nicest place in the world, but you'll be all right with me."

Halle let out a nervous laugh. She was a strong,

independent modern woman so why was she acting like a besotted schoolgirl every time Clayton paid her any attention?

Mercifully, the moment passed as they turned down towards the river. As they drove along the road towards the Pickford estate, the transformation was astonishing. John had mentioned it was a nice place in an otherwise deprived area, and he was right.

As they got to the edge of the estate, they entered a tree-lined road, a welcome flash of greenery that had been horribly absent on their drive. The main part of the estate opened out and they were presented with a beautifully landscaped area, full of trees and green spaces, interlocked with a variety of two-, three- and four-bedroom dwellings, with a modern well-kept feel.

Halle couldn't contain herself. "Wow, this is lovely. What a beautiful estate."

Clayton nodded approvingly and slowed the car down. "What's the number of the house we are going to?"

"Oh, er, 117."

Clayton eyed the numbers on the doors and set off clockwise around the main estate road, passing lots of well-tended gardens that were standing up well against the annoying wind which hadn't died down for nearly twenty-four hours.

They found the house at the top end of the estate, close to the river. Clayton parked up and they all bundled out. They gathered all the kit, Rod getting his camera equipment as ready as he could, to minimise set-up time. People didn't like cameras at the best of times, and the tragedy of this situation was not likely to make this easy.

Halle puffed out her cheeks and looked at both of them. "Okay, here goes nothing."

They pushed the bell and waited. A few seconds later, a woman appeared at the door, the recent trauma apparent in her face, which was pale and drawn. Her hair was tied up in a bun, trying to hide the fact that it didn't look like it had been washed in a while, and her ensemble of t-shirt, sloppy cardigan and tracksuit bottoms played up to a cliché of someone that had long forgotten about looking after herself. She eyed them suspiciously, lingering on Clayton, a look of disapproval apparent in her facial expression.

Halle looked at Clayton quizzically. What was that all about? Was she reacting to the colour of his skin? The sort of casual racism that was all too evident in current society. The type that people pretended wasn't there but was evident in the non-verbal mannerisms of the people that were guilty of it. Halle tried to cut across the uncomfortable vibe.

"Mrs Wyatt? My name is Halle Jacobs from Goldwin Productions and this is my camera technician, Rod, and my security man, Clayton."

She mumbled a response. "You'd better come in."

They all walked into the living room. Children's toys were still in evidence around the room, the sign of someone who hadn't or couldn't move on.

They all took a seat and Mrs Wyatt continued to eye Clayton suspiciously. Halle looked at him, concerned with the vibe she was giving off, but he seemed completely unfazed by her manner. She tried to focus Mrs Wyatt on the job in hand.

"Mrs Wyatt…"

"Call me Jen… please. Mrs Wyatt sounds so formal."

Halle was pleased. It showed she was up for a level of familiarisation that was going to be necessary if they were to move this thing forward.

"Okay, Jen. If possible, we would like to film our initial conversation as part of footage that we hope will ultimately become part of our *Tragic Britain* series, which is showing on Channel 4."

"Yeh, I've seen it, so you must think there is a story here."

"We really do. The number of responses you had to your Facebook appeal within this estate is a statistical anomaly. We believe there is something sinister at play here, and we need your help to find out what."

Jen allowed a pained smile to cross her face and the realisation someone was in her corner seemed to relax her. She stood up. "Okay, you set up your camera stuff and I'll make us all a coffee."

When Jen returned with a tray of coffee and biscuits, she had a spark in her eyes that wasn't there when she first opened the door. Halle grabbed her coffee and wasted no time in starting the interview.

The interview lasted for forty-five minutes and Jen spoke articulately about her experiences, in between bouts of emotion that made her stop and fight back understandable tears. She explained how her son, Jamie, had first suffered bouts of nausea, headaches and severe fatigue about a year ago, followed by a persistent cough. A few months in, she took him to the doctors for blood tests to be confronted with the earth-shattering news that he had developed leukaemia. They went straight onto a treatment programme but he died six months later. She explained that her husband worked away a lot and she had made the Facebook plea out of sheer desperation, needing something or someone to help deal with the loneliness of her grief.

As the interview came to an end, Halle sensed that the outpouring of information, whilst trying to contain her grief, had taken it out of Jen.

Halle stroked her arm in a feeble attempt to show some empathy but, in reality, she had no idea how Jen was feeling.

"Thank you so much for everything you have told us. That can't have been easy for you. We are going to do some further investigations into what might have caused your son and all these other children to develop cancer. We will be back in touch and keep you in the loop with our investigation. Do you have any plans to meet up with the people that responded to your Facebook post?"

Jen's eyes lit up, re-energised by the question. "Do you think that would help?"

"Well, we can go and speak to each one individually, but if there was an opportunity to meet everyone together, that would help us enormously."

Jen stood up and unexpectedly hugged Halle. "I'm gonna do that. I'm gonna get everyone together. I owe it to my son to find out if someone or something was responsible for his death."

They packed up their stuff and exchanged contact details. Jen promised to organise something as quickly as she could, and Halle was glad to have one solid line of enquiry.

As they got back in the SUV, Halle looked at Rod and Clayton. "What did you make of that?"

Clayton let out a grunt. "I'm desperately sorry for what that woman went through and I really hope we find out what happened, but it doesn't stop her being a racist."

Halle caught herself in a sharp breath. "God, Clayton, I'm so sorry. I thought she was giving off a bad vibe to you."

"Hey, don't worry about it. You get used to ignoring ignorant people like her. At least she wasn't calling me the N word."

They drove off and Halle felt really uncomfortable with what had just happened to Clayton. She couldn't find the right words and realised how unprepared she was for situations like this. Rod helped clear the uneasy vibe by chatting away about football and what his wife was going to get him to do at the weekend. She realised what a sheltered life she had led with her lovely parents in their typical white middle-class environment in the suburbs.

As they drove on, she closed her eyes and tried to process the morning's events. Was she really ready for this big grown-up challenge?

9

The loud music in the club was blasting out something relevant about 'bumping and grinding' as the stripper ground her arse into Edward's crotch, closely followed by her rubbing her fake pneumatic breasts in his face. He slipped a £20 note in her G-string and told her to 'fuck off'. She gave a smile as fake as her breasts and flicked him the finger.

He turned and clinked his champagne glass with his Uncle James, who was admiring the stripper defying gravity on the main pole at the centre of the dimly lit stage.

"So, tell me what you've found out about our Miss Parker. Andrew had a run-in with her the other day and said she ain't inclined to keep her nose out of our business."

"Well, it seems like her core business model is based on her buying up blocks of print advertising space from local and national newspapers, magazines and journals. Her team then sell this space on to a range of clients, acting as the broker between the client and the relevant print media. She also brokers social media advertising space with all the major online players."

"Where's the weakness in her business?"

"It seems she buys up the advertising space in advance, meaning she has to sell it all to make a profit."

"Ah, okay, so she has some financial exposure if she is left with advertising space she can't sell?"

"That's right."

"How can we hurt her?"

"She spreads the risk by having a wide client base, some regular customers and some ad-hoc, but there are a couple of bigger players that would cause her a headache if they suddenly decided not to work with her."

Edward poured them both another glass of champagne and fixed his uncle with a conspiratorial smile. "Find another advertising agency that would be willing to significantly undercut her pricing structure, oiled by a generous contribution from us to help with any inconveniences this may cause them. Let's start giving her something else to worry about, so she keeps her nosy beak out of our business."

"No problem. I'm on it."

"Oh, and make sure there is no trail back to us."

"Of course."

*

Andrew and Peter sat in the ALMS offices reading through the report on the Wapping site that Jeremy from PEMS had provided.

Peter shook his head. "Blimey, this one's the worst we've ever had. It looks like every pollutant known to man is on this site."

"I'm not surprised, little brother. Those old metalworks churned out all sorts of pollution, so it's not rocket science to conclude that the ground will be full of everything they processed."

"Okay, but can we realistically deal with all this stuff?"

"Yeh, no problem. Jeremy is suggesting the usual three-tiered approach of removing some of the contaminated soil, a washout of contaminants and clay barriers."

"Is that going to be enough?"

"Don't you trust PEMS? They have never let us down."

"I know, I know, but this site seems like one we should be walking away from. It's on a different scale to everything else we have ever done."

Andrew stood up. "Stop worrying, little brother. Jeremy will make it good. I can guarantee it."

Peter watched him leave. Once again, he had been put in his place. He hated the way Edward and Andrew kept calling him 'little brother', like they felt the need to constantly reinforce their hierarchical dominance. He swore to himself under his breath and went back to reading the report from PEMS.

Half an hour later, Peter decided to call it a day. As was often the case, it was dark outside by the time he had finished for the day, and he resolved himself to another quick microwave meal before the inevitable crash-out on the sofa.

As he packed up his bags, his phone beeped. A text message.

Peter, I'm just reading this latest environmental study from Jeremy about the Wapping site. I gather you project manage these from your end. Would like to speak about

the proposed work before we get started. Can you come
and see me tomorrow morning to discuss? Sophie Parker

Peter stared at the message. "Oh shit!"

10

Halle and Todd sat in the office watching the footage from the interview with Jen Wyatt. A tear rolled down Halle's cheek. The raw emotion evident in everything that Jen was saying, whilst she courageously stuck to the task in hand, overwhelmed Halle's senses. She brushed the tear away. "God, I'm sorry. What a wuss I am."

"Hey, don't worry about it. That's what is going to make you a great investigative reporter. Being able to feel empathy for the victims."

"Thank you. It's very kind of you to say but…"

Her sentence drifted off and she absentmindedly chewed her lip.

"Are you okay?"

"Oh, Todd. This woman has been through a level of pain and trauma I can't begin to understand, but I keep being distracted by the way she treated Clayton."

"What do you mean? What did she do?"

"Well, she didn't DO anything as such, but she kept giving him a really bad vibe. When we got back in the car, he called her a racist. I mean, I could sense she had a problem with him but it was all so weird. Clayton seemed to accept that some people were like that, but I don't know what to do about it. I don't want her or any of her neighbours treating him like some second-class citizen. It's just appalling."

Todd thought for a moment. "You are right, but I can guess what the bosses will say. That's not the story here. Focus on what you have been asked to investigate and get the job done. All you can do is confront the racism when it happens and move on."

Todd left to grab them both a drink and Halle stared out of the window. *Racists lose child to cancer.* Todd was right. She couldn't see the powerbrokers liking that as the strapline of her piece.

She regrouped when Todd returned, and focused the conversation on what they should do next.

"Okay, we need to work out our next steps. Jen has agreed to contact all the people on the Facebook group to see if we can meet them as a collective, which will save us a load of time, but we need some other angles of investigation."

"I agree and I reckon we need to get a medical opinion about this. I'm sure the kids' doctors are not going to speak to us about the specific cases, patient confidentiality and all that, but we need someone that can give us some indicators as to what might have caused all these children to develop cancer. My research confirms that the number of cases in this small population is way off the scale compared to the average number of cases across the country."

"How do we do that?"

"I think we are going to have to approach a private healthcare firm, one that will do anything for a bit of cold hard cash. There's one just down the road from here who has a cancer specialist. If you approve the possibility of some expenditure for this guy's time, I will see if we can set something up."

"God, yeah, go for it."

"Okay, I'll get that sorted ASAP and speak to Mrs Wyatt later to see if we can get back over there sooner rather than later."

Todd bounced out of the office like an excitable puppy. Once again, Halle found herself laughing at his infectious enthusiasm, but the self-doubt kept coming to her in waves. Her team were wonderful. If she couldn't succeed with great people like Todd, Rod and Clayton around her, she just wasn't cut out for this job.

She clicked on the footage again and watched Jen Wyatt pour out her heart about the little boy that was so cruelly taken from her. Halle shook her head. *Come on, Halle. You owe it to this woman to find out what happened.*

*

Peter decided to work from home at the start of the day. If he was going to see Sophie Parker, there was no way he was going to be in the office, open to difficult questions about where he was off to. His brothers and uncle would go 'ape-shit' if they knew he was contemplating meeting her. He had still not responded to her text but knew he couldn't ignore it. She was doing exactly what Edward didn't want her to do. Meddling.

He hadn't met her but her online profile confirmed what he had learnt from his meeting with Ross. She was a savvy businesswoman. She was also gorgeous with a cracking pair of…

He stopped the thought in its tracks. *Enough, Peter, have some respect.* Peter hated the way his father, uncle and brothers disrespected women. He hated himself for condoning the type of *banter* that he had almost repeated in his head without thinking. It was just easier to go along with it half the time. The hassle he would get for trying to educate their narrow minds and the constant accusations of being *a bender* were just not worth it. It was peer pressure of the most abhorrent kind.

None of the brothers were married or maintained any sort of long-term relationships. Their father's influence was all too evident in their approach to sex and relationships. Women were used as objects for sex or for cleaning their obscenely expensive houses.

Thinking about his brothers' objectionable attitudes helped him make a decision. He texted Sophie back and agreed to meet her at 11 am. He poured himself another coffee whilst simultaneously eyeing the bottle of brandy that was on the kitchen worktop, teasing him with the promise of Dutch courage. He shook the thought away and fired off an email to the PAs, telling them he was 'working from home' and would be in later.

After a relatively straightforward tube ride, Peter walked towards the entrance of PEMS, which was a two-minute walk from Wimbledon station. The early autumn weather was still erratic, switching from mild to wintry in a matter of minutes. He pulled his jacket around him as the wind continued to agitate anything that was not pinned down.

As he reached the entrance, he looked around, a moment of self-doubt creeping into his psyche. What if someone saw him walking in? How would he explain it away? Edward would not tolerate family disloyalty. He stood staring at the entrance for a few minutes, the devil on his shoulder urging him on.

He eventually worked through it and found himself at reception waiting for Sophie to collect him. A few minutes later, he saw her walking down the stairs towards him, a pleasant smile shaping a pretty face. She looked even more beautiful in the flesh, and he used all his willpower to keep his gaze fixed on her face. He was not going to be that person. It was time for him to be the person he was. Not the one initially shaped by his father's archaic attitudes or his brothers' determination to live out his legacy.

He leapt out of the chair and greeted her warmly. "Miss Parker. It's an absolute pleasure to meet you."

11

The familiar rumbling in her stomach told Halle that it was time for her to think about lunch options. As she contemplated the dilemma of choosing between a pastrami sandwich on rye from the local deli against a ramen noodle takeout box from the *Singapore Kitchen,* Todd bounced back into her office.

"I've done it, boss lady. If you can cover his £200 consultation fee, you have an appointment this afternoon with Mr Sadiq Jaffra, a consultant oncologist working at Redwing Healthcare, just down the road from here."

"Mr? Is he not a doctor then?"

"Oh yes, but you need to know their strange approach to salutations. They work all those years for the right to be called a doctor, but as soon as they become a consultant surgeon, they insist on being called Mr. It's bizarre."

"How odd."

"Yes, and don't get it wrong or they will correct you with heavily loaded contempt."

Halle pulled a funny face. "Okay, happy to cover his fees. When can we see him?"

"The appointments at 3 pm. I'll get back to his executive assistant and confirm. Can I come with you?"

"Yeh, I guess he won't be up for being filmed, so let's just use it as a fact-finding mission."

Todd left and she drummed her fingers on the desk. Todd was a whirlwind. He was driving the work forward faster than Halle could process it. She settled on the pastrami sandwich.

*

Peter settled into the comfy seat across from Sophie. Her mastery of small talk as they navigated the stairs and lifts up to her office had immediately put Peter at ease, and he found himself strangely drawn to her. Her assistant brought in their drinks and she wasted no time in getting to the point.

"Peter, I've been reading Jeremy's study of the Wapping site and I just wanted to make one hundred per cent sure you were happy with the proposal. I'm not an expert on these things and I haven't had much time to look through the previous work we have done for you, but this seems to be a particular challenging site from a pollution perspective."

Peter stared at Sophie. He was like a rabbit in headlights. Her soft tone was like silk on his eardrums, and he felt like closing his eyes so he could just listen to her speak. He suddenly realised she was looking at him, confused at his lack of response. He immediately shook himself out of his daze.

"Oh, sorry. Miles away. Er, yes, you are right, this is probably the worst site we have acquired from a pollution perspective. I did raise my concerns with my brother

Andrew last night, but he seems completely confident in the plan that Jeremy has proposed."

Sophie scanned through the pages again. "We are proposing to charge you £600k for this work. Is that normal?"

"Er, I think so. Andrew deals with all the commercials but it sounds about right."

A few unspoken minutes passed as Sophie concentrated on reading the proposal over and over. Eventually, she looked up. "Okay, I'll discuss it with Ross, but if you and your brother are happy with it, I'll guess we can sign it off."

Peter stood up, relieved she hadn't put him in a position that would have necessitated exposure of their conversation to his brothers. As he began to walk out of her office, a strange devilment overtook him. He spun round. "Would you like to come to dinner with me tonight?"

Sophie was taken aback and her initial expression left Peter hoping the ground would swallow him up. As he rapidly tried to work out how to extract himself from the excruciating situation, she floored him with her answer.

"Umm, yes, okay, that would be nice. It will give us more time to get to know each other. You can pick me up at 7.30. I'll text you my address."

Peter tried not to repeat his rabbit-in-headlights expression and played it cool. "Oh, great. I'll see you later."

As he was escorted back down to reception, Peter couldn't help the stupid smile that was fixed on his face. She was absolutely gorgeous and way out of his league.

He puffed his chest out and walked on but as he got out onto the street, his phone beeped with a text message from Edward asking where he was. The stark realisation of the situation suddenly hit him. *What have I just done?*

12

The lobby of Redwing Healthcare was exactly as Halle expected. All marble floors, trendy glass partitions, elaborate oversized plants and sharp-suited receptionists, manicured to within an inch of their lives.

They were greeted with the over-Americanised, overenthusiastic manner of people that had good customer care rammed down their throats from the second they joined the company. Halle guessed it was the kind of thing people who had the money for private healthcare were expecting.

They made their introductions and were invited to wait in the plush visitors' seating area, with one of those coffee capsule machines and a tray of Danish pastries tempting them to indulge.

The fifteen-minute wait allowed them to enjoy the hospitality before a stern-looking woman called their names and invited them up to the second floor.

They were ushered into a huge corner office, overlooking Hyde Park. An ageing gentleman with greying hair greeted them warmly. "Hi, I'm Mr Sadiq Jaffra, consultant oncologist. How can I help you?"

Straight to the point, thought Halle. *Time is money and all that.*

"Thank you for seeing us, Mr Jaffra. My name is Halle Jacobs and this is my researcher, Todd Barkley. We work for Goldwin Productions and are currently putting together a piece on an unusually high number of childhood cancers on a housing estate in East London. We were looking for an expert opinion on why so many of these children might have been affected in one small geographical area."

Sadiq rubbed his chin. "Well, it's difficult for me to comment without seeing the individual cases."

Halle didn't say anything, expecting more from him, but soon realised that was all he was going to say. "Oh, well, we realise that but we are looking for some broad indicators as to what might have caused this anomaly. There are around twenty cases, including two deaths, in children on one housing estate. The proportion of children affected is way outside the averages you would expect in the normal population."

Sadiq nodded as Halle spoke but initially offered no response. She desperately wanted to fill the uncomfortable space but eventually he spoke.

"Okay, despite the millions spent on cancer research, we still know very little about what causes cancer in children. We obviously understand the science of it, that bad cells are created when they replicate, but we have very little evidence as to what causes these genetic errors in the body. There is a clear genetic link to family members and this can probably explain away a percentage of all cases, but the rest are still a medical dilemma."

"There must be other reasons that research has identified."

"Well, yes. Social deprivation has been cited as a factor by some leading doctors. Is this estate in a poor area?"

"Actually, no. Although the general area of East London that it is in could definitely be cited as an area of social deprivation, the area where the housing estate is located is lovely."

"East London, you say? Where exactly?"

"Near Beckton."

Sadiq nodded. "I know the area well. Very industrial. Has a big old gas works and historically many power stations and metalworks churning out all sorts of pollution. I won't be quoted on this in your TV programme, but my best guess is that you need to look for environmental factors. If that housing estate was built on polluted land, I reckon that could be a key factor in these cases."

"Oh really? Why?"

"Exposure to high levels of pollutant gases and metals such as benzene or mercury will significantly increase the risks of developing many types of cancer, and children are particularly susceptible to this."

Halle couldn't hide the shock that she felt as she listened to Sadiq's theories. "But… but the estate is a real oasis in an otherwise horrible area. I can't believe it could be a factor."

Sadiq threw his hands in the air. "Well, Miss Jacobs, it's up to you what you do with what I've said. You asked for my professional opinion and based on the limited information you've given me, that is my best guess. I would strongly advise you to research the history of that site and, if possible, get some soil and water samples tested. If I am right, tests like that will give you a good indicator as to what you are dealing with."

As they walked out of the building, Halle's head was spinning with what Sadiq had said. She stopped outside the entrance and turned to Todd. "Do you really think he could be right?"

"I think it has to be a real possibility and gives us another solid line of enquiry."

Halle shook her head. "Jesus, Todd. Is this it? Is this my story?"

13

Peter looked in the mirror, casting a critical eye over the face that was staring back at him. He had no idea how old Sophie Parker was and he wondered whether she thought he looked like someone in his early forties. There was the merest hint of grey around his temples, but his complexion was holding up against the ravages of age and the poor air quality that he had to endure most days as he travelled around London. His penthouse flat overlooking Kensington Park was his solace and he tried to maintain his fitness by running through the park as often as he could.

He kept plucking and preening, weirdly nervous at meeting up with Sophie again so quickly. He had managed to blag his way out of a difficult situation with Edward by saying he was working on some project plans at home. Edward's ranting about Sophie's meddling made Peter nervous. Was this just more of the same or was Edward deliberating goading him because he knew what Peter had done? He eventually decided that Edward could not have known. His brother didn't do subtle. He was the most direct and disagreeable man you could hope to meet. If Edward had a beef, he would have dealt with it directly, probably with some violence thrown in. Peter shook his head at the thought and continued to fiddle with his hair.

As he began to leave the flat, he backtracked and started frantically tidying things up. It wasn't messy as such, but the sudden thought that Sophie may want to come back here made him paranoid about what she would think.

He eventually made it to his car and set off to pick Sophie up from her place, in a quiet suburb of Wimbledon, just along from the famous tennis venue. Peter was impressed.

Sophie glided out of her front door; class personified. She had gone for what you might describe as posh, smart casual. She was wearing a designer top, a tan leather jacket, expensive jeans and calf- length boots. Her hair was loose and tumbled sexily over her shoulders.

Peter tried not to repeat his rabbit-in-headlights look again as she neared the car. He went for a peck on the cheek and she responded warmly.

They had chosen a mid-range expensive Italian restaurant a few miles from Sophie's place, and the initial few minutes were calm and functional as they settled in, ordering drinks and food.

As they relaxed in each other's company, drinking a full-bodied Merlot, Sophie fixed her gaze on Peter. Her expression was confusing. It wasn't threatening as such but it wasn't warm. Peter tried to hide the non-verbals but Sophie picked up on his discomfort.

"Do I make you nervous, Peter?"

"Er, no. I'm fine."

Sophie giggled. "I'm sorry. It's just many of my so-called suitors have told me I can be a bit intimidating."

"Oh, right, no… I guess this is all a bit strange. It's been a while since I've done this."

"And what do you think 'this' is?"

"Er, well, I guess it's a date."

Sophie's expression changed to something more serious. "Oh, right."

Peter was mortified. Had he read the signals wrong? As he floundered around for what to say next, Sophie suddenly roared with laughter. "Oh, Peter, you are so precious. Don't worry, I'm winding you up. I do see this as a date."

Peter visibly relaxed and the mood was light and comfortable as they navigated their way through the starters and main courses.

As they waited for desserts, Sophie changed the conversation away from the polite small talk that had focused on their private lives, likes and dislikes, favourite films and people they admired.

"So, tell me a little more about our business relationship. Why does my father seem so obsessed about making sure we treat you as our best customer?"

"Erm, well, our fathers started working together over forty years ago and from what I can gather developed a really solid business relationship and friendship based on the business model we are still using today. We find brownfield sites to develop. You do the environmental studies and any clean-up to make them ready for sale to developers. It's been very profitable on all sides, so I assume your father wants to make sure this legacy is not eroded."

"Yeah, I get that but there's something else at play here. Dad seems unusually agitated about it. He is usually such a calm man but whenever he speaks to Ross and me about it, he seems troubled."

"Troubled?"

"Like he doesn't want to let go. It's almost like he doesn't trust us to maintain the relationship."

"I dunno what to say. Since my father... erm... died rather suddenly, my Uncle James and eldest brother, Edward, took over the running of our company and kept the relationship going. Maybe your father felt some extra responsibility to maintain the business relationship once my father was not around and is now nervous about leaving it altogether."

Peter felt a bit uncomfortable as Sophie took a sip of wine and stared at him. She seemed to be analysing him, looking for something in his demeanour that would validate whatever it was that was troubling her. She broke the silence.

"Why do your brothers object to my involvement?"

Peter put his head down, not wanting to meet Sophie's probing stare. He shook his head and eventually looked back at her, shame all over his face.

"Oh, I'm so sorry about this. My father was a horrible man. He had very archaic attitudes to women and treated my mother appallingly..."

"Is that why she killed him?"

Peter stopped in his tracks. "Ah, you know about that?"

"Yes, Ross told me. I'm sorry that happened to you at such a young age."

"Thank you, but it's the main reason why they object to you so much. Father would never do business with women and when my mother killed him, they saw this as some sort of sick validation that women were not worthy. They have never forgiven her, and I'm the only one that ever visits her in prison. His legacy is so entrenched in my brothers' psyche, as well as my uncle's, that they just see any woman as a sex object or someone to clean their houses. It's appalling and I've been powerless to change their caveman attitudes."

Sophie gave Peter a pitying smile. "Oh dear. Well, at least I know what I'm dealing with now."

"You do have one thing going for you."

"What's that?"

"At least you're white. The other aspect of my father's sparkling personality was that he was a terrible xenophobe. He refused to do business with any foreigners, insisting on working only with British businesses and employing British people. To this day, Edward will only employ people who are White British. I'm fully expecting to walk into the office one day and see everyone dressed in white KKK robes."

Sophie put her hand to her mouth, wide-eyed with shock. "My word, how can you be in that environment?"

"Oh, I wonder that every day. Every time I visit my mother in prison, every time they demean women by commenting on their great tits or arse, every time they reject a perfectly good candidate because they are foreign, a little part of my soul dies. I'm so ashamed. I am a multi-millionaire because of our business but it is built on hate and intolerance. I am up against five misogynistic, racist dinosaurs and have no way out. I find it really difficult to cope sometimes."

Sophie grabbed Peter's hand and gave it a reassuring squeeze. "Don't worry. You've got me now."

As the desserts arrived, Peter's head was spinning. Was Sophie for real? Was he being played? Was she stringing him along as she tried to reconcile what was unsettling her about their business relationship?

A few minutes later he got the answer as Sophie's phone beeped and a look of absolute horror filled her face.

14

Halle and Todd sat in her office, the previous day's conversation with Sadiq Jaffra front and centre in their minds.

"So, what the hell do we do with what Mr Jaffra said?"

Todd had his usual excitable puppy persona in play. "Way ahead of you, boss lady."

Halle couldn't help but smile every time Todd's face lit up with the excitement of the chase. She was learning that his reputation as the best researcher they had was well founded. The problem was, she was finding it hard to keep up with him. The tail was wagging the dog and she felt like she was trying to hold onto a Todd tidal wave.

Her self-doubt kept surfacing. She never particularly considered herself to be naïve or un-streetwise. She had done the university thing, got blind drunk more times than she could remember, had even done an E once. Sex and relationships... well, she had done enough to know pleasure and pain in equal measure.

She got the researcher job straight from university and worked hard, supporting various reporters who exposed her to some of life's most tragic people and circumstances. So why did she feel so out of her depth? The sudden responsibility of exposing whatever was behind these tragic childhood cancers weighed heavy on her mind.

The situation with Jen Wyatt and Clayton was also really bothering her. It was like all the hatred and intolerance, which she had always watched from the sidelines, was now in her face, shouting at her, expecting her to react, expecting her to be brave and confront it.

She must have been daydreaming for a while, fighting the demons in her head, because she suddenly came to at the sound of Todd's voice.

"Are you okay?"

She shook away the malaise and looked at Todd. "Am I doing a good job? I feel so out of my depth."

Todd once again gave that reassuring sparkly smile and pointed at his t-shirt. "Who's this?"

"Er, I don't know."

Todd sighed. "Oh, Halle, I'm going to have to educate you in the ways of the Marvel Universe. This is *Black Widow*, played by Scarlett Johannsen. This is you. The smart, beautiful feisty woman who is going to kick arse and crush the baddies."

Halle laughed and tried to refocus. "Okay, tell me what you've got."

"I did some research on the history of the site that the housing estate was built on. Sadiq was right that it was the site of an old metalworks. It was decommissioned in the early '80s and sat dormant for several years before the land was acquired by a company called Allcock Land Management Services. They worked with a company called Parker Environmental Management Services to clean the site up and then sold it to a housing developer called FZX Homes. They released the houses for sale in two phases at the beginning of the '90s."

"Okay, so there is every chance the site was polluted."

"Well, yes, there is no doubt they had to clean the site up to build on it, but I have checked the records from the council and the Environment Agency. The site was given development clearances based on a series of soil and water tests. It seems these companies did all the relevant checks and made the site safe. If they hadn't, there was no way that estate would have been built."

Halle frowned and rubbed her temples. "There must be something in this. It just seems to fit so well with what Sadiq said."

"I agree but the only way we can really prove this is to do what he said. We need to get some soil and water samples tested on that site now. We are going to need the co-operation of the residents and a specialist testing firm to help us."

Halle looked excited. "Come on. Let's call Jen Wyatt again. We need to get that meeting set up and tell them what we need to do. We have no time to lose."

*

Peter was in the office but he couldn't concentrate. As soon as she read the message on her phone, Sophie had left the restaurant abruptly. No explanation, no goodbye. He went to chase after her but had to quickly divert to pay the bill. By the time he got outside the restaurant, she was gone.

He drove back to her place but all the lights were off.

He tried her mobile over and over but she didn't answer. From the moment he woke he had been ringing her, but still no response. He contacted her office at PEMS but was told she was not in. He eventually surmised that she must be at her advertising company. This was mostly confirmed when he got the 'Miss Parker is not available at any point today' response from the person answering the phone.

He rubbed his face. What the hell was going on? What had made her react like that? As he tried to reconcile the hundreds of paranoid thoughts racing through his head, he realised Edward was standing in the doorway with an amused expression on his face. When Peter looked up, he spoke.

"Having a bad day, little brother?"

Peter frowned. There was something in his brother's facial expression and superior attitude that unnerved him. Did he know what was going on?

"Er... no, I'm fine, Edward. Is there something I can do for you?"

Edward stared at him for a bit, the arrogant smirk a permanent fixture on his face. He started to laugh. A loud, booming laugh that filled the corridors as he walked away from Peter's office.

15

Ross Parker looked up at the clock. It was nearly 7 pm as once again his new role at PEMS was causing him to work late. He joined the firm as a junior executive when his father's health began to deteriorate, but his father's decision to suddenly relinquish control had caught him off guard, and he was having to put the hours in to compensate for his lack of experience.

As he forced himself to shut down his laptop and prepare for a slither of personal time, his exit was disturbed by someone crashing through the door of his outer office. It was Sophie.

She burst into his office and slammed a set of papers down on his desk. "Do not sign off this work order for ALMS. We are not going to give those bastards another second of our expertise."

Ross was dumbfounded. "What are you on about? What has brought this on?"

Sophie was pacing around the office, metaphorical steam coming out of every orifice. "I can't believe I was so stupid, letting Peter Allcock get close so I would lower my guard. That family is toxic. I don't care what Dad wants. We are in charge now and we will not work with ALMS ever again."

Ross was struggling to keep up. "Sophie, you need to slow down. What has happened? What have they done to make you so mad?"

She stopped pacing and stared at Ross. Her face was a mixture of rage and tears. She poured herself a glass of water and slumped on the chair.

"I was out with Peter last night. He invited me to dinner after our meeting yesterday and I foolishly accepted. We were having a nice time until I got a message from the office. My two biggest clients have cancelled their contracts, which are worth nearly £1.2 million in annual revenues. I spent all day trying to find out what happened. It seems they are both moving to a tin-pot agency called Jericho's Advertising who have undercut my pricing by thirty per cent. My research on this firm suggests they don't have the market leverage to pull off such a deal, which leads to only one conclusion."

"What's that?"

"That Peter and his bloody brothers are deliberately trying to sabotage my business in some sick attempt to stop me snooping into our business relationship."

"Do you have proof of that?"

"Of course not. The execs at the two firms stonewalled me with excuses about needing to cut costs, but it can't be a coincidence that both of my biggest clients quit on the same day. Someone is oiling those wheels, and I know the Allcocks are behind this."

Ross rubbed his face. "We can't cancel a contract with ALMS that is worth £8 million a year to us. Our business will go under and we will need to lay off loads of staff. Are you really ready to do that?"

Sophie stared at Ross for a long time, thoughts racing through her head. She eventually stood up. "Fucking hell. Okay, let's be smart about this. I know they are responsible for this, but I need to hit back, play them at their own game. We'll carry on working with them, but I am going to be all over every aspect of this relationship. There's something off about ALMS and I'm going to find out what it is. I don't care if I have to work twenty-four hours a day. I am going to save my advertising business and be all over them like a rash. I will not let those bastards beat me."

With that, Sophie grabbed her stuff and stormed out of Ross' office.

*

Peter sat in his car outside Sophie's house. Rain was beginning to fall and the early autumn conditions were peppering his windscreen with fallen leaves blown about by the nagging wind. He had been there nearly two hours, having failed to track down Sophie anywhere else. He hoped that she would eventually turn up at home so he could find out exactly what had happened the previous evening.

As his eyes began to droop, he suddenly spotted a set of car headlights heading up the close towards him. It was her.

He leapt out and ran towards her car. As she got out, she screamed at him. "Fuck off, Peter."

"Sophie, Sophie, please. I just want to know what is going on."

She had begun to walk at pace towards her front door but suddenly turned and walked back towards him, anger emanating from every pore. She got up close and personal, spitting the words out in his face.

"You really are a piece of work. You butter me up with a fake date, whilst all the while your family is sabotaging my business. And for what? To stop me interfering with the working relationship between our two firms? Well, Peter, you can tell your brothers that it ain't gonna work. You have just made me ten times more determined to get involved in our little business arrangement and I will expose whatever is going on here. And that's a promise."

She didn't give Peter a second to respond, storming back to her front door and slamming it behind her.

Peter stood on her driveway absolutely stunned. What was she on about? *Sabotaging her business. Expose whatever is going on.* Where was Sophie getting this stuff from?

As he got back in his car, the horrible feeling in the pit of his stomach returned. Edward's manner when he left Peter's office, laughing like an unruly child, was odd... almost maniacal. Sophie's reaction was so immediate, so extreme, that something terrible must have happened. His mind was spinning but the more he thought about it, the more concerned he was. *Edward,* he muttered under his breath.

16

Halle's fingers danced over the keyboard. She didn't want to upset Todd by doing his work but she needed to get back to her comfort zone for a few minutes. Be a researcher again, not the big important investigative reporter role that was scaring the shit out of her.

Whilst they waited for confirmation of the meeting with Jen Wyatt, Halle was looking into the three companies that were involved in the creation of the Pickford housing estate.

She started with FZX Homes, who had built the houses on the estate. It didn't take long to find out that they were an active housebuilder in the '80s and '90s but folded as a company in the midst of the economic downturn in the early 2000s. Halle pondered the possibilities. Could their demise be due to shoddy work? Could they somehow have compromised the safety measures that had been put in place to protect the community from any residual pollutants?

She moved on to Parker Environmental Management Services. She found a long-established family firm, based in South London, whose core business was environmental studies and clean-up of brownfield sites. They were still trading and did the work that allowed sites to be redeveloped with all safety permits in place. Halle was interested to find that the founder of the firm, Bill Parker, had recently relinquished control of the firm to his children, Ross and Sophie Parker. A look at their client list on their website confirmed the connection to the third company on her list, Allcock Land Management Services. They were one of their major clients, a relationship that seemed to be long standing. Once again, she pondered the possibilities. Could they somehow have compromised the safety of that site?

She quickly focused her attention on Allcock Land Management Services, which had been set up in the late '70s by Edward Allcock. They had become a major player in land acquisitions around London and the South East. The curious thing was that the leadership team on the website had no mention of the founder. There was mention of an Edward Allcock but this appeared to be one of his five sons, who seemed to be running the firm with their uncle as chairman. *Hmm*, Halle thought to herself, *another male bastion*. She was curious about their turnover and looked at their company records. She gasped at the figures that confronted her. Year-on-year turnover was between £750 million and £850 million. She sat back in her chair, staring at the screen. There was something about big money and corruption that went hand in hand.

Halle realised she was treating these three firms like murder suspects. She needed to be careful not to jump to conclusions just because they fitted with one person's theory. Her bosses would not thank her if their exciting new TV series was undermined by shoddy unsubstantiated journalism.

As she stared out of the window watching the autumn leaves blowing about in a wind that didn't want to die down, she realised someone was stood in the doorway.

"Oh, hi. Sorry, I was miles away. I've just been looking into those three firms that were involved in the Pickford housing estate."

Todd put his hands on his hips and pulled a menacing face. "Hulk is angry."

For a split second, Halle was worried until she saw that Todd was wearing the latest line in his never-ending supply of Marvel t-shirts. She laughed. "Ah now, that one I know. Are you going to turn green on me, Mr Hulk?"

Todd smiled. "No, I'm good, but what are you playing at doing my work for me?"

"Do ya know, I just needed to be a researcher for a minute, remind myself what I'm good at."

Todd screwed his face up. "For crying out loud, stop with this self-persecution. You are great at this and I'm certain we are going to make a shit-hot TV programme."

Halle wanted to cry at his kindness but instead stood up and gave Todd a hug. Halle probably lingered a bit too long, revelling in the warmth and comfort she was getting from the physical contact. As she drew away, there was that weird moment between two people when you are both trying to work out whether you should go in for a kiss. The awkward moment was broken by someone clearing their throat in the doorway.

"Do I get one of those?" It was Clayton. Halle quickly extracted herself from Todd's grip, flushing with embarrassment whilst simultaneously flicking her hair and pushing her chest out. Todd looked at her quizzically with a *what-the-fuck-was-that* expression over his face.

Halle ignored the look and focused on Clayton. "I'm sorry, Clayton. I was just having a weak moment and Todd was giving me some much-needed reassurance."

Clayton held his hands up in the air. "Hey, no sweat. Whatever gets you through. You know we are all here for you."

There it was, once again, the ridiculous amount of support and kindness from her team. She shook herself out of her self-pity. Time to toughen up.

"What can I do for you?"

"I was just wondering whether you need me tomorrow. I understand we are going back to the estate."

Halle looked at Todd. "Yes, I have just spoken to Jen Wyatt and we are meeting most of the parents in their community hall at 5 pm tomorrow."

"Thanks, Todd. Can you make that?"

"Of course. I'll get the car ready for about 4 pm tomorrow."

With that, Clayton left. Halle left no time for awkward silences and cracked on.

"Right, I've only taken a preliminary look at these three companies and I don't want to influence your thoughts, so please do your own research and let me have your thoughts by the end of the day."

Todd was slightly taken aback by her sudden business-like manner but let it go. The hug was unexpected. The lustful energy that coursed between them was definitely unexpected.

"Of course, consider it done."

"Oh, there is one thing. Can you find out why Edward Allcock is not running Allcock Land Management Services? He was the founder of the company but doesn't appear anywhere on the website as being part of their current leadership team. I'm guessing he retired or something, but I'm curious to know why he is not still involved."

Todd left the office to get on with the work and Halle immediately picked up the phone to Rod. She had to discuss the footage she needed when they visited the estate again. She'd had her wobble. Now it was time to knuckle down and get this story in the can.

17

Peter sat in his office, peering through the glass walls. He could see Edward and Andrew standing in the main office. They were in deep conversation and Edward's body language suggested he was somewhat agitated.

Peter had wanted to crash straight into Edward's office and confront him about Sophie but, as usual, he had chickened out. He couldn't work out what Edward might have done, but he was sure he was responsible for her sudden rage.

As he sat there, frozen in procrastination, he realised they were both heading towards his office at speed. He quickly started tapping away at his laptop, trying to give the impression that he was busily working.

Edward wasted no time in barking at Peter as he and Andrew flew through his office door. "Why have PEMS not signed off the work order for the Wapping site?"

Peter continued to stare at his laptop, tapping away at nothing in particular, desperately trying to purvey an air of nonchalance when in reality his guts were turning over with the stress. He left it a few more seconds before looking up, trying to add to the dramatic effect.

"Umm, sorry. Just needed to finish this off. What was it you were saying?"

Peter was sure that he could see steam coming out of Edward's ears as his face reddened with rage. He moved nearer to Peter.

"I said, why the fuck has PEMS not signed off the work order for the Wapping site? Is that stupid woman playing some fucking power game with us?"

"Er, if by stupid woman you mean Sophie Parker, I spoke to her on the phone the other day..." the lies were now coming easily "...and she checked a couple of points with me, which were all good. She said she was going to discuss it with Ross and get it signed off."

Edward stood back up from his aggressive hands-on-the-table posture and shot a look at Andrew. Peter picked up on it immediately.

"Is there something wrong, Edward?"

Edward turned and stormed out of the office, not another word spoken.

Peter was now convinced. Edward's reaction suggested he was on the attack with Sophie Parker and she was biting back. The problem was that Sophie still thought Peter was involved in whatever sick and twisted game Edward was playing. He had to find a way to convince her that he was not involved.

*

Edward grabbed his uncle on the way back to his office and sat fuming there on an easy chair.

"I might have underestimated that woman. I'm sure she is deliberately delaying signing off that work order now that our little market sabotage has hit her firm."

James responded first. "Don't worry. She couldn't afford to give up our account even if she wanted to. We'll get that work order soon enough. Trust me."

Andrew pitched in. "I agree. I think she will be too busy trying to save her firm to worry about sabotaging our projects. Uncle and I will give Ross a call and get it sorted."

Edward calmed a bit and nodded. "Okay, guys. Get to it. We have those other three brownfield sites that we need to get started on. I am not letting that woman cost me any money. If she wants to fight, I will destroy her."

*

Sophie Parker arrived back at PEMS in the early afternoon determined to look deeper into the relationship with ALMS. She had earlier called an emergency breakfast meeting with her management team at the advertising agency. After copious amounts of coffee and a sugar-laden feast of pastries, the team had agreed a three-point recovery plan. Sophie had spoken to the two firms that were threatening to leave, matching the reduced rates that the new firm were offering. The account managers were tasked with generating new business quickly to mitigate the potential losses, and the commercial manager was tasked with checking all existing contracts to make sure other firms couldn't leave at the drop of a hat. She walked away from the meeting, quietly confident that her defensive strategies would work.

As she arrived at her office, she saw the large number of files that her PA had put on her desk. They contained the details of every project that had been completed with ALMS over the last five years. Sophie told her PA that she was not to be disturbed. She was going to find out what was going on, even if it took her all night.

18

Halle, Rod and Clayton arrived early to the Pickford housing estate. She agreed with Rod that they would do some links around the site, which could form some of the narrative for the TV programme. She knew a load of it would get edited out but the trick was to overprovide, to give the editors the chance to cut stuff out. She couldn't afford to go to them with insufficient footage or her project would be canned.

Clayton stood guard as they proceeded to do the links. Halle was still really concerned about the reactions he was going to get from the wider audience. Would they all have racist attitudes like Jen Wyatt?

They completed the links without incident and headed towards the community centre, which was on the eastern edge of the estate. The building was lovely. Very modern, with a light and airy feel. As they walked up to the front of the building, a plaque by the door caught Halle's eye.

"Oh, how funny. This place was opened on my birthday. Look. The 30th of November."

Rod and Clayton smiled at her childish enthusiasm for something so basic. She got the hint and walked into the foyer of the community centre. She could hear a low roar coming from the main room. The pitch and fall of numerous conversations going on between the residents. She immediately tensed up. The job was now getting very real. As she steeled herself to confront the crowd, Jen Wyatt appeared in the doorway. She gave a forced smile to Halle but once again eyed Clayton with suspicion. Halle shot a look at Clayton but he was staring past her into the main room.

Jen beckoned for them to come through. As they walked in, the crowd hushed, all eyes focused on their presence. Halle's stomach was churning but she tried to put on a friendly smile as she acknowledged the crowd. She chivvied Rod up to get the camera equipment ready. As she looked back at the crowd, which had mostly gone back to their conversations, she noticed a number of children playing outside in the playground. Her heart sank as she noticed the obvious signs of cancer in some of them. The bald heads stood out in the dusky light that was illuminating the space they were playing in.

She looked at Clayton for reassurance, his engaging smile instantly doing the job. As she looked back at the crowd, she had the weirdest sensation. The inner turmoil of feeling desperately sorry for these people was fighting for attention in her mind with whether she was in a room with a bunch of racists. She found herself perversely relieved when she realised that within the group were a number of black and Asian families. She hated herself for being relieved that these people were suffering just to suppress the risk of Clayton being racially abused.

Halle was snapped out of her self-persecution by the sound of Jen's voice calling the meeting to order. Rod was ready and had the camera rolling.

"Ladies and gentlemen. Can I introduce Halle, Rod and Clayton from the Goldwin Production Company who are making a TV show about our…" her voice cracked in the emotion of trying to say it and she had to pause "… children."

A number of pained, sympathetic faces stared back at Jen but before Halle could take the stage, a man stood up at the back.

"Why the hell are you here, exploiting our pain and suffering? You people are parasites."

There it was. Exactly what John Grayson had warned her about. Not so much the *lowlife scum* he had so eloquently parodied in her first interview question but the raw human emotion that comes from people suffering and the inevitable suspicion that comes with TV cameras being shoved in their faces.

The question had increased the low roar in the room as people reacted to what had been said. Halle let out a deep breath, stepped forward to the front of the stage and held her hands up for quiet. This was her moment. She caught the subtle move of the camera by Rod to focus on what she was about to say.

"Ladies and gentlemen, can I firstly say how desperately sorry I am for your suffering. I can't begin to understand what you are feeling but I hope by making this TV programme we can go some way to easing some of the pain and maybe explain why this is happening."

As she spoke, Halle instinctively looked out to the children in the playground, a gesture that was not lost on many of the crowd. "Let her speak," shouted one. A general nodding came from a number of the other people in the room. The man who had made the challenge shook his head and sat down.

The room was quiet and Halle started her pitch. The most important speech of her life.

"Thank you. My name is Halle Jacobs and, as Mrs Wyatt said, I work for Goldwin Productions as an investigative reporter. Rod is my cameraman who, with your permission, will record the interactions we have, which we hope will form part of the narrative for the final TV programme we are planning to produce and broadcast. Clayton here is my security detail, and I can assure you those muscles are all natural."

The comment was instinctive. She was goading the crowd, testing their reactions. Was she brave enough to walk away from this if the suppressed racism exhibited by Jen surfaced more overtly from others? She scanned the room. There were some half-smiles at the apparent joke, but there were also a few people leaning over to each other, making small talk. She was paranoid. What were they saying? Halle soon realised the room was quiet, waiting for her to continue. She grimaced. Todd's words stuck in her brain. Racism was not the story here. If she walked away, however right and noble that might be, her career would be over before it started.

She took a deep breath and continued.

"The basis of the show we are producing, which is called *Tragic Britain,* is to expose corruption and criminality—"

Halle was interrupted before she could continue. A woman at the front speaking up. "Hold on. So, you are saying that you think there is something criminal about our children developing cancer?"

The low roar returned but Halle ploughed on.

"The thing is, our researcher picked up your story when Mrs Wyatt posted about it on Facebook. The number of families that responded to her post citing the same awful experiences with their children developing cancer piqued his interest. It became a story that my boss was interested in when we realised that all the respondents lived on the same estate. Now, I don't want you to think I'm treating you as a number, but the incidences of childhood cancer on this relatively small estate are a statistical anomaly."

The man that had made the first challenge stood up again. "So, I'm right. You sniffed out a story and now you want to make money out of our pain and suffering."

The mob mentality was at play and a number of people looked round at him disapprovingly, telling him to shut up and sit down. As this played out, Jen Wyatt quickly whispered in Halle's ear that he was the father of the other child that had died. Halle was grateful for the intel and sought to quell his concerns.

"Sir, I'm so sorry for your loss and I promise you that our intentions are good. Of course, my TV studio will be delighted if we make a hard-hitting TV show that the public embrace, but our motivations are focused on what is happening here."

Another woman on the far side of the room piped up. "What do you think has happened here?"

Halle took another breath. This was the moment. The moment that would make or break her project.

"Whilst we haven't spoken to your children's doctors, we did seek out a specialist medical opinion from a cancer specialist. He was clear that a number of these tragic cases could be explained by genetics. If you have a history of cancer in your families, there is a high probability that you have been desperately unlucky in predisposing your children to developing cancer."

The faces staring back at her were serious and, in some cases, tear-stained, but there was no further interruption.

"However, our specialist agreed that the number of cases on one housing estate could not fully be explained by genetics. He suggested we look into the history of this site to look for environmental factors. I'm not sure if you are aware, but this estate was built on the site of an old metalworks, and he feels there is a strong possibility that some of the pollutants that were in the earth may be a factor as to why so many of your children have developed cancer."

The roar intensified. Looks of horror were all over the faces of the parents as everyone spoke at once, talking to each other and shouting at Halle. Eventually, one voice won through. "Are you saying that we are living on a polluted site? That we are all being exposed, every second, to pollutants that could kill our children?"

"We don't know that for sure but our expert believes it is a possibility. With your permission, we would like to bring a specialist team on site to test the soil and water in your individual houses and gardens."

The roar continued. Another voice. "You think someone is responsible for this? For killing our children?"

Halle responded. "That's what we are trying to find out."

The crowd was frantic. Loud, desperate conversations going on throughout the room. Halle was losing them. She tried to get them back but all that happened was people started talking louder and louder at each other, trying to make themselves heard. Another voice managed to cut through the noise.

"Is it safe to stay in our houses? Should we move out now?"

The crowd focused on what the man was saying. Others shouting in response. "Where can we go? I don't have anybody we can stay with."

The frantic conversations continued. Halle looked at Rod and Clayton, desperate for some idea of what to do next. Rod was lapping it up, moving the camera from group to group. No doubt the type of *gold dust* the editors would be looking for. Clayton stood there, unmoved. As Halle became desperate, her phone beeped. Her guardian angel had saved her. A text from Todd. He had found a testing firm that could be on site the next day.

Halle shouted at the top of her voice. Slowly, the noise abated. She held up her phone.

"I've just received a text from my researcher. We can have a testing team on site tomorrow."

There was a vacuum of peace before the room erupted once more. Looks of panic spread across most of the faces, accusing stares directed at Halle, people shouting and screaming. It hadn't worked. It was as though the reality of bringing a testing team on site had flicked a switch in people's heads. This thing was for real, and danger lurked in every corner of the estate they were living on.

People started streaming out of the community hall, running scared. The conciliatory, attentive crowd had changed into a vicious maelstrom of angry people, pushing and shoving to get out of the hall.

Halle looked at Clayton. "What are they doing? Why are they leaving?"

Clayton shrugged.

As the crowd started to file past where Halle was standing, the abuse started. People accusing her of ruining their lives, intruding on their grief. Wild, angry faces. Clayton instinctively pulled her away from the mob. She fought back tears as she allowed herself to be comforted by Clayton, his strong arms and warm body making her feel safe. She stayed put as the last few people walked out. Halle was shaking, her mind trying to process what had just happened. As she refocused, she realised the shouty man that had interrupted the start of her presentation was staring at her. His face was contorted with rage.

"I was right. You fucking people are just parasites. Exploiting the weak and vulnerable for the sake of a TV show. I'm just glad this bunch of losers finally saw you for what you really are. Now fuck off out of our lives and take your pet gorilla with you."

Halle burst into tears and buried her face in Clayton's chest. As her sobs abated, she looked up at him. "I'm sorry. You didn't deserve that."

He put both his hands on her shoulders. "Hey, don't sweat it. I've had much worse and I ain't gonna let one ignorant white man upset my day."

Halle stared at him. A rush of something coursed through her body, detaching her from reality. She moved in to kiss him.

He moved away. "Whoa, whoa. What are you doing? My services don't extend to that."

Halle stopped, her face dropping in horror. What had

she done? She pulled away, not able to look at Clayton. "God, I'm sorry. I'm such a fool. Please just take me home."

As they started to pack up, Halle consumed by embarrassment, she realised they were alone in the hall. Jen Wyatt had left.

They got in the car and Halle pushed her head back into the headrest. Closing her eyes, she tried not to think about the implications of what had just happened.

Without the families on the estate, she had no story.

19

Sophie had been looking through the files for nearly two hours and already she was spotting a pattern.

The environmental studies seemed robust enough. The relevant pollutants on each site had been clearly documented, with each location posing a range of different risks. What unnerved Sophie were the remediation plans. They were all basically the same.

Almost without exception, the remediation plans included a three-pronged approach. Removal of contaminated soil, an industrial wash of any contaminants that may be left after the soil removal and the creation of a four-foot protective layer of clay, supported by impermeable horizontal and vertical barriers.

She was no expert but this seemed odd. Surely, each site presented different risks and therefore needed different remediation plans. She opened up the search engine, hoping to find someone that could give her remediation 101. She was convinced there was something at play here and she didn't want to ask anyone in the firm, especially not her father. It was his manner every time they spoke about the ALMS account that had made her suspicious in the first place. He was usually such a calm and considered man, but every time the ALMS account came up, he was grumpy and agitated.

She started to read a range of articles on remediation work. The more she read, the more her head hurt. There was so much information about the subject, but nothing was really giving her a clear answer as to whether her firm's actions were valid.

She rubbed her face. Frustrated. Was she being overly paranoid? Were her suspicions unfounded?

She made herself another cup of tea and looked out of the office window, the bright lights of London dominant in the vista.

As she drained the last of the tea, she looked back at the piles of files strewn across her office. Something was not right. She could feel it.

She got back onto her computer and read some more. Eventually, she found something. An article that confirmed her suspicions. The author was an environmental and pollution specialist from King's College, London and was unequivocal in her conclusions. This was not a one-size-fits-all business.

Sophie's mind was racing. Why was her firm doing this? Why did they seem to be trotting out the same remediation plans for every site, when professional opinion seemed to fly in the face of what they were doing?

Sophie was no conspiracy theorist but she had watched enough films to know that there was one way to prove whether her paranoia had any foundations. *Follow the money.*

She grabbed a load of files that she had already reviewed and started to look at the financial details. The unnerving synergy she had found with the remediation plans was present in the financial analysis. The costs were generally between £500k and £700k, depending on the size of the site, and were distributed four ways. A fee to each of the firms that did the removal, clean-up and barrier implementation, with the same companies used every time. But what made Sophie stop in her tracks was the fourth recipient. A payment to a company called Bill Parker Holdings.

She shook her head. *Why is Dad paying himself for each piece of work?* She was manic. Page after page of financial detail. Every one was the same.

Sophie stopped and stared out of the window. Her gut tightened at the possibilities. She was convinced something was wrong here, and her father seemed to be at the centre of all of it.

20

Halle arrived back in the office, extracting herself from the uncomfortable situation with Clayton as fast as she could. She hoped to God she didn't bump into John. If he asked her how it was going, she wasn't sure what on earth she would say.

As she approached her office, Todd did his usual meerkat act, his head popping above the cubicle. She stopped by his desk and burst into tears.

Todd grabbed her and sat her down on one of the chairs in her office, kneeling down like some parent comforting a distressed child. "Hey, hey. What's up?"

Halle took a while to compose herself. Eventually, she raised her tear-stained face. "It didn't work, Todd. Telling the parents that they might be living on a polluted site was the wrong thing to do. It made them frantic and they accused us of exploiting their grief. When I mentioned the testing team, the room exploded into panic and they became horrible and abusive. Everyone left suddenly and I think many of the families were going to leave the site. It's a complete disaster. We've lost them."

Todd stroked her arm. "It's a knockback, but we can find another way."

Halle looked away from his gaze, trying to stem more tears. She placed her hand over her face. "It gets worse. I've made such a fool of myself."

Todd caught her gaze again but said nothing, the silence compelling her to fill the void. "I... I... oh God, I tried to kiss Clayton."

"What!"

"I know, I know, but he was being all protective when it kicked off. He was holding me as those horrible people were shouting abuse. One of them called him a gorilla. I was horrified. It was just one of those moments, where it all seems right but... I read it so wrong."

Todd couldn't help but smile. "What did he do?"

"He just said that his services didn't include that."

Todd couldn't hold it in any longer. He burst out laughing.

Halle looked at him, initially shocked that Todd seemed to be making fun of her. As she watched him revelling in the mirth of the story, she started to relax and the laughter came.

After breaking the tension, the laughter subsided and they both sat looking at each other. Halle realised that the Clayton situation was not the issue here. She would ride her embarrassment and apologise to him. The bigger problem still loomed large.

"What are we going to do? I've messed up so badly."

Todd looked at his watch. "Right, this needs a night of pizza, wine and Marvel films. We are going to my place for the evening and are going to forget about everything. We'll tackle this problem in the morning."

Halle was swept along in Todd's enthusiasm. Within

the hour, they were at his incredibly swanky flat tucking into pizza and were a good way through the first bottle of wine. As they ate, Todd grabbed the remote control and navigated to the Disney+ app on his TV. "Right, little lady. Your Marvel education begins now. We'll start at the beginning with *Iron Man*."

As the evening went on, Halle relaxed as the wine continued to flow. She even found herself strangely entertained by the nerd fest that was *Iron Man*.

After just over two hours of film and two bottles of wine, the film credits began to roll and Todd looked over to Halle, who was sat next to him on the deceivingly comfortable sofa.

"So, what do you see in him then?"

"Who?"

"Clayton."

"Oh, I don't know. He's just got that whole big cuddly teddy bear thing going on, coupled with that sense of safety and security every time you are near him."

"You know he's probably got a dick like a tree trunk. Do you think you could handle that?"

Halle put her hand to her mouth. "You can't say that. It's… it's… I dunno, racist or something."

"It's not racist. It's a fact that all black men have big dicks."

Halle slapped him playfully. "Does that interest you?"

"What?"

"Big black dicks."

Todd smiled. "Ah, the gay question. I get that a lot. No, I'm a straight-up pussy man, me."

Halle laughed. This was nice. Todd always seemed to

know just what she needed. She slid nearer to Todd and rested her head on his shoulder. It just felt right.

Todd didn't flinch. He adjusted his body to get more comfortable and stroked her hair. "Anyway, you don't have a chance with Clayton. I've seen him with a woman that looks like Beyoncé's sister."

Halle craned round to look at Todd without losing contact with his shoulder. She smiled and slapped him playfully again. He refilled her wine glass and fiddled with the TV. "Right. *Iron Man 2*."

21

It was just past 9 pm as Peter drove into the close where Sophie lived. He had to see her, convince her that whatever his brothers and uncle were up to, he had nothing to do with it. The autumn wind had finally died down, giving way to a colder, crisp evening; the heating in the car a welcome comfort against the chill.

As he approached her house, it was in darkness. Was she home? Had she gone to bed? He waited outside and watched for a few minutes. Nothing changed. He got out and rang the bell. It was one of those video doorbells and Sophie's voice crackled from the small speaker.

"What do you want?"

"I need to explain. Can I come in?"

"I'm not at home and have nothing to say. Goodbye."

Peter stood there, crestfallen. How was he ever going to make her understand if she wouldn't talk to him? He considered pressing the bell again but thought better of it.

He got in his car, closing his eyes and pushing his aching skull against the headrest. Hundreds of competing stresses raced through his head. How had he messed up his relationship with Sophie so quickly? He had become so downtrodden with the way his family did things. Sophie had been a breath of fresh air, a bright new flower amidst a den of thorns. He was the outsider in the family, the punchbag for his brothers, all because he didn't toe the line and still believed in his mother.

He eyed the bottle of pills that was in the well of the cup holder. It would be so easy.

*

Sophie was still in the office. She had been pacing around trying to decide what to do about the things she had found when Peter's call came in. She couldn't work him out. He did seem different to Andrew Allcock. Much of what he had said at dinner suggested he was genuinely uncomfortable with how his family behaved, but she just didn't know whether she could trust him.

And, there it was. The big question. Trust. Everywhere she turned at the moment, someone or something was making her suspicious. She didn't feel like she could trust anyone. She had been agonising over who she could ask about the financial arrangements she had found in the ALMS projects. Could she ask the finance manager? Ross? Or should she confront her father?

In the end, she knew she had to scratch this itch and set off to see her father. It was just after 9.30 pm when she entered his house. Because of his frailty, she had a key in case they needed to attend to an emergency. He was sat in the lounge watching TV, the home help having got him ready for bed and made him his evening drink.

"Who's that?"

"It's Sophie, Dad."

"What are you doing here at this ungodly hour?"

She walked into the lounge and sat down. He eyed her suspiciously.

"I need to talk to you about something."

"Couldn't it wait?"

"Er, well, no, not really."

"Okay, spit it out. What's on your mind?"

"What is Bill Parker Holdings and why do all the ALMS projects have money going into it?"

He took a swig of his cocoa and fixed her with a disapproving stare. "I told you to leave the ALMS account alone. Jeremy can run that account without your interference. You and Ross just need to sign off the work orders and let him get on with it."

"I'm just trying to understand the business better and you seemed so desperate to make sure that the ALMS account was looked after. I've been trying to learn more about it."

"You don't need to learn the business. Just let Jeremy get on with his job and ALMS will be fine. Haven't you got your own business to look after?"

"Well, yes, but I want to do both."

"You don't need to. Ross should be taking the bulk of the management role. You are there as a silent partner. Attend the board meetings, sign stuff off when it needs it and leave the rest to everyone else."

Sophie couldn't believe it. Here it was. The patriarchy alive and well in the 21st century. She was surprised at her father. He had always been supportive of her career and had never favoured Ross in any other part of their time growing up. It was now clear to her that the business was the line that he had drawn. He wanted Ross to run his business and she was supposed to kowtow to their demands.

She was going to leave it but as she stood up, the injustice of it all burned inside her. "Okay, Dad, you've made your feelings quite clear, but I still want to know what Bill Parker Holdings is. If it's part of the company, I need to know what it's for."

Her father's tone was terse but he answered the question. "It's the Research and Development account. As ALMS has always been the most profitable part of our business, I used the profit we made for R&D. The account is separate from the main operations accounts for that reason. I passed the management of it to Jeremy so you don't need to worry about it."

Sophie kissed him on the head and walked out. As she stood by her car, the same problem invaded her psyche. Trust. She didn't trust a word that had come out of her father's mouth.

22

Victoria Allcock lay on the bed in her cell, staring at the ceiling. Over the years, the cracks in the ceiling had begun to form into the shape of a letter E, like some sick otherworld message from her husband, Edward. He was still watching her, still haunting her every waking hour. She rolled over. There was still ten minutes before the screws started banging on the cells to start another day of hell.

Her mind was in turmoil. She still couldn't shake the tinge of excitement she'd had since Peter told her about old man Parker handing over his business to his children. Was this the opportunity to tell people what she knew about the relationship between Edward and old man Parker? But who would she tell? Apart from Peter, her sons had long since disowned her, but old man Parker had a daughter. Could she be the one to listen to her, to help her gain some sort of revenge on the Allcock men who had made her life a living hell? The problem was, she had no way of communicating with her. Peter visited occasionally but she still didn't really know whether she could trust him. Which left only one option. She had to get out. But therein lay the problem. The only way she could get out was to fawn to the parole board about how remorseful she suddenly was. The thought made her sick to the stomach.

The warden was *kindly* arranging a follow-up parole meeting in a few months' time. She closed her eyes, trying to resolve the demons that were battling for dominance in her head.

*

As usual, Peter was in the office bright and early, trying to get ahead of the workload before everyone else came in to disturb his peace and pile on more work. The situation with Sophie was on his mind constantly and he found himself daydreaming about what to do.

As the clock ticked round to 8.30 am, his musings were broken by the sound of his office door opening. It was the last person he wanted to see.

Edward was shaking a piece of paper. "Good news, little brother. We've had the signed work order from Ross Parker for the Wapping site, so get that work started today and then get those other sites moving."

He gave Peter no chance of a response, immediately slamming the office door behind him and walking back to his office.

Peter sat there. Confused. Edward had seemed convinced that Sophie was deliberately blocking the signing of the work order as some form of retaliation to whatever he was up to. So why had Ross suddenly signed it off? Was Sophie being marginalised?

He had to speak to her, convince her that his intentions

were good. He phoned her office number at PEMS. She wasn't in... or her PA had been given clear instructions not to let Peter contact her.

He slammed his fist on the desk in frustration. He had to find a way.

*

Sophie sat in the latest round of early-morning breakfast meetings with her management team at the advertising agency. The news was not good. The two big clients had refused her offer of lower rates and were sticking with their decision to move to the new agency.

Her sales manager had generated some new business, but it was not going to fill the hole made by the big two moving away. Her commercial manager reported positive news on the robustness of the other contracts that were in place, but Sophie knew it was not going to be enough. If they couldn't get more revenue coming in quickly, her business was going to fail. She tasked the sales team to redouble their efforts and set off for PEMS.

When she arrived in the office, her PA told her that Peter had phoned again. She felt so alone. Her father was a closed book and she didn't know if she could confide in Ross. She agonised over Peter's constant attempts to speak to her. Was he genuine? Could he really be the person that could help her out of this living hell?

23

Halle blinked one eye open, the sudden burst of light making her wince. Her mouth was as dry as a desert and her head felt like a herd of wildebeest were stampeding through it. She tried to reorientate herself. Where was she? She forced both eyes open. She wasn't in her flat. She looked under the covers. She was in Todd's bed. Fully clothed. Her inner monologue screamed at her.

What have I done?

A second later, the object of her guilt came bounding through the door to the bedroom. She sat up, pulling the covers up to her neck, trying to hide her embarrassment.

"Morning. I've made you some breakfast in bed."

Halle stared at the tray that Todd was holding. Orange juice, toast and a pot of coffee. It was so normal, like this was an everyday event for him. He put the tray on her lap and she drained the orange juice without saying a word, the sudden hit of vitamin C waking her senses.

She was mortified. Eventually, she formed the words. "My God… did we…? Shit, I'm so sorry…I—"

He cut across her. "Hey. Don't sweat it. Nothing happened here. By the time we had drained that fourth bottle of wine, we were both too wasted to do anything, so I put you to bed."

Halle put her face in her hands. "I'm so sorry. I'm supposed to be your boss. This is so inappropriate."

He smiled. "Look, you had a bad day yesterday and you needed someone to help you chill out. We had a great night, got a bit wasted but nothing has changed here. I was just happy to help. Now eat your breakfast. There are spare towels on the chair for you to have a shower and then you can go home, get changed and we can be in the office by eleven."

Todd left her to it. She poured a coffee and spread a piece of toast with jam. Todd had been amazing but she felt like she had let herself down. A line had been crossed which she may not be able to step back from.

She finished her breakfast, had a quick shower and re-dressed. She went downstairs where Todd was clearing up the breakfast things. He smiled. "Feeling better?"

Halle was about to answer when her phone beeped. She checked the message.

"Oh shit. It's from John. He wants to see me at noon today."

*

Halle did the walk of shame back to her flat. Mercifully, she only lived half a mile from Todd's place, and the walk in the sharp, frosty conditions helped to clear her head.

She whizzed around her flat, changing her clothes and slapping on the make-up to hide the bags under her eyes and the general lifelessness of her skin after last night's binging.

She got to the office at 11.30 am. Todd was in, seemingly coping with the effects of the previous night better than she was. She limited her interactions with him, still consumed with embarrassment. As she let the demons invade her psyche, she remembered there was someone else she needed to apologise to. Clayton. She texted him and asked him to come in and see her at some point in the afternoon. First, she had to get through the meeting with John.

*

Halle had taken some paracetamol, which were mercifully beginning to work on her thumping headache as she waited outside John's office. He called her in, bang on time.

She realised how utterly unprepared she was for the meeting, having no idea what he wanted to talk about. He launched right in, not giving her a second to think any more about it.

"I hear you had some trouble with the residents at the housing estate yesterday."

Halle looked perplexed. How did he know? Who was telling him this stuff?

"Miss Jacobs?"

"Oh… umm, yes… it didn't go well."

"What happened?"

"We… umm, I… decided to tell the residents about our theory that the number of cancer cases in their children might be linked to pollution on the site. My researcher had arranged a testing team to go on site today but as soon as I told them this, it all kicked off. The meeting descended into chaos, the residents started abusing us and streamed out of the hall we were meeting in. It seems like a number of them were so shocked by the possible link to the site that they are making arrangements to move out. It's a disaster."

John rubbed his chin. "What are you going to do about it?"

Halle was like a rabbit in headlights. She had no response.

John stared at her, waiting for a response. When one was not forthcoming, he stood up and turned away from the conversation. The tension was awful. Halle was paralysed. She was just about to speak when John turned around and addressed her.

"Miss Jacobs. Have I made a mistake in appointing you? This sort of situation happens every day in investigative reporting. I thought you were aware of that. You need to confront these challenges and sort them out. If you are going to fall at the first sign of trouble, then maybe you are not cut out for this job."

The speech sparked Halle back to reality. She sat up straight and fixed John with a firm, determined expression. "I'm sorry. Just a bit of first-night nerves. I'm past it and will find a way to sort this out. There is a story here and I'm damn well going to find out what is going on."

A few tense seconds passed before John's face changed from serious to a beaming smile. "There it is. There's the fire I saw at your interview. Resilience, Miss Jacobs. It's the most important skill an investigative reporter has. What we are dealing with here is personal pain and tragedy. People are not going to be nice, they are not going to appreciate people poking about in their lives and they are definitely not going to want to feel exploited by us. You have to build rapport if this is going to fly."

"I know, sir. You can rely on me. We are going to get right back on it."

John nodded. "Oh, I watched the footage that Rod uploaded last night. It's TV gold. You have to find a way for us to be able to use that."

The memory made Halle grimace.

"Something you want to say?"

"Er… yes, actually, I could do with your advice about something."

"Okay, fire away."

"Did the footage capture the racial abuse aimed at Clayton, as people were walking out?"

John shuffled in his chair, seemingly uncomfortable with the question. "Er… yes, but I did warn you this would happen."

Halle was taken aback by his response. "Well, I know, but it doesn't make it right. It was awful and I felt so sorry for him."

John rubbed his chin again, his expression changing back from the light happy persona of a few minutes ago to something more serious. "Is that the story here?"

"Well, no, but…"

"So, concentrate on the actual story. Everything else is peripheral."

John looked away and started tapping at his computer. The conversation was over.

Halle stood up and walked out. Her mind was

spinning. Why did no one seem to care about the racism that Clayton was experiencing? Was this how it felt to be a minority? To have people ignoring your persecution and making excuses for it? Halle had experienced sexism throughout her short career but this was on a different level.

She shook her head and walked back to her office.

24

Peter stood outside the PEMS office. His stomach was rumbling, breakfast a distant memory and no lunch plans. He felt like some lovesick teenager waiting around for a glimpse of his obsession. People started to give him strange looks as he stood on the path staring up at the building. What was he doing? What was his plan? Should he go in? Should he wait to see if she came out for lunch?

His phone beeped, snapping him out of his turmoil. It was Jeremy from PEMS confirming that the work on the Wapping site was starting. Peter rolled his eyes. Nothing changed. They would sort this site out and sell it for another obscene profit.

As he looked up from his phone, he suddenly caught a glimpse of something in the PEMS foyer. He adjusted his position. It was her. Sophie was leaving the building.

This was it. His only chance. He rushed towards the entrance, blocking her way as she exited the building.

Sophie stopped abruptly. "Move out of my way."

"No, you have to listen to me. Something is going on here and we need to talk about it."

Sophie stared at his face, her eyes darting frantically from left to right, trying to read him.

"Please."

Sophie's concentration was broken by one of the security guards. "Are you okay, Miss Parker? Is this gentleman bothering you?"

Sophie looked at the guard, looked back at Peter. A few seconds passed. Peter's expression became more pleading. The security guard went to make a move towards Peter.

Sophie put her arm out to stop him. "No, thank you, Tom. It's all fine here."

The security guard doffed his cap and walked away. Peter exhaled loudly. "Thank you, thank you. Let me buy you some lunch. I'm bloody starving."

The vibe was still tense as they walked up the street trying to find somewhere to eat. Peter kept glancing at Sophie, but she fixed her line of sight straight ahead. He was worried she was going to change her mind and bolt. He saw a little bistro up ahead and guided her quickly inside.

After an uncomfortable few minutes, the food was ordered and they sat opposite each other, neither saying a word. Sophie broke the tension.

"Okay, you've got me here. What do you want?"

"I want to know what's going on. We were having a lovely time the other night and you just stormed off with no explanation. You've ignored all my subsequent attempts to find out why you left and since then, my brothers and uncle have been acting strange, talking about you like war has been declared between our two firms."

Sophie did the darting-eye thing again. "How do I know I can trust you?"

"I'm not like them. Whatever they are doing to you, I know nothing about it."

Sophie took a swig of the orange juice she had ordered. "You're a good actor. You play the innocent downtrodden brother role really well. I fell for it the other night until that text came in and showed me what your family is really about."

Peter was becoming desperate. "I don't know what to say. I know my family are doing something to you but I have no idea what it is. I promise you. I don't know what else to say to you."

The food arrived and Sophie started to eat. Eventually, she spoke again.

"Okay, if I'm stupid enough to even contemplate trusting you, tell me everything that your brothers and uncle have said to you since our evening out and I will see if I am prepared to reciprocate."

Peter tucked into his BLT and started to talk in between mouthfuls.

"Okay, the morning after our meal, Edward came into my office all arrogant and superior, asking me if I was having a bad day. I dismissed it but he just left my office laughing. Never a good thing, which means he thinks he has the upper hand on something. When you shouted at me on your doorstep the following evening, you mentioned something about us sabotaging your business. The next morning, Edward storms into my office asking why you haven't signed off the work order for the Wapping site. It was then I got the impression he felt you were doing it as a retaliatory action for something he had done. I started to try and piece this together and concluded he must be interfering in your business somehow. I promise I have no idea what he is doing."

Peter had hardly taken a breath as he blurted it all out. By the end, Sophie's expression had softened.

"You've had the work order, though. So, what's his problem?"

"Actually, that's true. He was bouncing around this morning telling me the order had been placed and to get on with the work. Jeremy just texted me to say he has started work on the project today."

Sophie almost cracked a smile as she pursed her lips and nodded. "Okay, here's the deal. If you are serious about helping me, then you are all in. Your loyalties must be solely to our relationship and you must do everything I say."

"Er… fine. I'm sick of my bloody family. It's time to do the right thing."

Sophie smiled and looked at her watch. "I've gotta get back for a meeting, Peter. Come round my place tonight around 7.30 pm and we'll talk some more. In the meantime, carry on doing what you are doing at ALMS and don't let your brothers or uncle suspect anything is going on. Can you do that, Peter? Can you do that for me?"

25

It was late afternoon as Halle sat in her office with Todd. She had seen Clayton and apologised to him for her inappropriate actions. He had accepted her apology with good grace and given her one of his big teddy bear hugs, which just made her feel worse. Todd was being his usual bouncy self, not seeming to have any hang-ups about what they did the previous evening.

"Right, boss lady. Let's get back to it. Tell me about your meeting with John."

Halle grimaced. "To be honest, he gave me a massive kick up the arse. Asked me if he had made a mistake in appointing me. I think I just about rode it out."

"Good. You know you were made for this job."

Halle allowed herself to laugh, breaking the gut-tightening stress she had felt since she had woken up in Todd's bed that morning. Todd always seemed to know what she needed.

"Okay, we need to refocus and get this thing back on track. Tell me what you have done over the last twenty-four hours, and then I'm going to ring Jen Wyatt."

"Right, let me start with my work on the three companies involved in that site. I managed to track down the guy that ran FZX Homes. They aren't trading anymore and he is now running an import/export business. He seemed like a bit of a Del Boy character but was happy to talk to me about the site. He bought it from ALMS for £28 million, built the houses and made a tidy profit. He said the site was clear when they started building, all the permits were in place and they had no issues with residual pollution during the entire construction phase. Once they finished, they left each resident with a National House Building Council contract for any subsequent maintenance issues."

"Okay, so doesn't sound like our story is with them."

"No, I agree. I think these other two firms are much more interesting. Firstly, both these firms were set up in the mid '70s. Parker Environmental Management Services was set up by Bill Parker and developed a long-standing business relationship with Allcock Land Management Services, which was set up by Edward Allcock Snr. It seems that PEMS have done all the environmental studies on ALMS' brownfield site acquisitions for the last forty-odd years, as well as implementing the remediation plans to make the sites safe. For their part, ALMS put up the capital to find and purchase the sites, selling them off to developers once the sites are clean and all the relevant permits are in place."

"A nice cosy relationship, but where's the story?"

Todd smiled. "Well, in the late '80s, Edward Allcock Snr was murdered by his wife, Victoria. She pleaded clemency on the basis of years of physical and mental abuse, but the jury was having none of it. She is about thirty years into a life sentence."

Halle put her hand to her mouth. "Oh my God. What happened with the firm?"

"The Allcocks have five boys but they were all still kids when this happened. It seems their uncle took over the running of the business and is still there as chairman. Once the boys were old enough, they took over the running of the firm, and the oldest son, Edward Allcock Jnr, is now the CEO. The death didn't seem to affect the firm. They turn over around £750 million every year, by buying greenfield and brownfield sites, selling each one for a large profit. They only seem to work with PEMS on the brownfield sites. With the amount of money they make each year, they must all be multi-millionaires."

Halle's brain was spinning with all the new information. "My God, we always say that where there's money, there's a story. Can we get to the mother?"

"I don't know. We would have to make an application to the prison warden to see if they would grant us visiting rights. I do agree, though, she seems like she could be a really interesting subplot to this story."

"What about this Parkers firm?"

"Again, an interesting story. They are a much smaller outfit than ALMS and seem to rely heavily on the contract with them for a good proportion of their revenue. It seems until recently, Bill Parker ran that business pretty much on his own, overseeing everything and running a tight ship. He recently had to hand the firm over to his children, Ross and Sophie Parker, due to ill health."

"Interesting. I definitely think these two firms are where the story might be. Do you think we should front this out and go and talk to them both?"

"Hmm, I dunno. I think there is more digging here before we expose what we are doing."

"Okay, I agree. Do some more research and let me know what you find. Approach the prison to see whether we can get to the mother. In the meantime, I'm going to ring Jen Wyatt. I need to sort out this mess I created or we have no story."

Todd left her to it and she was relieved to have some time to herself. The blowout the previous evening, the awkwardness of waking up in Todd's bed, the dressing-down from John and having to apologise to Clayton had drained her mentally and physically. She really just wanted to go home, drink a hot cup of cocoa and curl up in bed.

She nipped to the washrooms and splashed her face with water. If she was true to what she said to John, she had to knuckle down and power through this difficult start to her investigative career.

She got back to her office and dialled Jen Wyatt's number.

The phone seemed to ring for a long while, making Halle think that Jen had joined the throngs of people leaving the estate. As she was about to give it up, a quiet voice said hello.

"Hello, is that Jen? It's Halle Jacobs from Goldwin Productions."

There was silence bar the faint sound of someone breathing.

"Hello. Jen."

"What do you want?"

"I wanted to apologise. I misjudged the mood of the residents. I didn't mean to spook them."

"Well, your apology don't mean shit. After your little performance yesterday, I'm a bloody pariah. Everyone's blaming me for bringing you into our community and frightening them to death. I've been ostracised. No one will speak to me unless it's to shout some abuse or other. Everyone else has just upped and left the site."

Halle couldn't help but feel a sense of balance when hearing what Jen had said. *Maybe you know what Clayton feels like,* she thought to herself.

She quickly shook it off. "Look, whether you accept my apology or not, I'm sure there is still a story here. I know I messed up big time, but the only way I can sort this out is with your help."

"I don't want nothing to do with you. As if my life wasn't shit enough already, you go and make me enemy number one in my own neighbourhood. Just fucking leave me alone."

"But, please let me help you. Think of your son. You have to get justice for him."

The pitch didn't work. Jen disconnected the call.

Halle put her phone down and placed her head in her hands. "Fuck!"

26

Edward, Andrew and James sat in the boardroom. Edward spat out what was on everyone's mind. "Why have we suddenly got that work order? Has Ross suddenly got some balls or is that woman playing us?"

James responded first. "I'm not sure. I spoke to Ross and he seemed surprised we hadn't already had it. He didn't mention any problems with Sophie."

"What about Peter? I'm sure that little shit is trying to get into her pants. Is he going to betray us like he has with Mother?"

"Don't worry about him. He's a lightweight. He's not got the best track record with women and, from the business side, Jeremy will keep feeding him all he needs to know about progress on the projects. We can keep him in blissful ignorance."

"I dunno. You need to keep an eye on him as well."

"I will, Edward. Don't worry about it."

Edward was still agitated and quickly turned his attention to his brother.

"What about our little intervention in her business, Andrew?"

"I've spoken to the advertising agency we are using

as a front and they say her two biggest clients are still committed to moving to them. It seems Sophie offered to match the new rates we offered them, but our financial compensation package persuaded them it was not a good idea."

"Okay, but I can't see her just rolling over. What else is she up to?"

"I don't know. From all accounts, she seems to be taking this in her stride."

Edward stood up and paced around the room. "I don't like this. If it was me, I'd be all over this like a rash. Why is she being so impassive? Are we worrying about her unnecessarily? Is Ross in full control of PEMS so we don't need to worry about her interference?"

Andrew was shaking his head. "I think we do need to worry about her. If she starts digging around our projects, there's no telling what she might uncover."

"What the hell? Bill Parker assured me that Jeremy would have complete control over our projects and that Ross and Sophie would not interfere."

"Well, she ain't listening. That woman is trouble. We need to take her out of the picture."

Edward looked at his uncle. "What do you think?"

"What would your father have done?"

Edward smiled and nodded his understanding. "He would have silenced her for good."

27

Peter drove up to Sophie's place, his gut churning with nervous excitement. He had spent a ridiculous amount of time getting ready, trying on outfit after outfit, each one seeming wrong for different reasons. He had finally settled on a plain blue shirt, black jeans and a leather jacket. He had primped his hair to within an inch of its life and splashed a subtle amount of cologne on his neck. He blew into his hand, trying to smell his breath. It seemed fine.

He sat in the car a few yards away from her house. What was she expecting of him? Would she be up for... he batted the thought away. He had to play this cool. He had finally got her attention and he couldn't blow it by having unrealistic expectations of what might happen.

He finally plucked up the courage to get out of the car and walked up to her door. It was just gone 7.30 pm.

Sophie opened the door, greeting Peter with a pained smile. Once again, she looked effortlessly elegant in a shift dress that celebrated her curves. Peter tried not to stare but he realised in that moment how much he fancied Sophie. He had been enchanted by her since the first minute they met, and his infatuation was not helped by being in such close proximity to her, and in that dress.

Peter tried desperately to control his growing erection as she invited him into the living room. Sophie noticed the strange walk he was doing. "Are you okay? You seem to be walking funny."

Peter tried not to blush. "Oh, it's nothing. Just an old sports injury playing up."

"Wine?"

Peter wanted to say no. Alcohol was going to make this situation worse but he had to keep her on side.

"That would be lovely."

She beckoned for him to sit at one end of the sofa. She poured the wine and sat at the other end. She fixed her stare on Peter. "I'm trusting you, Peter, because I have nowhere else to turn. There is something going on between our two firms and I'm damn well going to find out what it is."

"Okay, how can I help?"

"What do you know about the two biggest clients at my advertising agency suddenly moving to another firm?"

Peter pulled a confused expression. "Er, nothing. What has that got to do with our business relationship?"

"I'm pretty sure your brothers are responsible."

"Eh, how?"

"A few days after I went to the Wapping site to meet Andrew and find out a bit more about the project, I suddenly get notified that both my biggest advertising agency clients are moving to some tin-pot agency that is offering them significantly lower rates."

"So, what makes you think my brothers are involved?"

"Andrew was less than civil when I mentioned I wanted to oversee the Wapping project, to help me learn about

126

the PEMS business. He accused me of interfering and told me my father had insisted that Jeremy was in complete control and did not need Ross or I to get involved in any of the ALMS projects. It can't be a coincidence that a few days later, someone is trying to sabotage my business."

Peter mused on what Sophie had said. "I don't know anything about it, but it does sound like the sort of thing that Edward and Andrew might do. Did you get the notification when we were in the restaurant? Is that why you stormed out?"

"Yes."

Peter nodded his head. "I must admit that does make sense now. I told you that Edward was all smug one morning asking about my day and cackling at some private joke he was having with himself. I reckon that may have been linked to what you were saying. The odd thing is that he was back in my office a couple of days later berating me for not getting the work order off you. When I mentioned your name, I noticed a subtle look between Edward, Andrew and my uncle. There was some unspoken secret that was passing between them. If what you say is right, I reckon they were worried you knew it was them and were retaliating."

"I did speak to Ross but he just dismissed it. Said your account was too important to us to make any waves."

"Is that why we suddenly got the work order?"

"Yes. I decided I had to make out our business relationship was carrying on as normal so as not to raise their suspicions."

Peter blew out his cheeks. "Bloody hell. If this is all true, this is so messed up. What do they think they are going to achieve by sabotaging your other business?"

"I think it's a perverse attempt to keep me busy so I don't get involved in our projects."

"Is it working?"

"No, it bloody well isn't. I've got my leadership team at the advertising agency working on a recovery plan and I am still fully committed to PEMS, even if I have to work eighteen-hour days."

There was a brief pause in the conversation as they both tried to process the opening salvos in this new phase of their relationship. Sophie leant over to fill up Peter's wine glass, giving him a short flash of cleavage. It didn't help the constant stirrings in his trousers.

"So, tell me more about your brothers and uncle."

"Well, my uncle took over the running of the business when my father died…"

"…Was murdered by your mother."

"Yes, after my father was murdered, Uncle ran the business until we were old enough to join the management team. Edward became CEO, Uncle is now the chairman and Andrew is deputy CEO."

"What about the rest of you?"

"I'm in charge of project delivery, Philip looks after finance and Stephen runs the office."

"But you don't really have any power."

Peter grimaced at the comment but knew she was right. "We all attend the monthly board meetings but, you are probably right, the power sits with those three. I don't think Philip and Stephen are involved in any of the really big stuff, but they are intensely loyal to Edward and the legacy of my father. I'm the black sheep because I'm the only one that thinks my mother was wrongly convicted."

"Why do you think that?"

"My father was a violent, abusive man. The police took no notice of her testimony but I can tell you she was beaten and sexually assaulted by him on a daily basis."

"That's terrible. Did she ever try to appeal her sentence?"

"No, and she won't tell the parole board what they need to hear to let her out early."

The room fell silent again as they continued to process the new information they were gleaning from this new spirit of co-operation. Sophie's mood seemed to have relaxed and she launched back into the conversation.

"There's something else we need to talk about. What do you know about the detail of our projects?"

"In what respect?"

"How much do you know about the remediation plans?"

"Er, well, once Jeremy's team has done the environmental study, we get a report from you outlining any pollutants that need to be dealt with before the site can be made ready for sale to developers. The remediation proposal is always part of that paperwork."

"Okay, but have you realised that the remediation plans are all pretty much the same? I have been looking through about five years of our projects and the same remediation proposals are made in every one."

"Why do you see that as a problem? I just assume this is the standard approach to dealing with pollutants, and it clearly works because we have made millions selling off sites after the work your team has done."

"I'm not convinced. I trawled the internet for advice

on remediation and I found one article in particular that suggested this is not a one-size-fits-all business."

Peter flinched as Sophie spoke. "What is it?"

"You know, I really hadn't paid too much attention to the detail before. Jeremy always seems to have such a firm grip on it and I can coast along taking all the plaudits for each successful project that is delivered. But I did query the report about the Wapping site with Andrew because the levels of pollutants on that site seem exponentially bigger than anything I've seen before."

"And what did he say?"

"He told me not to worry about it."

Sophie stood up and started to pace around. "You see. Andrew is shutting you down and Jeremy must be involved as well. My father keeps shutting me down every time I ask a question about the ALMS projects, telling me to leave it all to Jeremy."

"Okay, let's say I believe you that something is going on here. What exactly do you think they are up to?"

"I don't know. I haven't worked that out yet but there is one more strange thing I found."

"What?"

"I looked at the financial breakdown on each of the ALMS projects. Generally, there are payments being made to the contractors that clear the site, clean it up and do the clay barrier work, but there is also a payment to an account called Bill Parker Holdings. I confronted my father about it and he told me it was the R&D account."

"Eh, that sounds odd."

"Exactly, and once again he shut me down by saying Jeremy had complete control over it. I don't understand why hundreds of thousands of pounds are being syphoned off outside of Ross' and my control."

Peter's body language gave away what he was thinking. "Peter?"

He looked at Sophie; the stress of years and years of playing patsy to his brothers spilled out of him in that moment. "Having seen the way my brothers operate, that can only mean one thing. I have a horrible feeling that money is being used to give a few backhanders."

28

Halle was in the office by 7.30 am. She'd hardly slept, agonising over her phone call with Jen Wyatt. How had she got it so wrong? She was determined to find a solution. She had to. Despite John's kind words at the end of their last conversation, she knew he would be watching her every move. She sipped at her steaming hot green tea and looked out of the window. Thinking.

She must have been staring out of the window longer than she thought because Todd was standing in the doorway as she heard the local church bell strike eight.

She swivelled round to face him and started speaking before he had a chance to say good morning. "That testing firm you had lined up. What's to stop them going onsite and collecting samples?"

Todd was taken aback by her abruptness but let it slide. "Well, nothing, I guess. They won't be able to enter the private residences without permission, which I assume we are not going to get at the moment, but that doesn't stop them collecting samples from the public areas of the site."

"Good. Get them over there. Tell them to be discreet but get it done quickly. I want to know the results as soon as they get them."

Todd had rarely seen Halle so focused, and decided to ride the wave with her. "Okay, boss lady. Consider it done. Anything else?"

"Yes, crack on with your research about PEMS and ALMS. Find those skeletons."

Halle swivelled her chair back to look at the view. The conversation with Todd was over and he left the room. As she stared out of the window, the problem of Jen Wyatt played through her mind. As she watched the bustle of rush hour gather pace, she spotted something. An advert for a charity on one of the billboards. "My God, that's it. That's how I can get Jen back onside."

She picked up her phone and dialled Jen's number. The butterflies were back. Jen answered after a couple of rings.

"Jen. It's Halle Jacobs."

"I told you I don't want to talk to you."

"Please. Hear me out. I know I have royally messed up, but I have an idea how to make it right."

There was an agonising pause as Jen didn't respond. Halle let the silence hang.

"Okay, I'm listening."

Halle punched the air. "By way of an apology for my actions, I want to set up a charitable trust in your son's memory. We'll set the trust up with a donation of £10,000 and you can decide where that money goes. We will help you promote the trust so we can get more donations. You may want to give some of the money to research into childhood cancers."

Halle winced as she waited for Jen's response. She had made two bad judgement calls with this investigation. She hoped this wasn't three for three.

The silences were killing her, but the fact that Jen was still on the line was a good sign. At least it meant she was considering Halle's pitch.

"What do you want in return?"

Halle tried to stifle the excitement in her voice. "There's just one thing. Will you let our testing team come onto your property and take some soil and water samples?"

"Yes, okay. Can you get them over here this afternoon?"

"Absolutely!"

Halle finished the call and bounded out to Todd. "I've done it. I've solved our Jen Wyatt problem. I'm gonna set up a charitable trust in honour of her son and start it off with a ten-grand donation. In return, she has agreed to let the testing team onto her property, but they need to go this afternoon."

"That's fine. I had already asked them to do the work today. I'll let them know they can extend their work to Jen Wyatt's place."

"Oh, and get Rod over there to film them whilst they are doing the testing. We desperately need to get some more footage, or we won't have enough in the can to fill an advert slot!"

Halle walked back into her office, once again staring at the view out of the office window. She allowed herself a fist pump.

Come on, girl, she thought to herself. *You're back in the game.*

*

Victoria Allcock paced around the outer yard, the same routine for the last thirty years. An hour's outdoor exercise in the featureless space, all walls and wire fencing, overseen by uninterested screws. It was a chance to see the sky but not much else. In her childhood, she would spend hours in the woods, watching nature, breathing in the fresh air and picking wildflowers to take back to her mother. It was a long-distant memory and one she was never sure she would experience again.

The weather was mercifully dry but cold. She pulled her coat tight around her and sat on the cold bench. "Y'all right, Vic?"

She looked up. It was Dolores, her best friend in this stinking shithole. They had bonded over their sentences, both killing their abusive husbands in final acts of desperation. They healed their mental and physical wounds by spending hours talking about their experiences. Victoria loved the irony that Dolores was a bold, confident woman proud of her Jamaican heritage, a person that Edward would have objected to her seeing on account of his abhorrent views on foreigners and women. It was one of Victoria's greatest regrets that killing Edward had alienated her sons and led them to become mirror images of their father with his bigoted views, inflammatory language and hatred for women. Peter was the only one who hadn't been completely moulded into an Edward Allcock clone.

She took a drag on her cigarette and smiled at Dolores. "What should I do, D? I need to get out of here, but I can't bring myself to tell that parole board what they want to hear."

"I hear you, girlfriend, but what is a few dishonest words against the chance to live the rest of our lives outside this nightmare? I did it. I just went on autopilot and told them what I knew they wanted to hear and now, in a few weeks' time, I am going to see my gorgeous granddaughter for the first time."

Victoria shook her head. "I dunno. If I say those words, it's like he wins all over again. Like I'm admitting that I deserved to be stuck in this hell for the last thirty years. I just can't do it."

Dolores stood up. "Well, that's your choice, Vic, but you is still young. You still has a chance at a life outside. I would think long and hard about that before you commit yourself to more time in here."

As Dolores walked away, Victoria stared at the sky, a lone seagull circling the compound and screeching its eerie call every so often. A metaphor for how Victoria felt every day.

The arguments for and against raged around her brain. The opportunity to tell someone what she knew about Bill Parker's and Edward's business practices was urging her on. With Bill out of the way, there was nothing stopping her talking to his daughter, but she could only do that if she was outside these walls. Was it enough, though? Was it enough to justify telling those bastards on the parole board that she was 'sorry' and 'full of remorse' for what she had done? The thought made bile stick in her throat.

As she finished her cigarette, she flicked the stub on the floor and thrust both hands back in her coat. As she did, she felt something stuck at the bottom of the pocket and fished it out.

It was an old crumpled picture, long since forgotten. The memory threatened to overwhelm her as tears welled up in her eyes. Maybe this was the reason she needed to get out of here.

29

Sophie was back in the PEMS office after another early breakfast meeting with her advertising agency leadership team. Progress was slow in recovering from the loss of her two biggest clients, but they were making inroads and she was confident they could ride it out.

She found it hard to concentrate on anything in that meeting. Peter's suggestion that the so-called R&D fund that Jeremy was in control of could be a front for giving people backhanders had blown her mind. If Peter was right, who were they paying off and for what reason? The gut-wrenching feeling of loneliness consumed her once again. She didn't feel she could tell Ross about this stuff and she was convinced her father was the chief architect of whatever this was. If she confronted Jeremy, she would play her hand too early. She needed someone that could look into this without being detected. She was okay at the internet stuff but was way off having the skills to find what was needed in the darker holes of the World Wide Web. She needed a technical expert.

*

After the breakthrough with Jen Wyatt, Halle had gone home the previous evening and slept for twelve hours straight. Now, she was back in the office, full of nervous excitement, desperate for news on the soil and water tests on the Pickford housing estate.

As soon as Todd came through the door, she was on him. "Did we get them? The results."

Todd looked bleary-eyed and less than enamoured at Halle's early-morning energy. "Whoa, whoa, boss lady. Let's get a coffee inside us before we even begin to think about work. You need to let my poor embattled laptop boot up first."

Halle stood there with hands on her hips like some spoilt child, playing up to the cliché by letting out an indignant huff and stomping back into her office.

Ten minutes later, Todd brought Halle a coffee. She looked up expectantly. "Nothing yet. Sorry. I've sent them a message."

"I need this. I need them to find something to cement this story."

"I know, I know. I'll let you know as soon as they come in."

Halle impatiently tapped away at her phone, doing nothing in particular. The waiting was killing her. She called Todd back in.

"Have you found anything else on PEMS or ALMS?"

"No, nothing that flags up any obvious alarm bells. I have had a look at the public documentation on both companies. ALMS is a monster, regularly turning over around £750 million annually, usually clearing £30 or £40 million profit a year. PEMS is much smaller, turning over between 20 and 30 million a year with modest profits of between 1 and 2 mill a year. They both seem to file their company accounts and VAT returns on time and have clean audit inspections of their finances."

"Is that normal?"

"Well, normal in the sense that any company that doesn't want too much external scrutiny by the revenue or customs and excise will be anal about keeping within the rules."

"What about the documentation on these sites they develop?"

"At the moment, I have been searching the stuff in the public domain and I can find records of several land purchases by ALMS and subsequent sales to developers. They do a mixture of greenfield and brownfield site acquisitions, working with PEMS on the brownfield ones only. On average, they seem to make between three and five times what it costs them to buy."

"Bloody hell, no wonder they are raking it in."

"Yeah, there's no doubt they are very successful at what they do."

"What about PEMS?"

"Again, the public domain documentation that is registered with the relevant local authorities shows PEMS' work on the environmental studies, the remediation plans for each brownfield site and their involvement in securing the development permits."

"This ain't exactly rocking my boat."

"No, and I didn't really expect anything else. If there are any skeletons to find, we ain't gonna find them in the public domain."

"So, go deeper. Do what we always do."

"As long as you're sure. If you condone me bending the law, there's no deniability on your part if the shit hits the fan."

"I'm not worried about that. We go full pelt on this. Whatever it takes."

They both sat for a moment, the adrenalin beginning to flow as they both felt the excitement of the chase. It's what they had been trained for. Finding the story and exposing the criminals.

As Todd began to leave, Halle threw more at him. "Oh, what about the Allcock mother?"

"I've emailed the prison asking if we can go and visit her. I don't suppose the response will be quick, but I will let you know as soon as we get something."

Halle stood looking out of the window for the umpteenth time that morning. Why did it feel like they were waiting on every avenue of their investigation? They were pumped up and ready. The waiting was killing her.

She wasn't sure how long she had been idly staring at the bustle of people going about their business on the street below, or watching the strange mating ritual of a pigeon bowing at its partner as it tried to get a shag, but her daydreaming was broken by Todd rushing into her office.

"We've got them. They've just emailed the results from the housing estate."

Todd quickly plonked his laptop on Halle's desk and they both held their breath as he clicked on the attachment on the email. They both read the text frantically. Within seconds, they both looked at each other, stunned by what they had read. Halle blurted out what they were both thinking.

"What the hell is this? These results can't be right."

30

Peter was finding it hard to concentrate on what he was doing. The revelation from Sophie the other evening had floored him. Could PEMS really be in the business of giving backhanders? Were ALMS involved?

Every time he saw the smug, arrogant expressions of Edward or Andrew, he knew the answer to that question. If there was something going on, you could bet that they were somehow pulling the strings. He hadn't wanted to consider the possibilities but had thought about little else.

It had always amazed him how smooth every project with PEMS had gone. His role in monitoring progress on these projects had always been a breeze and he had been grateful for that. But therein lay the problem. Project management was notoriously difficult. So, either Jeremy was the best project manager the world had ever seen, knocking down every hurdle that he faced, or there was something else at play here.

Peter realised this situation had been going on for as long as he could remember. He had been in this role for nearly fifteen years and he couldn't remember ever having any significant issues with the PEMS projects. The stark reality of the situation hit him. He put his hand to his mouth. How could he have been so naïve? He was a stool pigeon. Edward had put him in a role where he knew he couldn't do any damage, which meant ALMS were well and truly involved.

The possibilities were raging around Peter's head. If Sophie was right, Jeremy was the chief protagonist at PEMS and he had to be working with Edward or Andrew on whatever scams they were pulling. The problem was that every part of the business transaction seemed to be above board. All the documentation was in place and registered with the relevant authorities, thereby allowing the development permits to be issued. Neat and tidy. A clean, repeatable process.

Peter couldn't reconcile it. As he agonised over the possibilities, another thought came to him. If there was something going on, how far back did this go? Was this Edward Jnr's doing or did this start with his father?

Peter stood up, grabbed his coat and left the office. He needed some air. The realisation that something sinister could be going on right under his nose brought the dark thoughts flooding back. He stifled back tears. The possibility that this thing was initiated by his father made it worse. There was only one other person he could speak to about this.

He called the prison. He needed to speak to his mother.

*

Sophie walked into the IT office, trying to seem casual, like she was doing some management walkabout to inspire the troops. She tried some small talk as they eyed her suspiciously, all the time trying to suss out whether she could persuade one of them to do some extra-curricular activity.

The team were all relatively new and she wasn't sure how loyal they were to her father. The trust question was killing her. Everywhere she turned, she was seeing danger, suspicious of everyone and everything.

She made her excuses and left. It didn't feel right.

*

Halle and Todd read the report over and over again. The team had managed to secure soil samples from ten points around the housing estate, including Jen Wyatt's garden. All the samples showed some residual evidence of pollutants but not enough to breach safety standards. The one water sample they had collected from Jen's place was also within safety ranges.

"This doesn't ring true. Our story is premised on this site being polluted. I don't understand it."

"I dunno what to say. This company is one of the leading firms in their field. We have to trust that their results are correct."

Halle spread out the large site map of the housing estate on her desk, plotting where they had taken the samples. They had managed to do a decent job of collecting samples from across the site and by all accounts had not run into too much hostility from the residents.

Halle couldn't deny that this seemed like a statistically

valid piece of work, but the conspiracy worm kept burrowing away in her brain. She was sure that pollution was playing a part in all these children getting cancer. She just had to find the evidence.

31

It was early evening as Sophie began the short commute from her office to home. Her head was spinning with the stress of the situation. She was trusting Peter. She had to. There was no one else in her corner. No one else she felt she could trust. He was coming over later so they could talk some more.

As she continued to drive home, she noticed a dark saloon car with tinted windows was driving up close to her bumper, aggressive and impatient. She looked in the mirror. The driver's face was obscured by the glass. She sped up to try to create a gap but the car just kept driving erratically, speeding up to the back of her car, slamming on the brakes and then repeating the process.

She quickly dialled her home number, leaving a message for herself that contained the number plate of the car. The intimidating situation carried on for another mile until the turn that led into her close appeared on the left. She indicated, heart in mouth. What would she do if the car followed her?

She made the manoeuvre. The car sped straight on. She exhaled deeply.

She entered her house and poured a glass of wine to

calm her nerves. A second later, her doorbell rang and she jumped out of her skin. Fear gripped her. She quickly got the video doorbell app up on her phone. It was Peter. He was early.

She opened the door, her face as white as a sheet. "My God, are you okay? You look like you've seen a ghost."

She manhandled Peter inside, quickly scanning the close as she did so. There was no one else out there.

Peter repeated his enquiry. "Are you okay?"

They both sat down on the sofa. "It's nothing. I'm just a bit jumpy. I had one of those boy racers up my arse as I was driving home. He kept tailgating me. It was really intimidating. I've got his number plate. Maybe I should report it to the police."

"Yeah, maybe you sh…"

Peter's sentence tailed off, unfinished as he stared ahead, his brain in overdrive.

"Peter?"

"Oh, sorry, it's just a bit odd that this happens on top of everything else. I haven't found a lot out today, but the one thing that I couldn't shake all day is the stark realisation that Edward and Andrew will stop at nothing to protect the business. You need to be careful. I'm worried that was no coincidence."

Sophie bowed her head, trying to stifle the tears. What on earth had she got herself into? She looked up at Peter, his care for her seemingly genuine. She had to trust him; she had no one else.

She wasn't sure whether it was her heightened emotional state or the amusing recollection of the previous evening when Peter was trying his best to disguise his troublesome erection, but she stood up, unzipped her dress and let it fall to the floor.

*

Todd walked into his spare room. The technology hub that was the real reason he was so good at his job. He played the part of the geeky researcher with his company laptop whilst he was at work, but it was the set-up at home that really delivered results.

Multiple laptops, CPUs, screens and backup drives littered the room. Huge processing power at his fingertips to reach the darkest parts of the internet and hack into almost anywhere he wanted to go.

The company never really questioned where he got some of the stuff. As long as it was true, they were happy to use it.

His real speciality was hacking banks. So many of the conspiracies played up to the cliché that you would find the skeletons if you followed the money.

He was also an active member of Proton, a self-sustaining group of like-minded hackers that helped each other out. No names, no identities, just good old hackers supporting each other in getting results.

He logged on to speak to his best mate on the site – a legendary hacker called Krypto, who had gained national notoriety when he helped crack the 'cash for babies' scandal a few years back. Krypto was great at tracking people and what they were up to.

He typed in his username. SNAPDEVIL

32

Halle tried to watch some TV as she wolfed down a microwave lasagne, but her mind couldn't shake the latest knockback. Why didn't those results vindicate her theory? What else could explain so many childhood cancers? There was no way this could be bad luck. That just didn't make sense.

She agonised over how she was going to explain to John that she had committed ten grand of her budget to a charitable trust for Jen Wyatt's son. She had seen it as an investment in the investigation, securing Jen's support and giving them access to her premises so they could prove their theory. But it hadn't worked and she had wasted the money on a calculated gamble. The guilt continued to come in waves. In her desperation to get Jen on side, she hadn't even considered Clayton's feelings in all this. Jen's latent racism still bothered Halle and she felt powerless to do anything about it. Halle screamed at no one in particular. Why was she messing up at every turn?

She wallowed in self-pity for a while but eventually the memory of John's words refocused her. She had to find a way forward. John made it clear that she had to be resilient, confront every problem and find a solution.

She had given Todd the green light to do whatever was necessary to find some dirt. All the researchers bent the rules when it came to finding what they needed to know in the darker reaches of the internet and by all accounts, Todd was one of the best. She prayed he would deliver.

She cycled through the other lines of enquiry. The Allcock mother was an intriguing subplot. She would follow up Todd's email to the prison warden and see if they could get in and see her.

Approaching ALMS and PEMS before they knew what they were dealing with was a dangerous move, but she tried to balance up the risks and rewards. Of the two firms, PEMS seemed like the better option. The retirement of Bill Parker might present an opportunity to speak to one of the children. She grabbed her phone and searched *Sophie Parker*. There were lots of articles about her and Ross taking over the PEMS business but also a few references to her role as the owner of Parker's Advertising Agency. A quick search found them to be a mid-range player in a competitive market. By all accounts, she was an astute businesswoman. By comparison, Ross seemed to have been nurtured to take over the business, having spent all his working career at PEMS in various roles until his appointment as CEO when Bill Parker retired. Halle winced at more evidence of the patriarchy at work.

As the exhaustion of the day started to take its toll, Halle decided to grab an early night. Her instincts were telling her that approaching Sophie Parker was a calculated gamble. She just hoped this one paid off.

*

Sophie and Peter lay on the sofa, their naked bodies entwined in the glow of the frantic, satisfying sex that had just occurred.

Peter was shocked at the suddenness of the encounter, but Sophie dropping her dress and revealing sexy black lingerie had immediately dispelled any doubts. He was hard in seconds and she was on him, rocking her hips back and forward in a trance-like state until they both came with shuddering ecstasy.

He looked at her. "Well, that was nice. Does that mean we are proper friends now?"

Sophie sat up. The sight of her firm breasts made Peter hard all over again. She looked down at his erection.

"Well, someone recovers fast." She mounted him again.

*

Peter stirred. The post-sex sleep had been inevitable and he was disorientated as he tried to work out how long he'd been out. He heard movement in the kitchen. Sophie walked back into the living room with a cup of coffee for him.

He sat up. "Oh. You put your clothes back on. How disappointing."

Sophie handed him the coffee and gave an embarrassed smile. "I'm sorry about that. I don't know what came over me. I guess I just needed some comfort."

"Hey, I ain't complaining."

"Look, get dressed. We need to talk."

Peter gave a pouty, disappointed expression but did as he was told.

They sat back on the sofa and drank their coffee. Sophie launched in.

"I'm convinced the answer to whatever is going on lies with that so-called R&D account. I need to find a way to review the transactions in and out of that account, but unless I confront Jeremy about it directly, I'm not sure how I would do this. I need someone that can access it discreetly."

"What, like a hacker?"

"Yeh, I guess so. I did go down to our IT department to see if I could recruit one of them to help me but when I spoke to them, it didn't feel right. I just don't know them well enough to trust them with something so important."

"I don't know anybody. How would we find someone like that?"

"I have no idea. This is so bloody frustrating."

"I haven't done much at my end but I do have access to all the project paperwork between our firms. It's reasonable for me to take a look at it in more detail without raising too much suspicion. If I talk to Philip about the finances from our end, I might be able to find something."

"We have to start digging at both ends, but I fear this stuff is not going to be out in the open for anyone to find. If this thing is as bad as we think it might be, it's all going to be hidden."

"Look, my IT skills are pretty good. I'm sure I can search through our servers to find something. We have an ultra-secure space where all the confidential company information is kept. That has to be the place to start."

"Do what you can. I need to know what is going on here."

Todd started typing.

SNAPDEVIL: Yo, Krypto, need your help

KRYPTO: Always on it

SNAPDEVIL: Have another live one

KRYPTO: Cool, been a while

SNAPDEVIL: I know. Usual suspects

KRYPTO: Ooh, don't tease me. Greedy bastards, I'm
    guessing

SNAPDEVIL: Looks like it. Gonna do the bank thing.
    Can you do the people thing

KRYPTO: Sure. Put the brief in the usual place

SNAPDEVIL: There in five

33

Halle almost spilled her coffee as she read the first email of the day. The prison had come through. She had been allocated the next available visitors' slot to see Victoria Allcock. As she rewarded herself with a little sit-down jig, Todd walked into her office.

"Someone's happy. What's up?"

"Finally, something is going our way. The prison has granted us access to see Victoria Allcock, in two days' time."

"Wow, that was quick. We must have struck lucky with the visiting times. She can't have too many visitors if that slot was available at short notice."

"Hmm, yes, that's interesting in itself. What have you been up to?"

"I spent last night setting up the tools to do a deep dive into the financial transactions around these firms. I also procured some help from one of the best people I know to look into the Allcocks and the Parkers. He's one of the best at finding people's dirty secrets."

"I'm assuming I don't need to know who this person is and how you two are going about finding the dirt."

"I think best if you don't."

Halle smiled and nodded. "No problem. Whatever it takes."

Todd hung around, waiting to see if Halle had any more for him. She had drifted off in her thoughts, looking up suddenly, almost surprised he was still there. "Is there anything else?"

"Er, no. I don't think so. Is there anything else you need from me?"

The hundreds of thoughts competing for space in her mind cycled round. "I'm thinking of approaching Sophie Parker."

"Really? Is that a good idea? I thought we were waiting until we found out more about these firms before we played our cards."

"I need to do something else. We keep hitting hurdles and I need to have as many lines of enquiry open as we can. I just think she may be worth speaking to."

"Why? What makes her different to the rest of them?"

Halle smiled. "A very male response, Todd. Think about it. She is the only woman involved in this across both these firms. By all accounts, she is a very savvy businesswoman and I can't see her just accepting this macho-dominated world. I've got a feeling she might be the sort of person to ask some difficult questions. She just might be the ally we need."

"That's a huge leap of faith."

"I know, and my recent track record of calculated gambles has not exactly paid off, but I have a good feeling about this. I was reading up on her last night. It just feels right."

Todd held his hands up in mock defeat and left her office.

She took another slug of coffee. She hoped she was right about this one. She needed to speak to Sophie Parker.

Peter opened his emails. As he scrolled through the usual junk, he realised he had one from the prison. He quickly opened it. His jaw dropped. "What the hell?"

The prison had refused his request to see his mother in the next visiting slot. Someone else had been booked in.

Peter stared at the email, trying to make sense of what he was reading. No one but him visited his mother. Who the hell had nicked his slot?

He picked up the phone and dialled the prison, navigating the infernal options system to finally get through to the prison administration department that handled the visiting times.

"Oh, hello, my name is Peter Allcock. I put in an application to visit my mother on Wednesday this week but you have refused it."

The sound of keyboard tapping filled the brief silence. "Umm, yes, someone else has filled that slot. Sorry."

"I need to know who that is. I'm the only one who has ever visited my mother and I can't understand why you would give my slot away."

"We can't divulge that information. It's confidential."

"But… but that's ridiculous. I have a right to know."

"I'm sorry. It's prison policy. Anyone can apply to visit an inmate, but we can't tell you who they are."

"Can you at least tell me if it's a relative?"

There was another brief pause. "Er, no. It doesn't look like it."

34

Sophie tapped away at the keyboard, aimlessly searching the PEMS network for something that would vindicate the growing paranoia she was feeling. The paper files had given her an insight into how the ALMS projects were managed, including the revelation about the so-called R&D account. But it wasn't enough. She knew any dirty secrets would not be out in the open, easy for nosy people like her to find.

She clicked on a folder called ALMS. The most recent projects were listed in subfolders. She clicked through to some she had already reviewed on paper. The same documentation, the same financial reports were there. Digitised copies of the paperwork in the file. She looked at numerous subfolders but the same thing happened with each one. Nothing new. No dirty secrets.

She sat back in her chair staring at the screen, idly scrolling the list of folders. There was nothing that caught her eye.

She shoved her mouse across the desk in frustration. "What am I doing? This is hopeless."

She stood up, stretching her limbs, trying to reduce the tension that was ever-present in her body. Her agitated state was not helped when her office door suddenly opened.

"All right, sis?"

She looked around. Ross' goofy grin greeted her. She wasn't in the mood.

"What do you want, Ross? I'm really busy."

She noticed the eye-roll but didn't bite.

"Jeremy has sent through the work orders for two more of the ALMS sites. I need your sign-off."

Sophie tried to quell her rage. Ross was oblivious to what was going on, carrying on with their father's legacy, whatever that legacy really was. As she agonised over whether to say something to Ross about her growing paranoia, a horrible thought struck her. Did he know what was going on? Could their father have confided in Ross? The thought floored her. She stared at Ross, wide-eyed, trying to read him.

"You okay, sis? You seem a bit wired."

She moved towards him, grabbed the documentation, slammed it on the desk and signed it off. She threw it back at him and turned away from his gaze. He left with no further comment.

Sophie paced around the office, her anger growing. If she was right that Ross knew what was going on, she felt even more stupid. Did her father really think she was that insignificant that she couldn't be trusted to know the real truth about the relationship between PEMS and ALMS?

She sat back down, her mind full of different scenarios, every one seeming worse as she allowed her imagination to go into overdrive.

"Whoa, stop." The rational, sensible Sophie reappeared. "Come on you can't prove any of this. Focus."

The personal pep talk had worked. She closed her eyes and tried to relax her mind. After a few minutes she opened her eyes and picked up her mobile. It was time for action. She dialled Jeremy.

"Morning, Miss Parker. What can I do for you?"

Sophie realised how unprepared she was for the conversation. "Er, I've just signed off two more work orders for the ALMS projects. What are the next steps?"

"Oh, that's great news. I'll get the project teams moving and commission the site clearance and clean-up work."

"Will we use the same firms as before?"

"Yeh, we've been using them for years. Very reliable local firms. Never let us down."

Sophie knew she was skirting around the issue. "I noticed that when I was reviewing some old files. I've been trying to get a better understanding of how we run our projects with ALMS."

"Oh, okay. Is there anything I can help you with?"

Jeremy's tone was calm and considered. Not an ounce of tension.

This was it. Could Sophie risk exposing her hand? "I was looking at the f—"

The office phone interrupted her sentence. Her PA buzzed through. "Miss Parker. There's a Halle Jacobs on the phone. She is an investigative reporter from a TV company. She wants to speak to you about some show she is working on."

Sophie stopped in her tracks. What on earth was this?

She told her PA to hold the call for a second. She got back on her mobile. "Sorry, Jeremy, something's come up. I'll call you back."

Curiosity got the better of her. "Thanks, Jane, put her through."

*

Jeremy looked at his phone like it was some alien being. *How odd*, he thought to himself. *Why was Sophie Parker calling him and what was she about to say?*

He knew he had no choice. He scrolled through his phone and dialled Andrew Allcock.

"Andrew, it's Jeremy."

"What's up?"

"Sophie Parker's just called me. Seems she's doing what she threatened. Said she was trying to find out more about the projects between our firms. I felt like she was holding back, not really saying what she wanted to say. Then she was just about to ask me another question when she hung up. Said something had come up. It was really odd."

"That woman is trouble. I thought we'd done enough to keep her away from this, but I see we are going to have to ramp up our offensive against her."

"Okay, I guess you just want me to carry on as normal?"

"Yes, yes. She's not going to find anything at your end, is she, Jeremy?"

"No. If she looks on the PEMS network, she will just find the normal project documentation. All the stuff we don't want her to see is stored on Genesis."

"Good. We can't afford any slip-ups. Edward is going to be spitting chips that she is still sniffing around. Let me know if she contacts you again."

"I will."

"Oh, and Jeremy... don't forget your Christmas bonus is pending. I wouldn't want anything to jeopardise that."

"Don't you worry about that. My old lady is expecting that new BMW X5. I ain't gonna let anything jeopardise that or my life will be hell!"

They both laughed and ended the call.

Jeremy opened up his email to initiate the two new projects. He knew the Allcock brothers would deal with Sophie Parker. He did feel a tinge of regret but money talked, and he was not about to bite the hand that had made him a millionaire.

35

Peter shut his office door and logged on to the secure network. He started searching the folders. Board papers, financial statements, project documentation, sales. Everything in its place. Nice and ordered. A deeper search of folders he had rarely bothered to look at in the past gleaned little.

As he navigated back to the top level of the folder structure, he realised each of the brothers and his uncle had a private folder allocated in this part of the network. He clicked on his. There was very little in there. He rarely found a use for it.

He stared at Edward's name. Could it be that simple? Would Edward hide all his secrets in such an obvious place?

His mouse arrow hovered over the folder. Self-doubt was crippling him. It always did whenever he had to deal with Edward, the 'little brother' jibes a deliberate reminder of where the power lay in their relationship. Peter shook his head. Something had to change. He thought of Sophie and clicked on the folder.

PLEASE ENTER YOUR PASSWORD

Peter cursed. An obvious barrier. He stared at the

blinking cursor. He tried several options: *EdwardJnr,*
Allcock1, EdwardAllcock. None of them worked. He
screwed up a piece of paper and threw it at the mini
basketball hoop above his bin. It failed to hit the target,
just like his attempts to hack into Edward's folder.

*

The call was connected and Halle's heart flipped a beat.
The soft Home Counties tone of Sophie Parker's voice
greeted her.

"Oh, hello, Miss Parker. Thank you for taking my
call."

"What can I help you with, Miss Jacobs?"

"I'm an investigative reporter working for Goldwin
Productions. I'm working on a programme series called
Tragic Britain which looks at sad human-interest stories
and tries to expose who may be responsible."

There was silence from the other end. Halle wasn't sure
whether Sophie was about to hang up or was transfixed by
what she was saying. She powered on.

"We have come across a story from the Pickford
housing estate in East London. A number of children
on that estate have contracted cancer, with two deaths
in a very short space of time. The number of cases is
a statistical anomaly and we have been investigating
possible causes. We found that your firm was one of three
involved in the preparation and construction of that site
and I wondered whether we could meet to discuss it."

There was a long pause.

"Miss Parker. Are you still there?"

"Yes, sorry. When was this site built?"

"In the late '80s."

"How do you think I can help you?"

"I'm trying to find out why all these kids may have contracted cancer."

"I'm still not seeing how I can help with that."

"I'd rather meet with you face to face to discuss this."

"I'm very busy."

"Look, for what it's worth, I approached you because I thought you might be the one person who would be receptive to my enquiries. I am suspicious about the involvement of Allcock Land Management Services in all this, particularly due to the eye-watering amount of money they make on each deal. I know you have a long-standing relationship with them and I wanted to get your opinion on their business practices."

There was another long pause. Halle worried that her pitch was not working. Eventually, Sophie spoke.

"Do you have access to an IT expert that could find stuff in places that maybe people don't want you to go?"

Halle was surprised by the question but ran with it. Was this her in?

"Er, yes, I do actually. We each have a researcher allocated to our investigation team and mine is one of the best we have."

"Okay. I'll do you a deal. I'll meet you and if we decide there is some mutual benefit to us working together, I will tell you everything I know about ALMS, if I can have access to your researcher."

Halle couldn't believe it. "Deal!"

"Great. I don't want to meet here or in your offices. If

I send you my home address, can we meet tonight, around 7.30 pm?"

"Of course. I'll be there with bells on."

*

Sophie put the phone down. Her mind was racing. What on earth had that TV company found? She started frantically searching through the paper files that were strewn across her desk. The Pickford housing estate file wasn't there. She logged on to the network. No electronic folder either.

She buzzed her PA. "Jane, can you find a project folder for the Pickford housing estate. It was from the late '80s so may be in the archives."

She stared out of the window. Could this be it? Could this reporter help her find what she was looking for or had she done a deal with the devil?

She picked up her phone and texted Peter. He was supposed to come round to her place again that evening, but she wanted to meet this reporter on her own. She was beginning to trust Peter, but this was something she felt she had to do alone. She looked at the time. Seven hours until she found out whether she had just made a big mistake.

36

Peter stayed late in the office until everyone had left. Sophie had blown him off for their latest evening get-together, texting to say she was tired and wanted an early night. He was annoyed but made the best of it. He had to crack Edward's password.

He crept towards Edward's office and opened the door. He scanned the room, hoping for some inspiration, something that might give him a clue as to what his password might be. He sat at his desk and opened the drawers. He fanned through a few notebooks. Nothing. He looked at the pictures on the walls, the business magazines strewn across the coffee table. Nothing was clicking.

He got up from the desk chair and sat on one of the comfy sofas, picking up one of the business magazines. He started to idly flick through it. An article caught his eye.

"That's it!"

He raced back to his office and navigated to the secure network. He clicked on Edward's folder.

PLEASE ENTER YOUR PASSWORD

He typed in *GREEDISGOOD*. The article was about

Wall Street, Edward's favourite film. Gordon Gecko was his hero and his password had to be his favourite phrase.

The mouse icon blinked a few times as the system processed what he had entered.

The screen refreshed. It had worked. He was in.

The excitement of getting this far soon faded. There was only one subfolder and it was encrypted. It was called Genesis.

*

Edward sat in a corner booth of the strip club with Andrew and Uncle James, watching the girls on stage and batting away any attempts at a private lap dance. He took a big slug of his neat whisky and winced at the sharpness.

"How's our man doing with the Sophie problem, Andrew?"

"He followed her home the other night and shit her up by tailgating her."

Edward raised his eyebrows. "Is that it?"

"We're playing the slow game. We want to keep niggling away at her paranoia, make sure that every day she gets a little bit more frightened."

Edward snorted his derision. "Seems fucking lame to me, brother. We should be taking her out of the picture. Permanently."

"Andrew's right, Edward. We have to be careful."

Edward looked at his uncle. "Hmm… what about the business disruption?"

"We're still keeping an eye on that. The two firms are holding their line. She is going to have to generate new business quickly if she is to survive. That should be keeping her busy."

Andrew shuffled nervously in his chair, not wanting to rile Edward up further by telling him about Jeremy's call. Edward noticed the body language.

"Something to say?"

"No, no. We'll keep at it. She won't be a problem."

They could both tell he wasn't happy but mercifully the tension was broken by his phone beeping.

What he read didn't help his mood.

"Well, it seems our Sophie issue just became a two-person problem. Peter has just accessed my private folder on the secure network."

*

Todd's fingers were flying across the keyboard. He was in the zone, doing what he did best. Hacking the places people didn't want you to go.

He had easily navigated past the first layer of so-called protection on the ALMS network but was confronted with some sophisticated encryption that was protecting their secure server, the obvious place to start if he was going to find out what the Allcocks were up to. He would find a way past it. He always did. It just took time, patience and a little bit of maths.

As he threw code sequences at the server, his laptop beeped. It was a message on Proton.

SNAPDEVIL: Yo, Krypto, what's up?
KRYPTO: Starting looking at the money dudes. That
    Allcock family is one weird set-up

SNAPDEVIL: Why?

KRYPTO: Five brothers and their uncle. All multi-millionaires, living in big-arse houses in the most expensive parts of London. Driving around in flash cars but none of them married and not a single blemish on their lives. No parking tickets, no driving violations, no D&D, no drug possession. Every single aspect of their company management is A1. Everything filed on time, every bill paid on time, no VAT issues, a perfect audit record

SNAPDEVIL: So what?

KRYPTO: That ain't normal, dude. No business runs that efficiently and people with that much money can't be clean. I'm betting they are snorting enough white stuff up their noses to keep the local dealers in business

SNAPDEVIL: Maybe they're just very careful across all aspects of their lives

KRYPTO: All six of them? Unlikely. People with this much money pay their way out of trouble

SNAPDEVIL: OK, so what next?

KRYPTO: Gonna keep on it. I can smell scandal. Money and greed. There'll be something in their personal or business lives that they don't want us to find

SNAPDEVIL: Well, I'm just hacking into their network. Will let you know if I find anything

KRYPTO: Cool. Laters

Todd logged off and rubbed his hands. The game was on.

37

Halle drove into the close where Sophie Parker lived. A lovely quiet place in the suburbs, awash with mature trees lining the road and pretty well-kept gardens that were still blossoming despite the advent of winter.

She checked the time on her phone. She was a couple of minutes early. She walked up the gravelled path and pushed the doorbell. She was as nervous as hell.

A few seconds later the door opened, and Sophie Parker stood in the framed light of the doorway. She was stunningly attractive, looking effortlessly elegant in a wool jumper and jeans.

Her speech was clipped but she ushered Halle inside.

There was an awkward moment as they both stood in the living room, not knowing what to do. Sophie broke the mood. "Do you want a glass of wine?"

"Er, no thanks. Driving and all that."

Halle continued to stand as she watched Sophie pour herself a glass. Eventually, Halle was invited to sit down. She decided to go for it.

"Miss Parker…"

"Sophie, please."

"… er, Sophie, thank you for seeing me. I really need your help."

Sophie nodded but said no more. Halle ploughed on.

"As I mentioned in our brief conversation, I am working on a TV programme about tragic human-interest stories. I was assigned to an emerging story about childhood cancers on a housing estate in East London, where there are far too many cases in one small community to be just bad luck."

"I'm not seeing how I can help you, Miss Jacobs."

"Please call me Halle. The thing is, we consulted a medical expert who suggested that the most likely cause of so many children contracting cancer was pollution. That site, like many of the sites you work on with ALMS, was heavily polluted before it was built on."

Halle noticed an involuntary twitch in Sophie's face as she mentioned pollution.

"What do you think?"

There was a brief pause as Halle wondered whether Sophie was engaging in what she was saying or was about to kick her out of her house. Sophie leant forward and Halle tensed up. This was it. Fight or flight time.

"Do you have any evidence of residual pollution on that site?"

Halle winced at the question. "Not yet. Initial tests were inconclusive." She held Sophie with a firm stare, hoping her facial expression would not expose the lie she had just told.

"Once again, I'm struggling to see how I can help you."

Halle knew she was losing her. She changed tack. "Why did you agree to see me? You mentioned something about needing an IT expert."

Halle could see Sophie processing the question. She

was being understandably guarded in her responses, but Halle hoped whatever was driving her to be part of this conversation would win over. Halle waited nervously as she watched Sophie pour herself another glass of wine.

"Look, I'm new to the PEMS business so know very little about what we do. I do know that we are responsible for the environmental impact assessments on these sites and manage the clean-ups, but there is no suggestion in anything I've read so far that would suggest we have a problem with residual pollution on any of the sites we have worked on."

Halle knew she had to push it. "So, what is worrying you?"

Sophie pursed her lips but answered the question. "It's our relationship with Allcock Land Management Services that is bugging me. My father ran PEMS single-handedly for over forty years before ill health forced him to hand the business over to me and my brother. My father is one of the calmest, kindest men you will ever meet, but every time we discuss our relationship with ALMS, he gets angry and agitated. He keeps telling Ross and I to leave the management of the account to our project director, Jeremy Hogan, who has been working with ALMS for years. Every time I have tried to find out more about this business relationship, I'm shut down either by my father, Jeremy or one of the delightful Allcock men."

Halle was transfixed. She didn't know how exactly this information connected with her story but Sophie was spilling her guts and she urged her to say more. Sophie drew breath and Halle sensed the punchline was about to be delivered.

"The real problem is I'm convinced they are hiding something. I reviewed the financial breakdown on loads of our recent projects with ALMS and on every one a payment was made to an account called Bill Parker Holdings, my father's name. When I confronted him about it, he said it's for R&D and Jeremy manages the account."

"And you don't believe him?"

"Not for a second. There must be hundreds of thousands of pounds going into that account that Ross and I don't control. It's not right."

"How can I help?"

"I need someone to hack into that account. I'm sure whatever is going on will be explained if we can look at the detail of what goes in and out of that account."

"Do you have any theories?"

Sophie looked sheepish but continued to answer Halle's questions. "I've… I've managed to build a relationship with Peter Allcock. He seems different to all the other brothers and is beginning to agree with me that everything is not right here."

"Really, can you trust him?"

"I don't know, but I need someone else in my corner. I can't do this alone."

"What's his theory about this account?"

"He claims he knows nothing about the account but agreed to look at his end to see if he could get any answers. The alarming thing is, he has a theory about what that account might be being used for. He thinks we might be giving backhanders."

38

Peter was back in the office early the following morning. The excitement at cracking Edward's password had been short-lived, and his inability to work out what Genesis was and how to access it had given him a restless night.

As he necked his second cup of strong coffee, the door to his office opened. He tensed up. It was Edward.

"Hello, little brother. How the devil are you?"

Peter glanced up, not keen to meet Edward's eye but intrigued by his weird, enthusiastic manner.

"I'm fine. You?"

"Oh yes. I'm thinking of going fishing later. Always good to catch a slippery fish or two."

With that, he walked out of his office, doing the maniacal laugh that always meant he thought he had the upper hand on something.

Peter watched his progress as he walked back to the office, thoughts racing through his head. *What the hell was that? And what on earth did he mean about going fishing? He has never picked up a rod in his life.*

Peter was nervous. The thought hit him. *Does Edward somehow know what I did last night?*

Sophie arrived back at PEMS after another meeting with her advertising agency leadership team. Progress on the recovery plan was slow but she had to rely on them to sort it. The situation with the ALMS and PEMS relationship and that damn holding account were consuming her.

The meeting with the TV reporter the previous evening had been quite positive. She hoped she could trust Halle Jacobs, who had promised to speak to her researcher about doing some work on accessing the mystery account.

She continued to agonise over whether she had made the right decisions in trusting Halle and Peter Allcock. The feelings of loneliness and disempowerment when her suspicions were first raised about the situation was not somewhere she wanted to go back to, but she wasn't sure this scenario of having people in her corner was making her feel any better.

Her PA broke her concentration as she brought in the day's post. Sophie had a quick sift through the envelopes, stopping at a handwritten envelope with just her name on it. She opened it up and her heart sank.

STOP SNOOPING… OR ELSE

*

Halle sat in the car with Clayton and Rod. They were off to see Jen Wyatt to give her the bad news about the soil and water tests. She wasn't look forward to it. Halle had banked her reputation and £10,000 on this theory and it had blown up in her face.

As they drove into the estate, there was still a distinct lack of people around. Halle had no idea how many of the families at the meeting had followed through and left their properties, but the eerie stillness of the surroundings, framed by the late-morning fog, made it seem like a scene from a horror movie.

Halle had asked Rod to bring his smaller video camera. She wanted the footage of the meeting with Jen but didn't want all the fuss of setting up the large camera equipment. He had obliged with the latest in small hand-held 4K devices. He was fiddling in the back seat with it the whole way. She smiled to herself. Boys with their toys.

They got out of the car and knocked on Jen's door. She ushered them in. No refreshments were offered so they all sat down in the living room. Rod got the camera ready to roll.

Halle fixed Jen with as sympathetic an expression as she could. "Jen. I'm afraid I have some bad news. The results of the soil and water tests have come back negative, both from your property and across the estate. I'm sorry. I was sure that this was going to be the explanation."

Jen said nothing. She looked at Halle, tears welling up in her eyes. She flinched at the sound of the camera zooming in on her grief. She glared at Rod and back to Halle. "Does he have to do that?"

Halle looked round and gestured for him to stop filming.

"Look, Jen, we are going to—"

"Does he have to be here?"

Halle was taken aback at the interruption. Jen was looking straight at Clayton.

"It's bad enough that you've made me a pariah in my own neighbourhood, then bribed me to help you on a false errand, but do I really have to put up with people like him being in my house?"

Halle was gobsmacked. The latent racism that had been emanating from Jen on the two previous occasions was now out and in their faces.

She stood up. "Do you know, I'm sorry for what has happened to you and I'm sorry my hunch about the pollution didn't pay off, but I will not put up with you treating my staff with such bigotry and hatred. You can kiss goodbye to that charitable trust as well. We will solve this mystery without you."

With that, Halle ushered them through the door and stormed out.

As they sat in the car, Halle was fuming. Clayton looked over to her. "You didn't have to do that."

"Yes, I did. That woman has been giving off bad vibes to you since the moment we met her, and from our experience in the community hall, it seems a number of people on this estate share her abhorrent attitudes. I will not let you be exposed to that."

Clayton gave her the smile that melted her heart. "Well, thank you, but you shouldn't jeopardise the investigation to spare my feelings."

Halle shook her head. "We don't need her or any other of these racist bastards. I have a number of lines of enquiry on the go. I'll solve this mystery in spite of these people."

Rod piped up from the back seat. "That's all very noble, but at the moment, I can't see how we can use any of the footage we have shot from this estate. We don't have their consent to broadcast it."

Halle swivelled in her seat. "We'll find a way. We can justify infringement of privacy in the public interest. Can't we?"

"I don't know. You can if it relates to crime or public safety and if you can really find out what is going on here, I suppose there's a chance you'll get away with it. You'll have to convince the big bosses of that, which won't be easy."

Halle turned back and stared out of the car window. The fog was beginning to clear and a small shaft of sunlight broke through. She took it as a sign.

"Okay, guys, let's get back to the office."

As they began to drive out of the estate, they noticed a woman gesturing to them from one of the houses on their left.

Halle told Clayton to stop the car and wound down the window. The woman looked around nervously but approached the car.

"I need to speak to you."

39

Victoria Allcock lined up in the lunch queue for the daily game of 'guess the slop'. She asked for a burger, some insipid chips and an orange slop that purported to be mashed carrot. She got to her table and covered it in salt, hoping that some flavour might emerge.

Dolores sat down next to her. "All right, Vic. Come to any decisions yet?"

Victoria forked a load of chips and shoved them in her mouth. As she ate, she looked at her friend and welled up. "Hey, girlfriend, don't be getting all emotional on me."

"I dunno, D. I have to get out of here. There're so many things I need to do, so many things I have been too scared to confront. I can't do any of them if I'm stuck in here."

"Do it then. Tell those parole bastards what they want to hear. No one will know what you have said and I want you out there with me, living the next stages of our lives."

"Oh. I just don't know if I can. I will know what I said and I don't know if I can live with that."

They finished their food, both lost in their own thoughts. A few minutes later, their concentration was broken by one of the guards handing round details of their visiting slots. Victoria was mostly disappointed at this bi-weekly ritual, Peter being the only one that occasionally visited. She was surprised to see a paper slip chucked down in front of her.

She picked it up. The visitor wasn't Peter.

*

Peter rushed to the bistro. He'd received a frantic phone call from Sophie, pleading with him to meet her for lunch. He was glad to get away from the unsettling atmosphere in the office but he was filled with dread at what Sophie was going to tell him.

She was already seated as he entered the bistro. He took off his coat and quickly sat down. Sophie was shaking and the tears began to flow. He grabbed her hand. "What's wrong, Sophie?"

She shoved the piece of paper across the table. Peter looked at it in astonishment.

"What's this?"

Sophie tried to calm herself. "It... it arrived this morning. A handwritten envelope with the rest of the post."

Peter rubbed his face. "This is not good. I think we might be in trouble. Edward was in my office this morning, doing his stupid laugh like he knows something I don't and making some strange comments about going fishing. I think he might know that we are hooking up."

Sophie grabbed her head. "How does he know this shit? What sort of man does this to another person? He's a fucking psycho."

The other diners were starting to look over at them as the volume of the conversation and the emotional responses became more animated.

Peter noticed and grabbed Sophie's hand. "We need to get away, Sophie. Find somewhere to hunker down. The atmosphere in the office is awful and I would much rather not be there. I can work from anywhere and am owed some time off. Let's find a big hotel suite in London to hole up in and work out our next steps. I'm not going to let him win. Not again."

*

Halle's stomach was rumbling but she didn't want to miss the opportunity to see what this woman wanted. They parked up outside her house and trundled in.

They all sat down and she launched straight in. "My name is Marjit Gupta and I was at your presentation the other night. I'm sorry it went so wrong for you. Not everybody in that room objected to what you were saying but the mob mentality took over."

Halle smiled at her. "Thank you, Mrs Gupta, that's kind of you to say. Would you mind if Rod filmed our interaction?"

"No, no. Please carry on."

"Okay. Tell me about your situation."

Marjit bowed her head but ploughed on. "My son Sunil is four years old. He started getting ill about six months ago. Nausea, headaches, tiredness. It got worse and worse until we were forced to go to the doctor. He was diagnosed with leukaemia a month ago."

Halle grabbed her hand. "I'm so sorry, but this is why we are trying to find out what happened here."

"I know, I know, and as I said, there are a few of us that support what you're doing here, but the big loud voices in this neighbourhood have stirred everything up."

Halle grimaced. "Yes, we have just been back to Jen Wyatt's house this morning to give her some bad news. We managed to do some soil tests with her support but they came back negative for pollution, which I was banking on to explain this. She didn't take it well and said she had been alienated as a result of what we had done."

Marjit let out a snort of derision. "Ha, you must be joking. She's lying to you. Her and that other man that was rude to you the other night have been going around the neighbourhood stirring things up, and she was bragging about some cash she'd conned out of you. It's horrible around here at the moment and even worse for people like us."

Halle noticed the involuntary glance at Clayton.

"Well, if it makes you feel any better, I've told Jen Wyatt that we are not going to work with her on this investigation anymore or give her any money. She has been racially abusive to Clayton and I'm not prepared to give her any more airtime. I'm sorry for what happened to her son, but I can't work with people like that."

Marjit pulled a pained expression. "Yes, a daily occurrence around here. Our kids can play happily together but we are never far away from a snide look, a mumbled comment under their breath or parents ushering their children away when we turn up in the playground."

"What is wrong with people? I thought this community

would be rallying around each other in such desperate times."

"That's not how it is. The stress of this situation is tearing people apart."

There was a pause in the conversation and Marjit offered them some refreshments. Halle was grateful for the sustenance as the clock clicked through her normal lunchtime.

As they finished up, Halle focused back on how Marjit could help them. "Mrs Gupta. How many families are with you?"

"There are three more. We are willing to help you in whatever way we can."

Halle grabbed her hands again. "Thank you. I can't tell you how much this means to me. I want to get the testing teams back to take samples from your properties, if that is okay with you?"

"Of course, whatever you need."

Halle puffed out her cheeks. What a strange morning. After the stress of dealing with Jen Wyatt, she had finally caught a break.

40

Halle walked back into the office just after 2 pm and grabbed Todd.

She slumped in her chair. "I dunno about you but I've just had a very eventful twenty-four hours."

"Ooh, do tell."

"Get me some caffeine first and at least three of those chocolate biscuits. If this adrenalin I'm running on suddenly stops, I fear I might fall asleep at my desk."

The coffee and biscuits were soon devoured and they sat across from each other, nervous excitement buzzing around them.

"Gosh. Where do I start?"

"Wherever you want, my most favourite person in the world."

Halle was slightly taken aback by the language but ploughed on. "Okay, firstly my hunch with Sophie Parker paid off. She invited me to her place last night and after some initial awkwardness she opened up. It seems she is worried about the relationship between Allcock Land Management Services and PEMS. She has been trying to find out more about the business but keeps being shut down by various people, including her father, whenever she probes the detail. She discovered a suspicious account where a proportion of the cash from each deal with ALMS is syphoned off to, which neither she nor her brother, Ross, seem to have control over."

Todd's face lit up. "Now we're talking. A proper conspiracy."

"Well, based on Sophie's suspicions, it certainly seems that way, but if we are to keep her onside, I need your help."

"Okay, shoot."

"She wants you to hack into that account. She's convinced the account will uncover whatever is going on here."

"That's no problem. My speciality. I was in the process last night of hacking into the ALMS network but I can refocus on this."

"Oh, what did you find?"

"Not much. I got past their main firewalls without a glitch but then hit a heavily encrypted server, which is proving more difficult to crack. I have a programme running against their network which will eventually crack it, but it just needs time."

"Do all you can. We have a real impetus on this thing if we can keep Sophie with us."

"No probs, but did you get anything from her about our housing estate problem?"

"Actually, no. She was quite cagey about that. I'm sure we'll get more from her if we can get her some answers."

They both stood up to stretch their legs and refill their coffee cups. The buzz was still there as they sat back down.

"How did your visit go this morning?"

"Eventful! We went to Jen Wyatt's to tell her the bad news about the soil tests and it didn't go well."

"Oh shit. What happened?"

"She was horrible. Complained about being filmed and then racially abused Clayton. I wasn't gonna put up with her bigotry, so we left immediately and I told her that my offer of a trust fund for her son was withdrawn."

"Bloody hell. Are you sure that was wise?"

Halle frowned. "Why is everyone questioning my judgement on this? Her behaviour is abhorrent and we shouldn't allow this to happen."

"I know. I'm with you but don't forget John has made it clear that racism is not the story here."

"But it is, Todd. What is happening to these people is tragic, but we can't possibly ignore the context within which this tragedy is playing out. It has to be relevant."

Todd raised his eyebrows. "Hey, I'll support you, but it's not me you need to convince."

There was a brief uncomfortable pause before Halle spoke again.

"Anyway, we caught a break. We don't need Jen Wyatt anymore."

"Really?"

"Yes, as we were driving out of the estate, we were flagged down by a woman. She wanted to speak to us to say she was supportive of what we are doing. She claims Jen is a fraud and was stirring shit up in the neighbourhood despite telling us that we had made her a pariah. This lady also claims Jen was bragging about conning us out of the ten grand. So, you see, my instincts about Jen were right."

"Okay, but how is this woman going to help us?"

"She claims there are three more families on the estate who want to help. They are nervous about being seen to work with us due to the mob mentality, but said they were prepared to help in any way they could. I've got her contact details here. Can you arrange for the testing team to go to her property and she will talk to the other families to sort out their tests?"

"Of course."

"The other important factor is that they are an Indian family."

"And?"

"She made it clear that most of that estate is filled with ignorant racists. She said that barely a day goes by when they are not abused in some shape or form. You see, the racial context is relevant to our story."

The conversation tailed off and Todd left the office. The exhaustion began to hit Halle and she found herself strangely deflated. One of her gambles had finally paid off and they had caught a break with Marjit Gupta, but she felt like she was pushing water uphill when it came to getting people to accept that racism needed to be part of this story. She had a review meeting with John in a couple of days. It was time to convince him that this story was not just about childhood cancer.

41

It was early evening as Sophie and Peter walked into a lavish suite at the Savoy Hotel. They had both rushed home, grabbed everything they thought they might need for the foreseeable future and rocked up to the hotel as quickly as they could. They had told their respective PAs that they had decided to take a couple of weeks off but were still contactable by email.

As they stood in the amazing suite, taking in the opulence and amazing views, Sophie looked at Peter. "What are we doing here?"

"It's just a precaution. If my brother is responsible for that note and all the other suspicious things that have happened to you over the past few days, we need to remove ourselves from the firing line. This place is used to dealing with guests that require absolute discretion. He won't find us here."

Sophie kissed him and walked into one of the two bedrooms. Peter had decided not to be too presumptuous about the sleeping arrangements despite his overwhelming desire to repeat the amazing sexual encounter from the other evening.

As they settled down to some pre-dinner champagne

in their suite, whilst they waited for room service, Sophie's stress was still evident.

"This is all so horrible. I mean, what the hell is going on that your brothers think it's acceptable to sabotage my business and threaten me with notes like this?"

"I don't know. I didn't get very far last night but I did manage to hack Edward's password, which got me into his private folders."

Sophie leant forward, expectantly, ignoring Peter's involuntary glance at her cleavage. "What did you find?"

"Have you heard anyone at PEMS talk about Genesis?"

"What? The band?"

Peter laughed. "No! In a business context. The only file in Edward's private folder was an executable file called Genesis. When I clicked on it, I was hit with some form of fancy encryption. It's way beyond my capabilities to crack, but hugely suspicious."

Sophie chewed her lip, deep in thought.

"Sorry. I haven't heard anyone talk about Genesis at PEMS. Do you think it could be connected to this mysterious Bill Parker Holdings account I found?"

"It's possible."

Their deliberations were broken by room service arriving. They tucked into filet mignon and chips with a heavenly sauce, followed by the most delicious apple pie they had eaten in ages.

As they finished up, Sophie knew she had to tell Peter about the other thing that had happened since they had last been together. "There is something else."

Peter took a sip of the lovely merlot they had ordered with the food and gazed at her expectantly.

"I was unexpectedly approached by a TV reporter yesterday who is working on a programme that looks at tragic human stories. Apparently, they have come across a housing estate in East London where there are a high number of childhood cancers and they are investigating whether it's due to pollution. She approached me because it's a site that both our firms worked on."

Peter put his glass down, concern etched all over his face. "Which estate is it and when was it built?"

"I think she said it was the Pickford housing estate and it was built in the late '80s."

Peter screwed his face up. "Hmm, before my time, but I don't like the sound of this. I've always been wary of some of the sites we acquire. They are so heavily polluted, yet Andrew and Jeremy always reassure me that everything is okay."

Sophie shook her head. "There we go again. The same people telling us everything will be all right. We're being played for mugs."

"I tend to agree with you. Have they found evidence of pollution on the site?"

"Actually, that's the strange thing. She said the soil and water tests they had done came back negative."

"So why was she approaching you if her story has no legs?"

"Because, like us, I don't think she believes what she is being told."

There was a brief pause as they both tried to process the dialogue. Peter broke the silence. "Why did you agree to speak to her? Do you know if you can trust her?"

"I was sceptical at first but I got something out of the deal as well."

"Oh really? What?"

"She is giving me access to her researcher. Apparently, he is a hacking genius. He's going to try to hack into this mysterious Bill Parker Holding account and I reckon we could persuade her to get him to find out about this Genesis thing."

Peter fixed Sophie with a determined stare. "Let's do it. Let's trust this reporter. If something is being hidden from us, I'm bloody determined to find out what it is."

42

Edward sat in his usual booth in the strip club with his Uncle James, nursing a whisky and soda. He looked over to the entrance to see Andrew come crashing through it, shoulders hunched and a face like thunder.

"What's up? You look like someone's stolen your lollipop."

Andrew sat down and beckoned one of the waitresses to get him a beer. "We have a major fucking problem. Sophie Parker and our dear little brother have disappeared. Our man went to her house to shit her up a bit more, but she wasn't there. I did some digging and it seems she told her PA that she was taking a couple of weeks off but didn't say where she was going. Told her to email if they needed anything. I then discover from Peter's PA that he has done the same."

Edward rubbed his chin. "Well, well. I was right. Looks like Peter is hooking up with that bitch and betraying the family once again." The lines on his forehead deepened. "Okay, I'll play his game of hide and seek. Here's what I want you both to do. Get onto IT immediately and revoke all of Peter's access rights to our network and get one of them to put a trace on his credit cards. He's bound to give up his location that way. Also, let's see if we can ramp up the business sabotage on that bloody woman."

He stared at the latest dancer on the stage sliding up and down the pole. His rage was building and he subconsciously blurted out what was on his mind. "I'm not going to let them destroy my father's legacy. Not now. Not ever."

Andrew and James got the hint and both got on their phones to implement what Edward had asked for. A few minutes later, a man approached their booth. Edward looked up. "Ah, excellent. Make yourself comfortable. We have a lot to talk about."

*

Todd was back in his technology nest, the place that always got his juices flowing. He loved working with Halle and was willing to put in the extra effort for her by working in the evenings. It was a sad reality that he didn't have much else to do with his spare time. His hacking skills had made him more money than he knew what to do with, but it all meant nothing if he had no one to share it with. Halle was on his mind. Constantly. He didn't do office romances but she was testing his resolve.

He shook it off, reconciling himself to the notion that he was punching way above his weight for even contemplating getting with Halle. He opened up his laptop. Time to go digging.

He checked the programme that had been running against the ALMS secure network. It had done its job and he was able to navigate easily through various company folders, which did little but confirm the huge amounts of money they were making. Each of the brothers and the uncle had password protected subfolders, and his hacking programme made light work of the security. He found little of any substance in Peter's, Philip's or Stephen Allcock's folders, but with the other three he hit gold dust. In Edward's, Andrew's and James' folders there was one file. An executable called Genesis.

A preliminary investigation of the link presented further challenges. It had multi-layered encryption, far more sophisticated than their secure network. Todd rubbed his hands. He could smell corruption, and this was exactly the type of security that hid dirty secrets. He configured his hacking programme against the link and set it going. This was going to take some time, but he knew eventually he would find out what was behind this virtual door.

As he left the programme to do its work, he changed his focus to the PEMS network. Halle had asked him to find the trail to a mysterious holding account that was being managed by their project director, Jeremy Hogan. The security on the PEMS network was pathetic. He was in within seconds and navigated around the network with ease. A quick trawl of project folders confirmed the link to a variety of ALMS projects, but there was nothing of any great interest. He found the documents that Sophie Parker had referred to. Financial reports that showed a breakdown of payments. Every one had a large chunk going into an account called Bill Parker Holdings. Todd navigated to the personal folders and found the one for Jeremy Hogan. Again, his hacking programme made light work of the basic password protection. The moment he opened the folder, he knew he was onto something.

The only file in Jeremy Hogan's folder was an executable called Genesis.

43

Halle was in the office bright and early. The move from autumn to winter was well underway, and the increasingly darker mornings were making it harder to get out of bed each morning. She tried to allay her weariness by sipping a green tea, and focused on preparing for the visit she had with Victoria Allcock later that day. She was excited about the prospect of meeting her and finding the real story behind her incarceration. She had a feeling her story was going to be an interesting subplot to this mystery. As she started to jot down some notes, Todd popped his head round the door. "Morning, my delightful one."

Halle was once again surprised by the language but let it go. "Oh, morning, Todd. Anything to report?"

"Oh yes. I'll grab a coffee and be straight in."

Halle watched him leave. What a strange man he was. His constantly happy mood was lovely but was hard to take some mornings when all she wanted to do was go back to bed. She couldn't work out his vibe. Were his clumsy compliments his way of telling her he liked her, or was that just the way he was? She was still mortified by her actions on their drunken night together and her toes curled up every time she thought about it. Todd bounded back in before the self-persecution went too much further.

"What did you find?"

"Well, my hacking programme got me into the ALMS network. I also got into Jeremy Hogan's folder in the PEMS network. Look what I found."

Halle perused four screen prints. "What are these?"

"These are screen prints from the personal company folders of Edward, James and Andrew Allcock from the ALMS network and Jeremy Hogan's from the PEMS network. In each one there is only one file. An executable to something called Genesis."

"What is that?"

"It's the entrance to Ali Baba's cave."

*

Sophie Parker spread her toast with marmalade as she relaxed in her pyjama/bathrobe combo, gazing out over the rooftops of London. Peter's instincts had been right. They had to hide out and work out what was going on. The note had frightened her more than she cared to admit, but she felt safe holed up in this opulent suite. As she finished off her toast and poured herself a coffee, Peter walked into the main living space. He was also sporting the complimentary bathrobe chic, coupled with brilliant bed hair and puffy, just-out-of-bed eyes. "Morning."

"Morning, Peter. Sleep well?"

"Like a baby. You?"

"Yes. Probably the best sleep I've had for ages. Thank you for doing this. I do feel a lot safer here."

As Peter busied himself with breakfast, Sophie's phone beeped. She opened the message and gasped.

"What is it?"

"It's from that reporter. Her researcher has hacked into the network folders of Edward, Andrew and your uncle, as well as Jeremy Hogan's. She's asking if we have ever heard of Genesis. Apparently, the only thing in each of their folders is a link to an executable programme."

Peter grabbed the phone and perused the text. "Shit! So, Andrew and Uncle James have the same link I found in Edward's folder, and bloody Jeremy has it as well. I think this confirms everything we feared."

As he gave her back the phone, he screwed his face up. "We may have to think about dumping our phones. This means we could be in real danger, and I've got a horrible feeling that Edward will have someone trying to track us through our credit cards and phones. I made an advanced payment directly from my bank account to the hotel, so that there was no credit card trail of where we are, but if I know him, he will get someone to track our phones. We need to go and buy a couple of burners. I think we have to assume that we are now public enemy number one in his eyes."

As they finished off breakfast, both lost in the hundreds of thoughts that were competing for space in their stressed brains, Peter picked up his tablet and tried to log on to the ALMS network.

"What the hell is this?"

Sophie looked up. "What's wrong?"

"I think this confirms he's onto us. I'm locked out of the ALMS network. He's revoked all my privileges."

Halle got out of the cab that dropped her right outside the prison, the butterflies in her stomach framing the nervous excitement she was feeling about meeting Victoria Allcock. Sophie Parker had come back to her to say that neither she nor Peter Allcock knew anything about the Genesis executable they had found in all four of the antagonists folders, which just confirmed they were onto something. It heightened Halle's optimism that Victoria Allcock would be able to tell her something about the situation between ALMS and PEMS.

The reception to the prison was cold and clinical, all glass screens and formidable steel doors. It was staffed by serious-looking people who asked probing questions about your intentions and scanned every item you had on your person. Necessary security but actions that made Halle feel unnecessarily guilty. She was relieved when they let her through to the prison visitors' waiting room. A machine that was churning out various shades of brown liquid was available whilst they waited but Halle decided to leave it. The room was filled with an eclectic mix of stressed-out men, women and children of all ages and creeds, desperate to maximise the short time they would get with their incarcerated friend or relative.

After a ten-minute wait, they were ushered into the main visiting area, lined with small tables and seats on either side; a stereotypical prison visiting scene that made Halle wince. She sat down in the chair she was allocated and waited. She started to bite her fingernails. Why was she so nervous? A few minutes later, the inmates started to file in. She craned her neck to see if she could spot Victoria Allcock. A number of people passed her, sitting down at various tables around the room. Eventually, Halle caught sight of a person she was convinced must be Victoria. A woman with greying, slightly wild hair, a well-lived-in but still attractive face, shuffled through the door. She stopped for a minute, scanning the room, trying to work out where she was supposed to go. Halle did a half-stand and raised her hand. The woman fixed her with a curious gaze and walked slowly over to her.

As she approached Halle, she slowed her pace. Her face turned from curiosity to a look of absolute horror. She was ten yards away, frozen where she stood. A few seconds later, her eyes rolled and she collapsed on the floor.

44

Todd decided to work from home in the afternoon. Halle was visiting the Allcock mother in prison and his work laptop was woefully inadequate for what she was asking him to do.

He logged onto his home tech and checked the progress against the Genesis link. The hack programme had been running for nearly fourteen hours with little success. Some of the routines were looping, which was never a good sign. Todd had cracked many sophisticated encryptions in the past and he had to admit this was up there with the best of them. He decided to chew the fat with his tech buddy.

SNAPDEVIL: Yo, Krypto, you online?

KRYPTO: Always, dude. Have some progress

SNAPDEVIL: Ooh what?

KRYPTO: Been doing a deep dive into the habits of Ed Allcock Junior, through his spending. Seems to have a penchant for one strip club in particular, using it like some cliched gangster base. Hacked into their CCTV last night. Open this link

SNAPDEVIL: Ah, that's Edward, Andrew and his Uncle

James. Who's the other dude?

KRYPTO: Don't know but defo one of the gang

SNAPDEVIL: Actually hold on… yeh, as I thought. That's Jeremy Hogan

KRYPTO: What, the dude from the other firm?

SNAPDEVIL: Yes. We have him right in the mix and this confirms it. Ever heard of a programme called Genesis?

KRYPTO: No. Why?

SNAPDEVIL: I hacked their business folders and all four of these dudes have a link to an executable called Genesis. I've had the mathsworm programme running against it for nearly fourteen hours and I'm making little progress

KRYPTO: Sounds like a proprietary app, designed to store their dirty secrets. Can I help?

SNAPDEVIL: No it's fine, dude. Keep looking into their lives and include this Jeremy character in your digging

KRYPTO: Will do, dude. Laters

Todd watched the CCTV recording again. Jeremy Hogan meeting with the three musketeers. Clear evidence that he was balls-deep in this thing. He constructed an email to Halle with the link. He was sure Sophie Parker and Peter Allcock would be interested to see what was going on.

*

Halle got the cab to take her straight home. As she leaned against the kitchen worktop, chronic tiredness taking hold, she poured herself a glass of wine despite it only just passing mid-afternoon. Her mind was spinning. What on earth had happened at the prison? The guards had rushed over when the woman fainted. In all the drama, Halle had managed to confirm that the woman was in fact Victoria Allcock.

Halle couldn't shake the look on Victoria's face as she got nearer to her. Her face initially framed in curiosity had gradually changed as she walked slowly towards her... ending in a look of absolute terror.

She gave the guards her mobile number and asked for them to let her know that Victoria was okay. So far nothing. As she fiddled with her phone, she realised she had an email from Todd. She opened up the link and some of her stress dissipated. She watched the CCTV footage. Clear evidence that Jeremy Hogan was involved. She quickly forwarded the email to Sophie Parker.

*

Sophie and Peter were back in their hotel suite. They had nipped out to buy new phones, nervously looking over their shoulders the whole time they were out, paranoid that Edward or one of his cronies would find them.

As they began to configure the new ones, Sophie realised she had an email from Halle on her old phone. She opened the link and gasped, thrusting the images at Peter.

"Holy shit. If that's not evidence of our suspicions, I don't know what is."

*

Edward sat in his office with Andrew and his uncle. "Have we found them yet?"

Uncle James was first to respond. "No. The IT guys say Peter hasn't used his credit card for the last twenty-four hours. They've revoked all his access privileges and confirmed he tried to access the network this morning, but they have no way of tracking where he is by his laptop."

"Hmm, I think this proves he is involved with that woman. He's taking measures not to be found. Guilty, spineless, treacherous wanker."

"What about your mother? Do you think we could catch him visiting her?"

Edward grimaced at the mention of his mother. "Yes, that may be another way of tracking him down. Can you speak to the prison, Andrew, and find out when the visiting times are?"

"Of course."

"What about the Parker business sabotage?"

"I've got the firm we are using to approach a load more of her clients. I think we can be confident that we will give her a few more headaches before the week is out."

Edward nodded, seemingly satisfied with what he was hearing. He stood up, an indication to the others that he wanted them to leave. As he made himself a coffee, he stared out of the window, watching the wind tear at the trees and the birds fighting to keep their flight patterns. A storm was coming in more ways than one.

45

It was just past 9 am as Halle sat outside John's office, waiting for his meeting to end. The delay was not helping her stress. She had to get him to accept that racism was a relevant part of this story.

A further fifteen agonising minutes passed before Halle was finally invited in. John gave her no time to compose herself.

"I've had a complaint about you, Miss Jacobs. A lady called Jen Wyatt has contacted me to say you bribed her with £10,000 and then refused to pay up."

Halle took the body blow. "That's not how it is, sir."

"Well, how is it then, because at the moment you seem to be floundering from one disaster to another, and if you have lost our main contact, you have no TV show."

"She's a nasty piece of work. Initially, I needed to find a way to get her back onside and I did agree to set up a trust fund in memory of her son. This allowed us to get soil and water samples from her house but unfortunately, they came back negative for pollution…"

John shook his head but Halle ploughed on.

"…and when I went back to her house to update her on the results, she got angry, complained about being filmed and racially abused Clayton."

"For God's sake, Miss Jacobs, if she is refusing to engage with us, we can't use any of the footage you have in the can, which, by the way, would make brilliant TV."

"We can, sir. I've made real progress on this story. There is something deeply corrupt around two of the firms that were involved in the construction of that site, and despite not having any evidence yet of pollution, there is a big story here. My team is working round the clock to find the skeletons. I'm sure we will ultimately be able to use the footage on the basis of clear criminality and public interest."

John's face reddened. "Are you trying to tell me my job?"

Halle was losing him but she stood firm. "No, sir, and I'm sorry if you think I'm being disrespectful, but I will deliver you a story and a kick-ass TV show. I just need time to dig deeper."

There was an uncomfortable stand-off as they both engaged in a staring contest. Eventually, John's expression softened.

"I don't share your faith, but I accept you are showing me the sort of resilience I was asking for, so I expect progress by our next review meeting in a couple of weeks. You also need to find a way to placate this Jen Wyatt."

"We don't need her, sir. We have a new contact on the housing estate who is going to help us and she is linked with three other families. She said that Mrs Wyatt is a fraud and was bragging about conning us out of the money. The mood on the estate is really tense and she is nervous about helping us, but is determined to find out whether something or someone is responsible for her son getting cancer. We have the testing team back on site today and I have asked for them to be discreet. We don't want to incite the situation anymore."

John nodded; a more conciliatory action. Halle decided to go for it.

"The other thing, sir, is that this woman is of Indian origin and confirmed there is a real culture of racism on that site. She says they are abused in one way or another every day. With the way Jen Wyatt abused Clayton and his treatment at our event the other day, I think racism is a key part of this story."

John stood up, his face changing back to the disapproving expression Halle saw when she first walked in. "I don't agree. Focus on the core story. I'll see you in two weeks. I need to get to my next meeting."

*

Halle and Todd sat in their usual places in her office, either side of the modern ergonomic desk with a meeting table integrated into the design to allow seamless movement from the desktop to the position they were now occupying.

She rubbed her eyes. "Bloody hell. I don't think I can keep going at this pace, especially when everything I do seems to turn to rat shit."

"Oh, what's happened now?"

Halle sighed. "Well, I've just had another frustrating meeting with John. Apparently, Jen Wyatt has complained about me withdrawing the offer of money. He doesn't seem to understand that she is a horrible racist that doesn't deserve our sympathy. All he cares about is that we have lost our main contact on the site and we don't have a TV show without her consenting to us broadcasting our interviews."

"I did warn you that the big bosses wouldn't necessarily support your direction on this thing."

"I don't care. My next meeting with him is in two weeks. I'll bloody well show him that we have a story here, with or without Jen Wyatt. Have you got the testing teams round at Mrs Gupta's?"

"Yes, they should be there this morning and she has organised time with the other families. Let's hope these tests give us something different."

Halle nodded. "Oh, thank you for that footage yesterday. A nice bit of evidence that our Mr Hogan is well entrenched in whatever this thing is. I sent it to Rod to add to the footage library. If we can ultimately prove some criminality, I'm determined to get stuff like that as part of the show. Hopefully, Rod is over at the site today recording the testers' work."

"Yes, he should be."

"What else did you do last night?"

"Actually, not a lot. Apart from getting that footage, I spent most of the evening watching my hacking programme, trying to break that link to this Genesis thing. It wasn't making much progress and some of the routines kept looping."

"What does that mean?"

"It means we are dealing with a very sophisticated security set-up. When my routines loop, it probably means that the encryption keys are changing faster than I can crack them. In other words, just at the point when I might be cracking through a layer of encryption, their security set-up changes the key, meaning my programme has to start all over again. This is the type of stuff you only see on military or national security set-ups."

"Bloody hell. So, a sure sign that this Genesis link is a hot line of enquiry."

"Absolutely. If there is corruption in this story, we need to crack that link to find out what is going on."

"Can you do it?"

Todd smiled. "Oh, yes, I will get there but it is going to take some time."

"Good, keep at it. We need a breakthrough. I'm not going to give John the satisfaction of telling me I've failed."

Todd gave her a sympathetic smile. "What happened with the Allcock mother?"

Halle suddenly became more animated. "Oh shit. That was totally weird. I was sat down in the visiting room waiting for her to arrive. I saw this woman who I thought was probably her. I waved her over to where I was sitting and when she got to within ten yards of me, she keeled over. Fainted on the spot."

"Eh?"

"Yeah, it was bizarre. The guards confirmed it was her and then shipped her off to the medical centre. They promised to ring me to let me know how she was but I've heard nothing."

"How odd. What was all that about?"

Halle's expression turned to one of real concern. "The thing is, Todd, I will never forget the look on her face as she got close to me. She looked scared, I dunno… almost like she was seeing a ghost."

46

Sophie sat at the oak-panelled desk, which was perfectly placed by the window in the part of the suite designed for people who wanted to get some business done. She had been trawling through the PEMS network trying to find something that would help their investigation.

She suddenly felt Peter's hand on her shoulder. The touch was gentle, intimate, but Sophie flinched at his touch. He took his hand away and she looked up at him, embarrassed by her involuntary reaction. "I'm sorry, Peter. I guess I'm still a bit jumpy."

He fixed her with those deep brown eyes that seemed to penetrate her soul. "It's fine."

She tried to divert attention away from the uncomfortable vibe. "What are we doing? I feel so useless. I've been searching through our network for something else that might explain this thing but I can't find anything. I can't just sit here doing nothing whilst we wait for that reporter and her researcher to solve our mystery."

"We have to be careful. You don't know what my brothers are capable of."

"I think I'm beginning to find out, Peter, but I refuse to be stuck here like a prisoner. I need to go to my advertising firm to sort some stuff out. I won't be long, and I'll meet you back here later this afternoon."

She picked up her bag and left, ignoring Peter's protestations.

*

It was a little after 2 pm as Sophie emerged from the building her advertising agency was located in. She looked around for a cab, but as her eyes scanned the immediate area the hairs on the back of her neck stood up. A primal instinct. A fear response. Straight ahead was a long blacked-out limousine.

As she frantically searched for a cab to hail down, her arm was gripped tightly from behind and she was bundled towards the limo. Before she could shout any sort of protest, a hand was put on her head and she was navigated into the passenger seat.

"Hello, Miss Parker. I don't think we've properly met. I'm Edward Allcock Jnr."

Sophie was horrified. How had he found her? "I've nothing to say to you. Let me out of this car. Now!"

"You're free to go whenever you want, once you answer one question."

Sophie was trying not to show her fear but she was beginning to shake, and his smug, arrogant expression told her that he had noticed. She tried to front it out. "What question is that?"

"Where's my brother?"

"Which one?"

"Oh, come now. Let's not play silly games. Peter. The

one who I assume is trying to get into your pants..." he eyed her up and down, mentally undressing her "... and I can see why."

Sophie tried to brush it off. "I don't know what you mean. I've no idea where he is."

Edward laughed. "You're not a very good liar. I know you two are plotting against me. I'm guessing you've found something in our private folders that you think is suspicious. Well, let me tell you that you really need to stop fishing. There's nothing to find. How about you leave business to the grown-ups? Let the men get on with what they're good at and you can flirt around with that little ad agency you have running."

"I would if you stopped trying to sabotage my business."

Edward held his hands up in mock surrender. "Hey, any business problems you are having are nothing to do with me."

"Let me out."

"Not until you tell me where Peter is."

"I told you. I don't know."

Edward grabbed a cigar and lit it. Sophie started to choke with the stench.

"Not a smoker then? Gives us men that sexy, gravelly voice that you birds so love. At least, in my experience."

"You really are a total wanker. I've no idea why we continue to work with you."

Edward let out a booming laugh. "You really are a naïve bitch. It's money, Miss Parker. Fucking money and lots of it."

"Let me out."

"Where's Peter?"

"I don't know."

"I can do this all day. I've nowhere to be."

"Let me out."

There was a short pause. Sophie went for the door handle but it didn't give. Edward looked at her with amused curiosity, like a lion stalking its prey. He pushed a button and the car started to move.

47

Peter stared at his new phone, willing it to ring, desperate for Sophie to call to explain why she wasn't back, that she was running late for some reason. The tightness in his gut was getting worse. Something bad had happened. He called her on the new phone. The third time in an hour. No answer.

He paced around the hotel suite, lost and confused. Why hadn't Sophie listened to him? Something must have happened at the ad agency. There was only one explanation. Edward or one of his minions must have found her and... Peter couldn't bear to think of the possibilities. His mind spiralled, every scenario getting worse in his mind. If Edward had caught up with her, how far would he go? Would he hold her to ransom to lure Peter out of hiding? Would he torture her to get her to tell where Peter was? The final thought sent chills down his spine. Could she be... dead?

The darkness consumed him once again, negative thoughts invading his psyche. *Why am I such a massive failure at life?*

He sat down, exhausted by the situation. The plan to hole up only worked if Sophie was with him. He cycled through his options. He wondered about Ross. Surely he would be concerned if his sister was in danger? With all the focus on Jeremy, they hadn't considered where Ross fitted in with all this. Could he be part of the corruption? It would follow that old man Parker would want someone to protect the dirty secrets. Had he put all his trust in Jeremy or was Ross in on it? Peter shook the thought away. Ross was too risky.

His mind turned to his mother. What did she know? He suddenly remembered the visiting slot the previous day, the one he was going to use to talk to her, to see if she could tell him anything about what was going on but... someone had taken the slot. Who the hell had done that?

He fought the demons. He had to stop wallowing and do something. He had only one option. The reporter and her researcher. They were on their side, motivated to find a story. Peter had no idea how the housing estate they mentioned tied in with what was going on, but they had found the suspicious links to this Genesis programme and proved with the CCTV pictures that Jeremy was in the thick of this thing.

Peter had never met them and had no contact details. The only way he could get to them was staring up at him from the coffee table. Sophie's old phone. They had turned their phones off the minute they got the burners, hoping that Edward had not already been tracking them. Peter knew he had to access her phone, to find an email or a phone number. The risk of Edward tracking Sophie's phone was lower than his. Was it possible that Edward didn't know her number? He knew that was a fanciful thought. If Edward was determined enough, he would have found out what it was.

He picked up Sophie's phone, turning it over and over in his hands. He made a decision. He had no choice. He turned it on. There was no code and he navigated to her emails. He found the last email from the reporter. Halle Jacobs. He quickly typed a message back to her, inviting them to come to his suite. There was no time to lose.

*

The prison doctor held Victoria's arm, taking her pulse. After a minute, he laid her arm back down on the bed. Victoria lay motionless, her eyes open, staring at the ceiling in the medical ward. They had revived her after her fainting spell but since she had come round, she had said nothing.

"Mrs Allcock. Can you hear what I'm saying?" There was no response. The doctor looked at the nurse in attendance, concern all over his face. They walked away from her bed.

"Sister, medically, Mrs Allcock is perfectly healthy. She has a good consistent pulse, her blood pressure is fine and her temperature is stable. But mentally, she seems to be in some sort of paralysis, like her body and mind have experienced some massive trauma. Do you have any idea what happened when she fainted?"

"According to the guards, she was walking towards her visitor, stopped when she was about ten yards away and just collapsed on the floor. She has been completely unresponsive since she came round."

"Okay, give her hourly obs and call me if anything changes."

*

It was a little after 7 pm when the butler assigned to Peter's suite announced he had two visitors. He beckoned them in. An attractive young woman and a geeky-looking guy wearing a Captain America t-shirt stood in the doorway, both wide-eyed with the opulence of the hotel suite they were being ushered into.

Peter stepped forward and offered his hand. "Hi, I'm Peter Allcock. I'm sorry about all this. It's a bit over the top but a necessary extravagance at the moment."

The young woman took his hand. "It's amazing. I'm Halle Jacobs and this is my researcher, Todd Barkley."

Peter asked them to sit and got the butler to order up some food and drink. He steeled himself. "Thank you for coming at such short notice. It's so great to meet you."

Halle continued to take the lead as Todd watched on. "Likewise, but why all the urgency and the secret location stuff?"

"Sophie Parker is missing."

"Missing? How?"

"I don't know but she went to her ad agency this morning and hasn't returned. Ever since she started to dig into the relationship between our two companies, strange things have started to happen."

"Like what?"

"She had someone following her home the other night, tailgating her in the car and then she received this note."

Halle and Todd looked at the crumpled piece of paper.

"I got worried that it was the work of my brothers so we decided to hide out here, whilst we tried to work out what is going on."

"Why did she leave the hotel?"

"Her ad agency is in trouble. She thinks my brothers have been trying to sabotage her business and she had to meet with her team to manage the situation."

"Oh. Why didn't she take her phone?"

"We bought burners. We were worried that my brothers might be trying to find us. I've rang it loads of times but there is no answer."

Halle looked at Todd and he fired his laptop up. "Give Todd the number and we can see if we can locate it."

They sat in silence as Todd tapped away. "The phone's off but its last known location was near Bishop's Park in West London, around early afternoon."

Peter put his head in his hands. "That's near where her ad agency is. What has happened to her?"

Halle tried to put on a sympathetic face. "The best thing we can do is to put everything we know on the table and see if we can work out what's happening here."

The butler knocked with the food and drink. "Come on, Peter. Let's eat something and get on with this. Sophie is depending on us to find her."

48

Her eyes blinked open. Her head was thumping. Everything was blurred. She was lying on a bed. She tried to force her eyes to focus. The shape of the room began to form. She was in a square room, all white walls with no windows. She forced herself to sit up. Where on earth was she?

She looked around. The bed she was laid on was against the back wall, with a bedside table next to it. On the other side of the room was a single lounge chair. There was a glass of water on the side and she guzzled it down to ease the soreness in her throat.

Her limbs were heavy but she forced her feet onto the floor. She stood up unsteadily, her mind beginning to form the memories of what had happened. Edward Allcock. The limo. The argument in the car. The locked door. When she refused to answer his question about Peter's location, he had driven off and then... Sophie couldn't remember. He must have knocked her out with something and now she was incarcerated in this room.

As she stood in the centre of the room, she realised something else. There was no door. She started to frantically paw at the walls. How could there be no way in? What the hell was this place? As she felt along the wall on the opposite side of the room, a panel moved with her probing. She gasped and pushed harder. A whole section of the wall moved inwards. Was this her way out? She stepped through the gap, hoping for some reference to where she was. The optimism left her immediately. It was a bathroom. A toilet, sink and a shower. Fresh towels, shampoo and shower gel lined the shelves.

*

"Holy fuck. Just what the hell do you think you are doing?"

Edward stood by the floor-to-ceiling window in the huge living space of his penthouse apartment, staring out at the London skyline, trying to ignore his uncle's disapproval.

"Edward? Are you for fucking real? Don't you dare ignore me."

Edward turned around. Apart from his father, his uncle was the only man that he allowed to speak to him like that. A father substitute who had guided them through the troubled years after their mother killed their father, a devastating emotional period in Edward's life that he wouldn't have survived without his uncle's support and guidance.

"I had no choice."

"You what! You had every choice. You should have let her out of the car. Been smart. Got someone to follow her to where Peter is hiding."

"It's done. I just need time to think, with her out of the way. I can't afford for her to find out what's been going on for all these years. I will not destroy my father's legacy. Not for anyone. You do understand that."

His uncle's face contorted with rage. "You patronising twat. I was the one that protected that legacy, nurtured it to make sure I could hand it over to you and your brothers. To make sure that you could all enjoy the financial trappings that came with it and to keep my promise to your father. So, don't you dare ask me if I understand."

Edward sat down, rubbing his face in frustration. "How exposed are we? How much do they know? Peter has found the link to Genesis. If they have someone who can crack that link, we're dead. Every single thing we've done that we don't want people to know about is documented in that programme. Years of…"

His uncle's mood softened as he filled the void left by Edward's unfinished sentence. "You need to be smart. They know nothing, and Genesis is protected by the most sophisticated security money can buy. All they have is their suspicions. We can ride this out whilst they play detective. They won't find anything. Trust me."

"Do we still have the 'kill switch' on that programme?"

"Yeah, of course we do, but that has to be the last option. If that programme doesn't exist, you lose all the leverage you have built up over all these years. Can you really afford that on the slight possibility that they somehow hack that programme?"

Edward poured himself a whisky and downed it in one, wincing as the sharpness hit his throat. "We have to consider it. We can't afford for that information to be out there, and anyway, the people who we are using that information against wouldn't know it's gone. We've shown them what we've got and the fear of exposure should keep them sweet."

"It's a risk, but I guess we have to consider it. We can kill it with one phone call."

Edward poured himself another whisky and walked back towards the window. After a few minutes, he turned back to look at his uncle.

"What about the current projects? She's already been on site with Jeremy. What if she insists on supervising the remediation work? She'll soon find what she's looking for if she does that."

"Well, we won't let her. Say it's about safety or something."

Edward let out a frustrated scream. James stood up and grabbed his arm.

"Look. The bottom line is that you made a mistake in locking her up. You can't possibly think you can keep her here indefinitely. We need to trust in what we've been doing all these years. She and your pathetic excuse for a brother are not going to find anything. You need to let her out."

49

Fully refreshed, the three of them got comfortable in the lavish living area. Halle tried to get them to focus. "Right, as I said, the only way we can help Sophie is if we all lay everything out on the table. You start with what you know."

Peter took a deep breath, the stress of losing Sophie etched all over his face. "Okay. The bottom line is that Sophie thinks there is something iffy going on between our firms which goes all the way back to when my father set up ALMS and started doing business with Sophie's father, who set up PEMS. She got suspicious because her father kept telling her to leave the ALMS relationship alone when he handed the business over to her and Ross. She said he was normally such a calm guy but was very agitated every time he spoke about it. He kept telling her that Jeremy had it covered. Now that we have evidence that Jeremy has been speaking to Edward at his skin palace, we're sure they're hiding something."

"Do you have any idea what it's about?"

"Not really. The only other thing she found was this weird bank account called Bill Parker Holdings which had large chunks of money going into it after each ALMS project. She does not have access to the account or the funds in it. When she confronted her father about it, he said it was for R&D and was managed by Jeremy."

"And she didn't believe him?"

"Would you?"

"No, I guess not, given what we suspect about Jeremy's involvement. How much money are we talking about?"

"Umm, I dunno. She said hundreds of thousands. I mean, from memory, PEMS charge us about £500k to £700k for their work on each site. I guess a good chunk of that money must be their profit margin, which I assume must be a couple of hundred thousand per deal."

Halle blew out her cheeks. "Wow, I can see why Sophie is concerned. What's a typical deal look like from your end?"

Peter looked embarrassed but didn't step away from answering the question. "Obviously, it varies depending on the site, but a typical average-sized brownfield site might cost us £5 million. We probably spend another million or two getting any buildings on the site demolished and the ground levelled. As I said, PEMS charge us about half to three quarters of a million for their work, meaning a total cost of seven to eight million."

"And you sell it for how much?"

"Probably about three to five times that. If a developer picks up a site for around £25 million and builds two or three hundred houses at London prices, they are still making a good profit."

Halle shook her head. "I can see why your firm makes so much money, Peter, and I can also see that it's something your family would want to protect at all costs."

Peter put his head in his hands. "What have I done? What have I been part of all these years? And now, I've put Sophie in danger."

"Look, there's no point moping over the past. If we are going to find Sophie, you need to tell us everything."

Peter perked up and took a long slug of the red wine he had ordered with the food.

"Okay, so after all the weird shit that's been happening to Sophie, we decided to hole up here to give us time to think and get out of the firing line. The problem is, we feel a bit hamstrung. I managed to hack my way into Edward's private folder and found this Genesis thing, but that's been about my limit in terms of hacking. It's why she was so willing to speak to you two. We desperately need your help."

"That's what we're here for. Anything else you can tell us? What about your family?"

"What can I say? My brother Edward is a nasty piece of work, very much in the image of my father. A woman-hating, xenophobic racist who will stop at nothing to make a few quid. Andrew follows him like a lapdog. And my uncle has been the substitute father, making sure we all knew how important our father's legacy was to him. Stephen and Philip are intensely loyal to Edward and my father but are basically harmless. If there's something going on here, I can guarantee that Edward, Andrew and Uncle James are pulling the strings."

"You've been around them all this time. Why didn't you spot that something odd was going on?"

Peter shook his head, the comment shaming him more than he cared to admit. He sighed heavily. "I'm so ashamed. I've been so naïve. I was happy to coast along doing my job and enjoying the ridiculous wealth that it brought me. I know now that I have been played all these years. Edward had me doing a job that was so easy to do because he made sure that people like Jeremy Hogan told me what I needed to know. I never questioned it. I was lazy."

"Is that why you're here now? Because you want to make it right?"

Peter gave Halle an embarrassed smile. "Er... I'd like to say that I finally got some balls but in reality, I wouldn't have done this without Sophie, she's..."

Halle filled the awkward silence that was left by Peter's unfinished sentence. The look on his face, when he spoke about Sophie, was one she recognised all too well. "Oh, so you two are..."

Peter stood up and walked to the window. "I don't know. I don't know what we are. I just know I've never met a woman like her. Maybe it's some schoolboy infatuation but at this moment I can't bear to think what might be happening if Edward has her."

Halle walked over to the window and put an arm round Peter. "Come on. Let's have another drink. We've still got a lot to get through."

They had a short break, letting the tension ease a bit before they reconvened in the living area. Halle knew she had to crack on.

"What about your mother?"

Peter once again shook his head. "My mother. Another victim of my father and his horrendous legacy. He abused my mother for years. One day, she finally cracked and

227

stabbed him to death. I was only nine at the time, not really understanding what was going on. Uncle James took us in and looked after us, ultimately nurturing us to take over the business and continue my father's legacy. For years, I didn't know anything better, but when I was old enough to start thinking for myself, I went to visit her in prison and she told me her side of the story. To this day, I'm the only one that thinks she's innocent and the only one that visits her."

Halle winced at Peter's final sentence. She knew she had to fess up. "Umm, Peter. I've something I need to tell you."

Peter looked at her expectantly.

"I went to visit your mother yesterday but something weird happened."

At first, Peter said nothing. Halle could see he was processing the information. His expression changed from quizzical to something more enlightened. Like something had dropped into his brain. "Ah, so it was you that nicked my visitor slot."

Halle looked embarrassed. "I'm sorry. The more we looked into this mystery, the more I got intrigued by how your mother's story fitted into all this. I made an application to the warden to visit her and they agreed. I'm so sorry if I stopped you seeing her."

"It's fine. I don't go every time. She probably wasn't expecting to see me anyway. So, how was she?"

"That's the thing. It was weird. As she approached the table I was sat at, she stopped in her tracks, staring at me like she'd seen a ghost. A few seconds later, she fainted, and the guards whisked her off to the medical room. I asked them to let me know how she is but they haven't called."

Peter immediately picked up his phone and dialled the prison. He walked out of the room.

Halle looked at Todd, who had been quietly tapping away on his laptop the whole time they had been talking. "Shit. What have I done? Do you think he's mad with me?"

"I doubt it. He's just worried about his mum. Give him some space. I'm sure he'll be back in a minute."

"God, I hope so. Have you got any good news for me? What about the hack on this Genesis thing?"

"To be honest, I'm struggling. I've rarely seen security this sophisticated. I might need to get my cyber buddies to help me. My normal programmes are not working and we might need to do a co-ordinated attack on the site to crack it."

"Okay, do what you have to do. I guess…"

Halle's concentration was broken by Peter walking back into the living area, concern etched all over his face. "Is she all right?"

"I dunno. They say that since she fainted, she hasn't said a word. Medically she's fine but mentally they say she seems like she's in some form of post-traumatic stress. She just lays on her bed, not saying a word and not responding to any stimulus."

"My God, that's awful. Was it my fault?"

"The doctors don't seem to know. They've agreed to let me visit her tomorrow."

As they all stopped to take in what Peter had said, there was a sudden commotion at the door to the suite. A few seconds later, they all gasped at the sight of the person standing in front of them.

50

Marjit Gupta turned the corner that led into the Pickford housing estate, her legs weary from another eight-hour shift in A&E, with rarely a second to rest. She pulled her coat around her, the sub-zero temperatures already pricking at her exposed skin as darkness took hold. She began to walk along the narrow alley that came out a few yards from her house when she was aware of a presence behind her.

She stopped and turned around. Two masked people were in her face. She instinctively turned to run but one of them grabbed her and smashed her hard against the wall.

"Let… let me go."

The assailant that had grabbed her and was pinning her against the wall spoke first. A man's voice. "Listen, you bitch. Stop dealing with those bloody reporters or we can't be held responsible for what might happen to you."

Marjit was terrified but tried to front it out. "I… I don't know what you're on about."

He pulled her forward and smashed her hard against the wall. Pain coursed through her back. Tears welling up. "Why are you doing this? I've done nothing wrong."

The second assailant spoke. A woman. "Nothing

wrong! Those bloody reporters don't care about us. They just want their story and you're helping them."

"Leave me alone."

The man relaxed his grip, giving her one more shove. The woman spoke again. "You've been warned. Stop talking to those reporters or worse will happen to you. Why don't you do us all a favour and fuck off back to your own country."

Marjit stood for a moment, letting the pain in her back subside a little. She knew who they were despite their stupid disguises. Jen Wyatt and the man who had lost his daughter to cancer... Graham something from the other side of the estate.

She understood their grief but she could never understand their hatred and ignorance, just because of the colour of her skin. The 'back to your own country' insult always made her laugh, if it wasn't such a hateful thing to say. She was born in Bermondsey and her son had been born whilst they lived on this estate.

She moved gingerly, debating whether to call the police. They had bruised her back but otherwise she was okay. She started to walk back to her home. As she opened the door, the sitter greeted her, noticing her wincing as she walked across the threshold.

"Are you okay, Mrs Gupta? You look like you are in pain."

"I'm okay, Ali. I slipped and jarred my back. Nothing a good night's sleep won't cure."

Marjit paid her and watched her leave. Had she been right to lie? Was she inadvertently condoning the behaviour of those racists?

She shook the thought away and walked up the stairs. Sunil was in bed but stirred as she hovered at the door. "Mama!"

Marjit walked in, trying not to well up at the sight of the wispy bits of hair that remained on Sunil's head as the chemotherapy took its toll. "Hello, sweetheart. I'm sorry to wake you. Are you okay?"

"I'm tired, Mama, and I feel sick."

"I know, Sunil, but the stuff we are doing at the hospital is trying to make you better."

"I know, Mama. Hug me."

As Marjit went to move, she pulled up in pain.

"Mama, are you okay?"

She gritted her teeth. "Yes, yes, Sunil. I just hurt my back earlier. It'll be fine."

They hugged for a good few minutes before Sunil began to get sleepy. Marjit laid him down and left his room.

She made herself a tea and popped a couple of painkillers. Her phone sat on the side staring up at her. What should she do? Would the police do anything?

She took her tea and sat down in the living area, the comfy chair easing the pain in her back. As she scrolled through her emails, she realised she had one from Halle Jacobs. She was going to pop round in the morning to update her on the soil and water tests. She smiled to herself. That's how she would make these racists pay. She would tell her story to the TV people and expose them for the ignorant assholes they were.

She finished her tea and closed her eyes. Tomorrow was another day.

51

"Sophie!" Peter ran across the room to embrace her. "What... what happened to you?"

Sophie walked slowly to the couch, poured herself some water and grabbed a leftover sandwich, devouring it in seconds. They all looked on, expectantly. She eventually looked up, a questioning glance at Todd as she surveyed the scene in front of her.

Halle picked up on the non-verbals. "Oh, this is Todd, Sophie. He's my researcher."

Sophie nodded without saying anything and ate another sandwich. Peter was wound up like a coil, desperate to get her to explain, but she kept her head down as she ate. In the end, the tension got too much and he touched her knee. "Sophie. Are you okay?"

She flinched at his touch. As she finished the sandwich and took a long slug of water, she spoke, shaking her head as she did. "Your family, Peter. They are unhinged. Does your brother think he's some sort of East End gangster?"

Peter was still frantic with worry. "I'm sorry. Did he find you? What did he do to you?"

She took another sip of water. "I don't really know. I was trying to hail a cab outside my offices, after I finished my meeting. It was around two. The next thing I know, someone is bundling me into a stretch limo and your delightful brother Edward is in the back. He wouldn't let me out. Kept asking over and over where you were. When I refused to answer him, we drove off. The next thing I know, I wake up in some weird room with no doors or windows…"

"He held you in his panic room?"

"…er …I dunno. Was that what it was?"

"He has a panic room in his penthouse apartment. Kept bragging about it when he got it put in. It's completely controlled by an App on his phone. It definitely sounds like the room he held you in."

Halle and Todd had been sat there quietly lapping up all the drama but Halle couldn't hold back any longer. "Why did he let you go?"

She turned her gaze to Halle. "How should I know? The man is a fucking psychopath."

"Shouldn't you report him to the police?"

Sophie stared at Halle, the trauma still evident in her pale, drawn expression. She didn't answer, just stood up and walked towards her bedroom. They all watched her walk away as they exchanged quizzical glances at each other. Peter went to follow her but Halle grabbed his arm. "Give her some space, Peter. It's still early. If she comes back, we can continue going through everything we know, because I think your brother has just drawn the battle lines."

They waited for over twenty minutes but Sophie didn't re-emerge. Halle took that as a sign that the evening was over. "I think we should go. Can we meet back up here tomorrow evening and finish off what we started tonight?"

"Yes, yes, I guess so. I'll try and talk to her in the morning and let you know if she's still not up to it."

"Call the police. Your brothers need to be stopped."

With that, Halle and Todd left. Peter sat in the living space. Shocked. Stunned. Paralysed with fear and indecision. He couldn't involve the police. Could he?

*

Sophie lay on her bed staring up at the ornate chandelier that was hanging in the centre of the room. The crystals were catching the light and she watched the reflections and shadows dance on the ceiling. She was numb. Questions kept flying through her mind. Why had her father got involved with Edward Allcock? What little secret scheme had they cooked up that was still going strong forty years later? Were they really paying people off from that mystery account? What did Ross know? Would they all go to jail if this thing turned out to be illegal? What was this Genesis thing hiding?

She turned over and buried her face in the pillow, stifling a scream. Their lives had always been so straightforward. Their father ran the company and their mother looked after everyone. They never seemed to want for anything and her childhood memories were generally good. As Ross went to work for Dad, she got interested in advertising and PR, leading to her starting her own company when she was twenty-five. So why, all of a sudden, had her life been turned upside down? She never really wanted to run PEMS but saw it as a new challenge, a chance to learn about the business and put her own stamp on it. But her father's behaviour was odd from the minute he announced he was standing down, and now she felt like she'd opened Pandora's box.

She rolled back over and shuddered as the memories of what happened with Edward Allcock came flooding back. She had never met anyone so... so evil, so wrapped up in his own self-importance that he couldn't see his behaviour was just wrong. The problem was, she couldn't, or wouldn't, allow herself to contemplate how bad this thing could be. Her father wasn't a criminal... was he? The Allcocks had demonstrated their potential to work outside the law, but she couldn't reconcile this with her sweet, caring father.

The problem was, they were no nearer to finding the answers. She didn't know why Halle Jacobs and her researcher had been here this evening, but she was not ready for a full-blown interrogation. The experience with Edward Allcock and the realisation that he was so desperate to silence her had scared her more than she cared to admit. Which still left the most pressing question.

Why did he let her go, and could she really navigate this thing without involving the police?

52

The next morning, Halle, Todd, Rod and Clayton were on their way to see Mrs Gupta. Todd had been promised the results of the soil tests on her property and the three others that had agreed to help them. Halle knew she had to get more footage and hoped the interaction with Mrs Gupta would be as compelling as the stuff she'd recorded with Jen Wyatt. The nagging mental reminders that she still didn't have enough evidence to use that footage without Jen's consent were stressing her out.

They parked up outside her house and walked to the door, Rod carrying all the necessary equipment to record the discussions. As Marjit Gupta opened the door, Halle could see she was in pain.

"Are you okay, Mrs Gupta?"

She gestured them in and invited them to sit down. Coffee and biscuits were already laid out. Marjit gestured at Rod. "Get that thing set up. I want what I'm about to say on your TV programme."

Halle looked concerned but chivvied Rod to get the camera set up. A few minutes later, they were ready to roll and Halle prompted her to tell her story. "What happened here?"

Marjit changed positions to get more comfortable. "I was assaulted last night by Jen Wyatt and that other bloke, Graham... oh, I don't know what his name is, but he's the other parent that lost a child. The one that was shouting at you at that thing we had in the community hall."

"Are you okay? Did you report it to the police?"

"He shoved me up against a wall and bruised my back quite badly. It'll be fine in a few days."

"Why did they do it?"

"They told me to stop helping you whilst adding in a bit of racial abuse for good measure."

"You didn't call the police?"

Marjit rolled her eyes and looked at Clayton for empathy. "You don't know much about the police round here, do you? People like us don't tend to get much sympathy from them. It's always our word against the white folk, and when most of the police officers are white, you kinda feel like there's no point. No, I'd much rather get all this on film and tell the world what it's like to live on this estate with these people."

There was a brief uncomfortable pause, which Marjit broke by offering to pour the coffees.

Having got over the shock of what they had walked into, Halle got Marjit to retell the story about her son Sunil developing cancer and their history of living on the estate. The raw emotion was evident throughout, and Halle was privately pleased that the footage would be the 'gold dust' that John had been looking for. Halle was pumped to find that two of the other three families were available and were coming round to Marjit's house within the hour. She was concerned at the threats from Jen Wyatt and her cronies but was impressed with the resilience that Marjit and the other families were showing.

As the interview trailed off, Todd gestured to Halle that the report had come through about the soil and water tests. They bundled around his laptop and read the report.

Todd provided the narrative. "Oh, the tests on your house, Mrs Gupta, and two of the other properties show only mild traces of pollution. All within safe limits. However, the tests from number 43, Mr and Mrs Chambers' house, show much higher levels. Now, the guys who did the testing said that whilst these are just within safe levels, they are much higher than most of the other tests we took."

They all looked at each other. Marjit spoke. "What does that mean?"

Todd rubbed his face. "I don't know. I can't work out why that one property is different to all the others. Where is it on the estate?"

"I think it's right over on the other side, on the eastern perimeter, near the community hall."

Halle studied the report. "Do we have that map, the one that shows where they took the samples?"

Todd tapped away. "Yes, here it is. Number 43 is a bit away from all the other sample sites we took and is stuck right on the perimeter of the site."

Halle's brain was racing. "Could that mean that the pollution is coming from something bordering the estate, something we hadn't considered?"

Todd fired up Google Maps and started to scan the area adjacent to that side of the estate. "I can't see anything obvious but maybe we should get the testing guys back to test just outside the estate, see if the pollution gets worse as you head east."

As the nervous energy coursed through Halle, her focus was distracted by the doorbell ringing. Two of Marjit's neighbours came in. Halle desperately wanted to follow this new lead but couldn't miss the opportunity to get their stories on tape. It wasn't the neighbours from number 43 but the two separate parents who spoke about their experiences with the same gut-wrenching pain that Halle had heard too often. Great TV but personal pain and tragedy that were beginning to wear her down.

As they got back in the car, Halle was exhausted but pleased they had got such a good amount of footage for the TV show. It might just get John off her back for a while, as he seemed to be checking on her footage library more regularly than she was comfortable with.

As Clayton began to drive out of the estate, Halle's mind was spinning with the results from number 43. She turned to Todd, who was sat in the back. "Can you get the testing team back to do some perimeter testing?"

"I'm on it like a scotch bonnet, my gorgeous one."

Halle tried to ignore his current obsession with cringeworthy flattery and shut her eyes. Something about those results was nagging in her mind. A feeling that she had the answer but just couldn't get it to the front of her brain.

She settled in for the drive back to the office, letting the brain worm fester away.

53

Peter parked up in the prison car park. Sophie was still sleeping when he left, so he had no idea how she was or whether she was up for seeing Halle and Todd later.

He'd spent most of the journey staring in his rear-view mirror, paranoid that someone was following him, but as he drew into the car park, nobody seemed to be interested in what he was doing.

He hurried into reception and explained the nature of the special visit he had been granted. A few minutes later, a prison officer escorted him to the medical wing.

As he entered, the doctor that was treating his mother stopped his progress. "Mr Allcock, I just wanted to speak to you about your mother before you go in."

"Oh yeah, of course."

"The thing is, medically she is perfectly fine but mentally she is... well, I can only describe it as a severe mental breakdown. She isn't speaking and doesn't respond to any normal stimulus. It's like she's in a living coma. Her eyes are open but she just stares ahead. It's the sort of thing we see in severe cases of post-traumatic stress. I'm hoping that your presence might snap her out of whatever paralysis she is under."

"Okay, well, I'll do my best."

The doctor escorted him into the private room. His mother was laid on the bed staring at the ceiling.

"Does she sleep?"

"Yes, it seems she sleeps when her body needs her to, but when she wakes up, she remains still and staring at the ceiling. We are dealing with all her bodily functions and feeding her through a drip, but other than that we have nothing we can do."

The doctor left and Peter sat by her bed. He picked up her hand. "Mum. Mum. It's Peter. Can you hear me?"

There was nothing. He stood up and got in her eyeline. There was no movement. No response. He called her name again. Nothing. He shook her lightly. Nothing. He sat back down and stared at her almost lifeless body.

A few minutes later, the doctor came back in. "No luck?"

"No, she is not responding to anything. I've got right in her eyeline, even shaken her lightly, but nothing is working. What the hell is going on?"

The doctor checked her vitals and shook his head. "There's nothing medically wrong with her, but mentally she is someplace else. Do you have any idea what has triggered this episode?"

"All I know is it happened when this reporter came to visit. She said my mother stopped as she was approaching her, had a really weird expression on her face and then fainted."

"Does she know this person?"

"No. I didn't know she had arranged to visit my mother and as far as I know, they have never met."

"Did you ask this reporter whether she recognised your mother?"

"Well, no, but I'm sure this is the first time they have met."

"Your mother's been in here a long time and I know she is up for parole. Has she said anything to you about getting out?"

"A bit. I know the last parole hearing went badly because she wasn't prepared to tell them what they wanted to hear. She feels her conviction was a gross miscarriage of justice and she isn't prepared to offer the remorse they are looking for."

"Do you think it could be why she has gone like this? Has the trauma of her time in here and the realisation that she won't get out unless she admits her crime sent her over the edge?"

"I guess it's possible but I still don't see how that relates to the visit by the reporter. She said my mother looked scared when she saw her. I just can't see the connection between the two scenarios."

They carried on 'chewing the fat', trying to find an explanation for why Victoria Allcock had disconnected with the world.

As the conversation trailed off, Peter looked back at his mother. Nothing had changed.

"Okay, Doctor, thank you. It doesn't seem like there is much else we can do here. Keep me up to date with any progress."

The doctor agreed and they moved towards the exit of the room. As they did, they heard a faint moan followed by the quietest of words… *Peter.*

They stopped in their tracks, looking at each other to validate if they had both heard the noise. They rushed back to her bedside. She was still staring up at the ceiling, but as Peter got closer, she turned her head slightly and looked at him. Her voice was barely audible but Peter could just make out what she said.

"Peter. That girl. I want to see her."

54

It was just past 6.30 pm as Halle and Todd rocked up to the Savoy Hotel, entering the mirrored lift that took them up to the lavish suites that Peter and Sophie had chosen as their hiding place. As the butler once again announced their arrival, they were met with stressed facial expressions.

Halle desperately wanted to crack on but she needed to keep them onside. She directed her empathy towards Sophie. "Are you okay? We don't have to do this tonight if you don't want to."

Sophie looked at Peter, some sort of reassurance needed, before she glanced back at Halle. "It's fine. I'm not going to let that psycho bastard intimidate me. His actions have just confirmed we are onto something and I'm bloody determined to find out what it is."

"Did you contact the police?"

"No. I need more. If I approach the police now, he'll brush it off as a misunderstanding and probably pay someone off to sweep it under the table. We need to be clever. We need to find more evidence of what he is up to. There will be a moment when the police go and arrest that bastard and I'm determined to make sure the case is watertight."

Halle was impressed with Sophie's resolve. She turned her attention to Peter. He met her gaze, his expression strange and unfriendly. "What did you do to my mother?"

"What? I didn't do anything. She fainted before she reached me."

"So why has she asked to see you?"

"Er… what? Has she come out of her… well, whatever was wrong with her?"

Peter's frown deepened. "She only uttered one sentence the whole time I was there. She said she wants to see you. What the hell is going on with you two?"

"I don't know what you mean. I've never met your mother before. I admit, I was intrigued by her story and I'm sorry I tried to see her behind your back, but that's where it ends."

There was a stand-off. Peter's accusing tone hung in the air. Halle looked at Sophie, her expression neutral but not doing anything to diffuse the situation.

Halle turned around and made for the exit, looking back briefly. "I can see it was a mistake coming here tonight. We don't need you to make our TV show and you should remember it was you that begged me for help. Maybe when you've calmed down, Peter, you will see that I've done nothing to your mother. You should look much closer to home for that one."

As they rode down in the lift, Todd smirked at Halle's face, all rage and confusion. "Go girl."

*

Edward sat on his own in his usual place in the strip club, surrounded by girls with wide pupils, spaced out on whatever drug was currently doing the rounds. They fawned over him, trying to illicit money to feed their habit. He mostly ignored them, consumed by the events of the previous day.

He still had no idea where Peter and Sophie were hiding out, but his uncle kept telling him to ignore their stupid game of hide and seek. He was pleased they felt threatened enough to hide out but he had no control over what they were doing, especially now they knew about Genesis. Could he really trust his uncle's judgement that the programme could never be hacked? Edward didn't like relying on other people. He simply did not leave things to chance.

His instincts with Sophie Parker had been to take her out of the game, but again his uncle's disapproval of his approach had forced him to let her go, and the stupid goons he employed had failed to follow her to wherever she was hiding out.

The girls continued to drape themselves over him, pawing at his groin and thrusting their breasts in his face. His shoved them off and told them to go. He needed to be completely alone.

He gestured a waitress for another whisky as he swilled the last of the golden mixture in the glass he was currently focusing on. His thoughts turned to his father. Uncharacteristic emotions welled up as he thought about the moment as a fourteen-year-old boy he was told his mother had murdered his father. The man was his life and that *bitch* had stolen the opportunity for him to learn more, to be more like him, which made Peter's betrayal all the more sickening. Siding with his mother and now

247

working against him with Sophie Parker, after all the years that the Allcocks and Parkers had worked together.

His anger deepened. The scenarios rolled around his head. In business, he made things happen. He paid people to do what he wanted and he took out his competitors. Genesis held the leverage he used to persuade people to his way of thinking, and he was damned if he was going to let his pathetic brother and a bloody woman mess that up. His whisky arrived and he downed it in one.

He made a decision. He was the head of the family and there was no way he was going to let his father's legacy be destroyed. He didn't care what his uncle thought. It was time for him to do what was necessary. He had to find Peter and Sophie and take them out of the game.

55

Sophie stared at Peter. "What the hell was that? You've just let our only chance of finding out what this thing is all about walk out that door."

Peter stood at the window, turning to face Sophie's rage. "They can't be trusted. They're bloody reporters, after all, looking for a story so they can make their TV show. She's lying to us about my mother. If she claims she's never met her before, why is mother asking to see her and why did her presence send her into some mental shutdown?"

"I don't know, but that's no reason to start accusing her of something you can't substantiate. Why didn't you ask your mother why she wanted to see her?"

"Because she's locked in whatever trauma that woman put her in. It was the only thing we could get out of her."

"Bloody hell, you need to start being smart. They want to help us. You admitted yourself that we don't have the skillset to hack that Genesis programme. Her researcher was confident he could hack it and now we have no control over what they are doing."

Peter's face was red with rage. "I don't care. You made a huge mistake in trusting that reporter. Didn't you realise she was just after a story? You're so naïve. I'm not letting anyone upset my mother, not after everything she has been through, and I'm sure as hell not going to let that bloody reporter go and see her."

Sophie stood up and set off for her bedroom. "Maybe when you calm down, Peter, you'll see some sense, but I can't be around you at the moment."

*

As they reached the lobby of the hotel, Halle grabbed Todd and dragged him into the bar. "Come on. I need a drink."

She ordered a vodka and tonic and Todd got a gin and lemonade. Halle winced at the prices but charged it to the company credit card. "It's about time John started paying for some of my stress."

They both took big slugs of their drinks and Halle could sense Todd's agitation. "Something to say, Todd?"

"Do you think that was wise?"

Halle looked at Todd, trying to read his mood. Was he showing disapproval? She tried to ignore it. "Oh, I dunno. He really is a prize asshole. Like the rest of his family. I mean, what the fuck was he accusing me of? I've never met his mother in my life. I have no idea why she went loco or why she wants to see me. I mean, what the hell am I meant to do about that?"

Todd put his hand on Halle's arm. "You're so cute when you're angry."

Halle screwed her face up. There it was again. What the hell was Todd playing at? He picked up on the vibe.

"Look, I'm sorry. Maybe this isn't the right time but I'm… er… shit, this is difficult… but I'm really into you."

"What?"

"I really like you, Halle. You are smart, you are funny, you have such a kind heart. You're amazing and I can't stop thinking about you."

Halle's gasp was so loud that it drew attention from people around them. "Todd, this can't happen. I'm flattered but I'm your boss, for God's sake."

Todd tried not to be too crestfallen. "I can't stop how I feel about you."

Halle fixed him with an enquiring gaze, her head spinning with what he had just said. "And you thought now was a good time to tell me!"

Todd finished his drink. "Well… I thought, why not?"

Halle finished her drink and ordered another round. She stared off in the other direction. Eventually, she re-engaged. "Look, I can't deny that there could be something between us in the future, but I just can't concentrate on that now. Can we just keep this on the level, get this TV show in the can, and then I might have the headspace to work out what this thing is between us?"

Todd leant over and kissed her on the cheek. "Of course, boss lady. I'll wait."

*

It was a little after 9.30 pm when Todd got back to his flat. They had left after the second drink and gone their separate ways. Todd felt a sense of relief. His feelings for Halle had been growing every day and he was bursting to tell her how he felt. He knew she may not follow through on her promise, but he was cheered by the fact that she accepted it was a possibility.

He fired up his tech and checked on the Genesis hack. It had made no progress. The programme was still looping. "Damn it!" Todd had hacked multinational corporations, major banks and even some military networks, but he had never come across security so sophisticated. *The Allcocks must be hiding some serious shit to have this level of security,* he mused to himself.

His frustration was interrupted by a ping on his laptop. He had a Proton message from Krypto.

KRYPTO: Yo, dude. How's the Genesis hack going?

SNAPDEVIL: It's not. Programme has been running for nearly two days and just keeps looping. I've never seen security like it

KRYPTO: Wowser. What's your plan?

SNAPDEVIL: Think we are gonna have to get a gang together and do some co-ordinated attacks. Looks like the encrypted keys are changing so fast that the hack programme can't solve them fast enough

KRYPTO: OK, let me know when you wanna do it

SNAPDEVIL: Will do. What progress have you made?

KRYPTO: Been busy. Got interested in this Jeremy dude. He's defo dodgy. Has spending habits that are way above what he earns at his firm. He is getting large sums of money on a regular basis and splurges it on holidays, cars and a big-arse house

SNAPDEVIL: Interesting. I think he's pivotal to whatever is going on with ALMS. Anything else?

KRYPTO: Yes. Finding out about Jezza made me do what we always do and I followed the money

SNAPDEVIL: And?

KRYPTO: Ooh, get ready, my sweet princess. Your prince charming is about to make your day

SNAPDEVIL: Ok, dude, a bit weird but go on

KRYPTO: You wanna look at the officials in the councils that are issuing the development permits to PEMS after they've implemented the remediation plans. I've only gone back about ten years but there is clear evidence of these people exhibiting similar spending patterns to Jezza

SNAPDEVIL: Wow, so the theory that people are being paid off from this dodgy account has some legs

KRYPTO: I'd say so, dude. These people are getting money from somewhere and it's a good bet it's coming from our dodge companies

SNAPDEVIL: Any theories about why they are paying people off?

KRYPTO: Not yet, but I suggest we try and find out!

56

Halle had once again got in early, needing some headspace before Todd arrived at his annoyingly regular time of 8 am on the dot. Every day was a rollercoaster of emotions and now Todd had expressed feelings for her, confirming some instinct that Halle had been trying to ignore. She hoped she had parked that for now. Too much was happening too quickly and she needed workhorse Todd, the invaluable sounding board and kick-arse researcher, not the love-struck teenager.

She had stewed all night on the Victoria Allcock situation. Why did she want to see her? Was it simply that she wanted to tell her story to someone other than Peter and seeing a new face overwhelmed her? Halle chewed it over. The reaction didn't seem to fit the theory. She had looked scared, not relieved, that someone else was coming to see her.

She made herself a tea and tried to calm her addled mind. As she walked back into her office, the other thing that was competing for space in her mind came to the fore. The housing estate. The treatment of Mrs Gupta by those racist bastards. She felt a little ashamed that Marjit did not feel able to go to the police about her assault. There was an angle here that she was determined to get into the final show. John was resisting it but the environment within which this tragedy was playing out was relevant. How could he ignore the fact that people going through such unimaginable tragedy could still not see past their ignorance and prejudices? It was incredible.

Halle idly flicked through the most recent report on the soil and water tests at Mrs Gupta's and the three other houses. The higher pollution levels on that one property were intriguing. She stood up and spread out the A1-sized map they had of the estate. She started to manually plot the locations of both sets of tests, checking it against the electronic version that the testing team had sent them. The sites were reasonably spread out and covered most of the site, although the one with the higher levels was slightly further away and was at the furthest extremities of the site on the eastern side. What was it about this particular property that was vexing Halle? They had discussed the possibility of the pollution coming from something bordering the site, but for some reason, Halle didn't believe this was relevant. There was something she had heard or something she had seen that was stuck in her subconscious that would give her the answer. What was it? She let out a frustrated scream.

"Ooh, I hope that's not about me."

Halle turned. Todd. Happy, smiling and... Christ, she hated to admit it but a little bit adorable. She quickly shook it off and tried to get back to a professional footing.

"No. Not about you. I've just been plotting the test sites on the big map. There's something about the location of this house with the higher pollution levels that is doing my head in. There's something stuck in my mind that I can't get out."

"Well, try to forget about it or go and sit on the loo for a while. I do all my best thinking in there."

"Eww, TMI."

"Sorry, anyway, boss lady, I have some massive news. My cyber buddy who has been looking into the characters around this scandal had a major breakthrough last night."

They both sat down. "Go on."

"He started looking at the spending habits of Jeremy Hogan. He is definitely in the thick of this because he is spending way above his salary level. Has been buying cars, going on expensive holidays and has a massive house. There is no evidence that he has inherited any money or won the lottery, so the only explanation is that he is getting big wodges of cash from somewhere."

"Can we prove that?"

"We can certainly get his credit card bills to show the spending patterns, but I suspect the bank trails are hidden in that Genesis programme."

Halle let out a huge breath, trying to process the implications of what she had just been told.

"That's not the best bit, though, Halle."

"There's more?"

"Oh yes. He decided to dig a bit deeper into this scenario and found countless council officials involved in the issuing of the development permits exhibiting similar spending patterns. He only went back ten years but found a trail of corruption."

"What does this mean?"

"Well, I've been working on a theory since last night,

connected to Peter Allcock's idea that the money in that PEMS account is for giving backhanders. I reckon whatever scheme ALMS and PEMS have been running, it might involve paying off council officials to issue development permits."

"For what reason?"

"I don't know exactly but there's something about the sites they are developing that needs officials to turn a blind eye. I'm convinced they are cutting corners on the site clean-ups and somehow bribing officials to not look too closely at what they've done."

"Okay, do you think the Pickford housing estate could be one of the sites affected by this? Does it go back that far?"

"We don't know yet, as he's only gone back ten years, but it follows that this could have been going on since the fathers set up the firms."

Halle screwed up her face. "I don't know. What are they gaining from this?"

"Come on, don't be naïve. It's about the money. The Allcocks haven't all become millionaires by chance. If they've been running this scam for forty years on every brownfield site they developed, they've made millions by cutting corners. I'm sure of it."

"Okay, but what is it they are doing?"

"Look, think about what Peter told us about a typical deal for a brownfield site. ALMS purchase the land and do the demolition. I don't think the scam can be with those steps, as PEMS are not involved, and we know that Jeremy Hogan and Bill Parker are definitely in the thick of this. So, it has to be something in the three major steps that PEMS deliver for ALMS. They do the environmental review, then they develop and implement the remediation plans, and finally they obtain the development permits from the relevant councils and water boards."

"It has to be the last stage then, if your mate thinks they are bribing council officials."

"Well, yes, but I still think we have to look at what the council officials are signing off against. I did a quick bit of research last night and it seems that to issue a development permit, they have to be satisfied with the final soil and water tests, and validate that the remediation plans have been implemented as per the specification."

"Go on, I can see you've developed a theory by that excitable puppy look you have on your face."

Todd laughed. "Ah, you know me too well. Yes, I do have a theory. Let's assume that the Pickford housing estate is one of the sites. Based on what we've found so far, we are not really finding any evidence of soil pollution at ground level. If you research chemical pollutants, they hang around for years, which is why so much effort goes into robust remediation plans. I think there is something dodgy about their implementation of the remediation plans, leaving the problem buried deeper underground."

"Okay, let's follow this theory. How does the money play into this?"

"Let's assume that the remediation plans that PEMS put together are, on paper, robust enough to deal with the pollutants that are identified. I reckon they present these plans as part of the permit sign-off but actually implement a different plan. One that costs them a lot less money. I reckon they are bribing council officials to turn a blind eye to what they have actually done."

Halle stared at Todd, transfixed by what he was saying. Could this really be true?

"What about the health aspects of this? Are they really that callous that they are prepared to risk people's health to make a few quid?"

"You know, I really believe they think the risks are low. It seems to me that they will stop at nothing to make money, but I can't see them leaving themselves exposed. It seems as though sites like the ones they are developing have clear guidelines about how the ground is used and accessed once the remediation plans are implemented. Nobody is supposed to be able to drill down below the protective layer, meaning any household extensions or additional building developments are very much restricted. I reckon ALMS and PEMS know this and took a risk that any pollutants they buried would never be disturbed."

"Which just leaves the 64-million-dollar question. What's happening at the Pickford housing estate?"

57

Sophie was up at the crack of dawn. What she needed to do required the stealth of an early-morning raid, and she had to get away from Peter.

A little after 8 am she was where she needed to be and stormed through the corridors of the ALMS building. She had made light work of the receptionist and was now pounding her way to Edward's office. No one stopped her progress. No one seemed to care.

As she reached the outer office of Edward's domain, his PA seemed unfazed by her presence. "He's expecting you. Please go in."

The accommodating nature of her welcome had taken the wind out of her sails. The rage and associated adrenalin that had willed her on to confront Edward had started to dissipate and her courage was draining. She stood for a moment, steeling herself for the confrontation. She walked in.

"Ahh, Miss Parker. How lovely to see you, but I'm afraid you are a bit late to interview for the PA job. We gave it to a nice girl with massive jugs. Not that you don't meet that criteria. I mean, with a body like that, you could earn thousands a night at my strip club."

Sophie shook her head. "You really are a disgusting man. I suppose the girl you appointed was white. It's like a meeting of the Ku Klux Klan in here."

Edward leant forward, suppressed anger evident in his tone. "There's nothing wrong with protecting British jobs and maintaining British values. All these bloody immigrants stealing the jobs that good hard-working British people should be doing is a scandal. A lesson that my father taught me very early on, and one which your father strongly believes in too. You would be well placed to respect our fathers' legacy."

Sophie was trying not to lose it. She had a purpose for being here and she needed to remain calm and professional. "I'm not here to discuss your archaic attitudes to women and foreigners, Edward. I want to know what you want."

Edward's face turned to one of surprise. "What I want? What a curious question. Please enlighten me as to what you mean by that."

"I'm not scared of you, and all your minions that have been trying to frighten me. I'm done hiding. What is it you want to stop persecuting me and my business?"

Edward stroked his chin and leant forward, trying to up the intimidation. "Okay, here's the deal. I want three things. Firstly, I want you to stop snooping around in our business relationships. There's nothing to find."

"What about this Genesis programme?"

"The Genesis programme holds highly confidential business information about our work. It's my system and I control who has access to it. It protects highly sensitive commercial information that we do not want other firms to see. If you had any head for business, you would realise that this type of stuff needs to be protected from unwanted hackers who are trying to infiltrate our business and damage our success. Your father understood this and entrusted PEMS access to this system to just himself and Jeremy Hogan. As I think your father has told you on a number of occasions, you don't need to worry about it."

Sophie tried to ignore the patronising tone. "What else?"

"Well, that's simple. As I mentioned when we had that little bit of a misunderstanding in my car, I want to know where Peter is."

"You mean when you kidnapped me."

"As I said, a misunderstanding, and I'm sorry for any inconvenience I caused you whilst you were staying with me."

Sophie gritted her teeth. She had to remain calm. She had to know what Edward really wanted.

"And the third thing?"

"Ah yes. The third thing. I want your business. I can see that you are not cut out to run PEMS and it would make it so much easier if I had complete control over the business activities our two firms have been successfully collaborating on for years... at least, when your father was in control. I'll give you £20 million to walk away from PEMS and sell me the whole business. You may also find that your advertising business suddenly perks up."

Sophie couldn't take any more. She stood up and began to walk out. She had got what she came for. Now she knew what Edward was really after. As she walked out of his office, he continued to goad her.

"The sum of £20 million, Miss Parker, and the location of my brother's hide-out, and this all goes away. I'll give you a week to decide and then the offers off the table."

58

Peter stirred. It was almost nine. The stress of the previous evening had exhausted him and he slept much longer than he intended. He cocked an ear. The place was silent. He jumped out of bed and pulled on his robe. Rain was lashing against the window, making everything seem darker and more foreboding, just like his mood.

He walked into the living area. Sophie wasn't there. He walked to her bedroom. The bed had been slept in but Sophie was nowhere to be seen. He cursed to himself. He knew he had been harsh on her the previous evening but he felt like such a fool, trusting that bloody reporter.

Thinking about his mother spurred him into action. He picked up the phone and rang the prison. He was connected to the warden's office and was unequivocal in his message. No one but him was allowed to visit his mother, especially not Halle Jacobs or anyone else from her firm.

He made himself a coffee and sat down. What the hell should he do now? It looked like Sophie had left. All her stuff was gone. What on earth was she playing at? If she wasn't hiding out with him, Edward would find her and... he didn't like to think about it.

He tried the new phone. He tried her old phone. Nothing. No response. Just voicemail.

He phoned the prison back. He wanted to see his mother. To shake her out of whatever trauma that bloody reporter had put her in. He needed answers.

*

Halle and Todd went down to the canteen for a bacon roll and strong coffee. Todd's theory about what ALMS and PEMS may have been up to had blown their brains. They needed some time to process what it all meant. As Halle finished off her bacon roll, Todd got his serviette and wiped a blob of grease off her chin. The act was so soft, so caring, so intimate that it made Halle's heart flip. What was this man doing to her? Once again, she tried to brush it off and concentrate on the business in hand.

"How can we prove if your theory holds water?"

"I can contact the firm that has been doing our soil tests. I think they have a division that deals with this stuff. I can try and arrange for someone to come in later today, so we can test out our theories."

"Yes, do it. I don't want to go down a rabbit hole with this one. If we can get an independent opinion on this, it gives me much more leverage with John, because I can take the angle that there is something criminal or within the public interest on this case."

"So you can use the footage from Jen Wyatt and your eventful community hall meeting without people's consent."

"Exactly!"

They both refilled their coffees, nervous excitement coursing through their veins.

"What do you think has happened at Pickford?"

"I dunno. If you follow my theory, it suggests that something has disturbed the protective layer on that site but maybe only on the eastern side where the higher levels are. Unless, of course, the problem is with something bordering the site."

"But we couldn't find anything obvious, could we?"

"No, but I will have to look at it again. See if there has been any development near the site that might explain it, particularly as the perimeter soil tests were inconclusive."

Halle gripped her cup tightly, trying to ease the tension. "We're getting close. I can feel it."

They drained the last of their coffee and started to make their way back to their office. Halle's phone beeped. She stopped to read the text.

"What is it?"

Halle looked surprised. "It's from Sophie Parker. She wants to come and see us this afternoon."

*

Peter drove into the prison car park, after spending another trip constantly looking in his rear-view mirror, paranoid that one of Edward's minions would be following him. There was no one around.

Within ten minutes, he was through security and entering the medical ward. The same doctor grabbed him before he went in to see his mother. "Mr Allcock, I'm pleased to say your mother seems to have come out of the worst of her trauma. She is sitting up and having basic interaction with the staff. She has eaten a light breakfast and is just having a cup of tea."

Peter was stoked. He burst into her room. His mother was sat up in bed but her face dropped as soon as she saw Peter. "What are you doing here?"

"What! I'm worried about you, Mum. You've been in some sort of trauma paralysis. Do you not remember lying in bed, staring at the ceiling, not responding to anybody or anything?"

"I'm fine. I just had a shock. That's all."

"What did that girl say to you to make you go so weird?"

Victoria looked away from Peter and stared out of the window.

"Mum?"

Victoria looked back at Peter. "She didn't say anything to me."

"So what happened? Why did you faint?"

"I had a shock. That's all."

"Why did she shock you? What did she do?"

"I told you, she didn't do anything."

Peter raised his voice, frustration growing. "What the hell. Stop playing games with me, Mum. There must be some reason that you went weird when you saw her."

"It's none of your business, Peter. I want to see her again."

"But why? You know she's a reporter. She's sniffing around about our relationship with PEMS. Thinks she's found some story about kids getting cancer on a housing estate in East London. It was one of the last ones Dad worked on and she wants to talk to you about it."

For the first time, Victoria allowed herself a faint smile. "Is she now? Well, I definitely want to see her then."

Peter's volume rose further. "If there's something going on, you need to tell me. Not a bloody reporter."

Peter's rant was interrupted by the doctor. "Mr Allcock, I must ask you to lower your voice. Mrs Allcock is not well enough to be barked at by you. If you don't refrain, I will have to ask you to leave."

Peter gritted his teeth and looked back at his mother. She rubbed her face. "The doctor's right. I don't need your bad attitude. Just leave. If you are not going to arrange for that lady to visit me, I will sort it myself. Goodbye, Peter."

*

Edward's phone rang and he picked it up immediately when he saw who it was from. "Speak."

"I got lucky, boss. I was staking out the prison like you suggested and he turned up to see your mother. I followed him and found out where he's staying."

"Where?"

"He's at the Savoy Hotel."

59

It was a little after 3 pm when Sophie arrived at the offices of Goldwin Productions. Within a few minutes of arriving, she was ensconced in Halle's office, feeling like a zoo exhibit as Halle and Todd stared at her expectantly. Halle broke the tension by asking why she was there.

Sophie said nothing for a minute. She looked at Halle and Todd, trying to judge whether her initial instincts were right. To trust them. Or was Peter right when he was ranting at her last night? Were these people just out for the story, not caring who they hurt on the way?

Her memories of the way Peter had spoken to her were still fresh in her mind, and the experience with Edward that morning had cemented her hatred of the Allcock men. She knew she had no choice. She had to trust these people.

"I made a mistake trusting Peter Allcock. I don't know what he said to you the other evening when I was... indisposed, but I want to sort this out. I need your help to take these bastards down. Something is badly corrupt with our relationship and I'm not going to let it lie."

Halle tried to hide her excitement at this development. "So, you are not hiding out with Peter any longer?"

"No. The way he spoke to me last night was… just like the rest of his family. I really thought he was different, but when the chips are down, the Allcock genes come flooding out. I need to distance myself from that whole family and find out what is going on."

"Don't you feel exposed? I thought Edward was gunning for you and that's why you decided to hide out in the first place."

Sophie winced at the memories, but a hard, determined expression formed on her face. "I decided that I wasn't going to be intimidated by that family anymore. I went to see Edward this morning to confront him about everything he's been doing. I made it clear I wasn't scared of him."

Halle was mesmerised. "Wow. That's ballsy. What happened?"

Sophie let out a faint laugh. "Do you know, I hate that family, but I have to say I was taken aback by what Edward had to say."

"Stop teasing us. What happened?"

"I asked him what he wanted to leave me alone."

"And?"

"He said there were three things he wanted. The first two were predictable. For me to stop snooping and tell him where Peter is hiding. The third one I was not expecting. He offered me £20 million to sell him PEMS."

There was a brief pause as Halle tried to take in what Sophie had said, shooting a look at Todd. He nodded, seemingly picking up on where her thought processes were going.

"My God, he's covering his tracks."

"What do you mean?"

"Todd had a breakthrough last night."

"With Genesis?"

"No. His cyber mate has been investigating Jeremy Hogan and found his spending patterns do not match the salary levels you pay him at PEMS."

Sophie was wide-eyed with shock. Halle cracked on. "He also followed the money trail and found that there are numerous examples of council officials with similar spending patterns. The ones that were involved in issuing your firm with the development permits."

"What does that mean?"

"We think it confirms your earlier suspicion about what that money going into that account is for. People are being paid off."

"For what, though?"

Halle looked at Todd. "Do you want to explain?"

All attention was focused on Todd. "I have a theory. I think your firm has been presenting robust remediation plans to the council and water boards when requesting the permits but implementing different plans. I think Jeremy is overseeing this work and you are paying council officials to look the other way when they do their final checks before they issue the permits."

Sophie's face crumpled, fighting back tears. "This can't be true. Why?"

"It's money, Sophie. I think Edward Allcock Snr and your father cooked up some scheme which would implement substandard remediation plans, thereby saving thousands of pounds on each deal. They invested some of that saving in paying Jeremy to protect their little secrets and to bribe council officials."

Sophie let out a wail, unable to supress the horror of what she was hearing. She tried to calm herself. "Can we prove any of this?"

Todd put on his most sympathetic face, leant forward and grabbed Sophie's hand. "Not yet, but we will. Trust me."

Sophie looked at Halle, disarmed by this strange man and his unwavering certainty that everything would be okay. Halle smiled and nodded. An act of support that Sophie took as confirmation that she had made the right decision.

"Okay. What can I do to help?"

Halle smiled at Todd. Sophie was back on their side.

"Okay. Tell us everything you know."

*

Edward called Andrew and his uncle into his office.

"We've found him."

Andrew leant forward, like a prowling tiger. "Where is he? I want to beat the living daylights out of him."

Edward smiled. "Patience, little brother. It seems his little alliance with Sophie Parker may have broken down. She came to see me this morning, asking what I wanted to stop persecuting her."

Andrew looked stunned. "Really! What did you say?"

"I said I wanted her to stop snooping, to tell me where Peter is hiding and to sell me her business."

James pulled a confused expression, cutting across the brotherly engagement. "Where did that come from? Don't you think you should have discussed something like that with me first?"

"The opportunity was there. I was surprised at her front in coming to see me, so I thought on my feet. It's a perfect opportunity to cut her out of this situation without… well, let's say, any more unpleasantness."

"How much did you offer her?"

"The grand sum of £20 million to walk away and to comply with my other requests."

"But you know where Peter is now."

"Which means she only has two things to do."

"She won't go for it."

"We'll see. I've given her a week to decide. If we owned PEMS, it would give us all the protection we need and protect my father's legacy."

Edward could sense Andrew was annoyed at being sidelined and was fidgeting in his chair. "What's wrong?"

"That's all fine and dandy, Edward, but what about Peter? We need to confront him whilst we still know where he is."

Edward drummed his fingers on the table. "Do you know I'm inclined to let him stew. If he has fallen out with Sophie Parker, he'll be stuck in that hotel room wondering what to do next. We know what a spineless twat he is. I have a feeling that without her support, he won't know what to do. Let's leave him alone for now. I'll deal with him when the time is right."

Andrew looked at his uncle, not happy with what Edward was saying. He got nothing back. Edward's expression told them both the meeting was over.

As they left, Edward smiled to himself. He was back in control. He was untouchable.

60

Sophie poured her heart out. Everything she knew, every emotion she had experienced since the day her father had told her that he was handing over the company. The suspicions, the lies, the sense she was always being sidelined. Her uncertainty over Ross' role in all this. The Allcocks and her ill-considered relationship with Peter. By the time she was finished, she was exhausted.

As Sophie ran out of steam, Todd launched in before Halle had a chance to process it all.

"I'm sorry to say this, but everything you say just reinforces my theory. I think we have a ticking time bomb here. Your father and Edward Allcock Snr have taken a calculated gamble. They've implemented substandard remediation plans on the basis that they never expected the problem to surface, if you can excuse the pun. I reckon they gambled on the possibilities that any residual pollution problem would take so long to appear that no one would connect it back to them or your firms. I'm absolutely convinced that the Pickford housing estate is the first of what could be a long line of trouble for you and ALMS."

Sophie and Halle stared at Todd, disarmed by his

words. He looked at them quizzically, trying to work out whether they disagreed with his stance or were just dumbstruck by the realisation of what might be happening.

Eventually, Halle leant forward, fixing Sophie with a concerned but determined expression. "I tend to agree with Todd. We've been scrabbling around trying to find something on the Pickford housing estate that would explain all these children getting cancer. We just need to find the evidence on that site that backs up this theory."

Sophie started to cry, the mention of the children overwhelming her. She spoke in that jerky fashion that accompanies uncontrollable sobbing.

"I... I... just can't... believe it... my father... is not a bad... man. He would... never do... something that would... endanger... children."

Halle gestured Sophie to stand up and gave her a long hug until the sobbing subsided. As Halle pulled away from the hug, she grabbed Sophie's arms and fixed her with another determined look. "We will expose whatever's going on here, and stop everyone that's involved in this horrendous scam. I have parents on that estate who are relying on us to find out what happened and, with your support, we are going to do it."

Sophie sat back down, a pained smile on her face. She wiped away the tears. "I'm going to prison, aren't I?"

Halle looked shocked. "What? No! Of course not. You have not been part of this and if you co-operate with our investigation, we will make sure, when the time is right, that the police know you have helped crack this case."

"Shouldn't we go to them now? Surely it would be

better for me if we told them what we know sooner rather than later."

There was an awkward look between Halle and Todd, the unspoken body language confirming what they each knew. Halle pushed on, desperate to convince Sophie that she had to go with their plan. "Er, I'm sorry to say this, Sophie, but I think the people paying my salary will want this story in the can before we go to the police. We also need to make sure we have all the evidence to back up our theories, or they won't be interested."

This was the moment. Halle knew she was treading a fine line between doing the right thing and protecting her career. The paymasters would not want to lose such a sensational story if their theories were right and they could prove it, but Sophie was in a fragile state. Halle could tell she was an honest, caring soul and was going to struggle with not engaging the police's help. Halle waited for the bombshell. Her fledgling career could hang on the next thing that Sophie Parker said.

61

It was a bright but cold afternoon. Sunil had been badgering Marjit to go to the playground. Her back was still painful and she was reluctant to walk around the estate, given what had happened to her the other evening, but Sunil's pleading had finally worn her down. She wasn't sure how long he had, or whether the miracles of modern science would save him, but she realised she had to think of her precious son first and foremost.

She wrapped him up in hat, coat, scarf and gloves and set off for the park on the other side of the estate. The place was still eerie. Ever since that meeting in the community hall with the reporters, a number of families had moved out, despite the news getting around about the negative soil tests. Houses that had previously been full of life and laughter were now shut up, dark and foreboding. Marjit had no idea whether this was a temporary situation. No one seemed to have estate agent signs up, indicating their decision to move.

They walked on. A few people were around and Marjit caught the usual looks and behind-the-hand remarks. It seemed most of the estate were with Jen Wyatt and Graham, her little stooge. Sunil was skipping along, unaware of the tension coursing through Marjit's body.

As they neared the park, her heart sank as she saw several children playing. Children of parents that were not in her camp. Sunil picked up speed as he bound towards the entrance to the playground. Marjit went to grab him but missed. She reluctantly went in after him, veering to the left-hand side of the playground, away from all the other parents.

She tried to seem relaxed, scrolling idly through her phone, all the while trying to see what was going on in her peripheral vision. The children's squeals and laughter filled the air, but all Marjit could focus on was the huddle of parents now forming on the other side of the playground.

She smiled at Sunil as he implored her to watch him going down the big slide, but her fear response kicked in as the small mob started to walk towards her.

One of the fathers, who she didn't know that well, took the lead as the group stood in front of her in an intimidating U-shape, blocking off any obvious escape routes. "You're not welcome here."

She stared at all of the faces, pinched with rage and intolerance. "It's a free country the last time I looked," she retorted.

The man took a slight step forward, forcing Marjit to flinch. "Our country. Not yours. All you fucking immigrants think you can come over here and do what you want. Taking our jobs and threatening our livelihoods. And now you think it's okay to side with those scum reporters."

"You'll thank me when they expose what's going on here."

The man screwed his face up, the frown lines deepening. "That's not what Jen says. None of you bastards can be trusted."

There it was. Jen Wyatt's influence and bigotry spreading across the estate.

"Leave her alone."

Everyone turned to see who had interrupted their 'discussion'. It was John Chambers, one of the parents helping Marjit, the one with the house that had higher pollution levels. He ploughed on.

"Go on. Piss off and leave us alone."

There was a brief stand-off. Eventually, the group exchanged amused glances and wandered off, racial slurs evident in their language as they walked away.

Marjit looked at John. "Thank you."

"It's no problem. Always best to stand up to bullies."

They watched as John's daughter Arabella and Sunil played quite happily with all the children, not affected by the intolerance and ignorance emanating from their parents.

"How is Sunil?"

"Oh, he's having a good day today, which is why he kept badgering me to come to the playground. We have to grab these moments when we can. Most of the time, he's so tired from the chemo. What about Arabella?"

"Likewise. She goes in for her next round of chemo in a few days. I'm not looking forward to it. She tries to stay positive but they shouldn't have to deal with this shit at their age."

They both drifted off into their own thoughts, their aching hearts eased by the few moments of pleasure their respective children were managing to glean from this short respite.

John looked at Marjit. "We're doing the right thing, you know. I'm convinced those reporters are going to find out what this is all about. These people are just stupid and scared. We'll show 'em."

*

She doesn't want to see you. Peter played the words over and over in his mind as he poured himself another whisky. He was desperate. Sophie had abandoned him; he had burnt all the bridges with his brothers and now his mother was refusing to see him.

He couldn't believe how his whole world had collapsed around him in just a couple of days. His head was fuzzy, the effects of three quarters of a bottle of whisky in one bingeworthy afternoon. He sunk another one, topping it up immediately with increasingly unsteady hands.

His eyes began to droop. He tried to refocus. What had he done? What on earth could he do now? He had nowhere to go and no one to help him. Maybe it was a sign. Maybe it was time for his pathetic, worthless life to end.

62

"Okay, let's do it your way."

Halle breathed a sigh of relief. They had Sophie Parker back in their corner.

Sophie got her emotions in check and was ready for the fight. "Okay, you two. What do you need me to do?"

Halle spoke first. "Are there any records in PEMS that might help us prove what is going on?"

"I really don't think so. I trawled through the paper and electronic files. The only thing I found was this reference to the Bill Parker Holdings account. If Todd's theory is right, the remediation plans will, on paper, be robust. However, I did think it was strange that we always seem to implement the same type of plans. I did some research and it suggested that this is not a one-size-fits-all business."

Halle looked at Todd. He interjected. "I think that does support my theory. If the remediation plans seem fine to the casual eye, they have probably been trotting out the same thing over and over, because it doesn't reflect what they've actually done."

Sophie let out an exasperated sigh. "How do we prove it then? I can't find anything more concrete."

Todd gave her his most sympathetic smile. "It's got to be this Genesis programme. It can't be a coincidence that all our main suspects have the same link in their secure folders."

"Haven't you cracked it? I thought you were an IT whizz."

Todd smiled. "Not yet. This programme has some of the most sophisticated security I've ever come across, comparable with bank and defence security. I am going to have to organise a co-ordinated attack with some of my cyber mates to have any chance of cracking it."

"When are you doing that?"

"I don't know yet. These people are... well, let's just say they are free spirits. It will take a bit of co-ordination."

The conversation drifted off. The tension in the room was eventually broken by Todd's phone beeping. Halle and Sophie looked at him expectantly. His fingers danced over the screen. "Oh wow. The guy from our testing firm is five minutes away. He said he can pop up and see us now."

As Todd confirmed they were available, Halle brought Sophie up to speed with what the testing team had done on the Pickford site and the reasons they had asked to see them. Nervous energy was coursing through Sophie's body, but she agreed to sit in on the meeting. Like a child spinning the handle on a jack-in-the-box, she wasn't sure whether she wanted to see what happened when the metaphorical box opened.

Within twenty minutes, they were all settled in the meeting room, steaming hot cups of coffee and chocolate digestives well on the way to being consumed.

The guy from the testing firm introduced himself

as Terence Bingley, one of the partners. A strong South African accent complemented a well-toned physique. "It's great to meet you all. How can I help?"

Halle took the lead and explained the wider background beyond what Terence already knew about the work his firm had done with the onsite testing. Sophie filled in the gaps, and her assertions about the remediation plans being the same on every site piqued his interest.

"I tend to agree, that it does seem odd that your firm rolls out the same remediation plans for each site. There is no doubt that a site clearance, pollution wash-out and impermeable barriers, supported by a four-foot clay layer, are perfectly reasonable steps for a polluted brownfield site. However, there are other things you can do and I would expect remediation plans to be adjusted to reflect the types of pollutants that are being dealt with and the type of soil that the land is built on. Both these things make a huge difference to how the site should be treated."

Sophie leant forward, her body language engaging this charming man. "Do you think the council officials issuing our development permits would know this?"

"Absolutely no doubt. The scrutiny on these types of sites is usually very stringent."

Todd said what the others were thinking. "So, you think our theory that ALMS and PEMS are paying people to look the other way holds water?"

"Yes. I really do. I can't believe that the type of remediation plans they are submitting would pass scrutiny on every site that has been developed."

Todd carried on. "But it's more than that, Terence. We

283

don't think they are even implementing the plans they are submitting."

"Well, that makes your theory even more solid. All sites are fully inspected before permits are issued. There's no way that a flaky remediation plan or one that has not been implemented to spec would pass those inspections."

The room went quiet. Halle broke the silence. "Bloody hell. What have we stumbled on and how on earth have they been running this scam for so long?"

There was no response as they all took in the gravity of the situation.

Halle ploughed on. "The Pickford housing estate. Is there any way we can survey what is under the ground on that site? We're sure this is the first example of where something has compromised the shoddy work that ALMS and PEMS have done, even though the site is over thirty years old. We know the soil tests have been inconclusive, but we desperately need to find some evidence to back up our theory and explain why all those poor children have got cancer."

Terence nodded. "Yes, there's lots we can do. My suggestion is that we complete a full underground scan on that site. It will tell us what is under there and, assuming there is a clay barrier, whether there are any splits in the installation."

Sophie remained quiet, hurt by every mention of PEMS' alleged wrongdoing, but what Terence was saying just made her more determined. "How quickly can you do this, Terence? I need to find out once and for all what my firm…" she hesitated as she spoke "…what my father has been up to all these years."

"I can start the work tomorrow and have the results in a couple of days."

There was a general sense of excitement in the group. Whilst Sophie was clearly nervous at what they might find, they all knew this could be the breakthrough they were looking for.

Halle went into organising mode. "Get us a quote tonight, and I will sign it off straight away. Are your team okay to go onsite again? I know the locals are a bit feisty."

"It's fine, the team did get a bit of aggro last time but with this, we can use technology that doesn't require us to be digging up the ground."

"Oh really?"

"Yeah. This can all be done with drones."

The meeting was over and as they all began to pack up their stuff and get on with their days, Sophie's phone beeped. She read the text message and gasped.

Halle reacted first. "What is it?"

She took a minute to compose herself. "It's a message from Ross. Dad is in hospital. Ross says the doctors think he only has a few hours to live."

63

Sophie was in complete turmoil. Her father lay in the hospital bed, heavily sedated, as the ravages of his poor heart condition were finally taking their toll. She needed to speak to him, to shake him awake and ask him why he had done these terrible things. Ask him why he had not had better judgement about his relationship with Edward Allcock Snr and why he had been seduced by greed.

All the while, the machines beeped and pumped, keeping him alive. Ross was staring at his father, oblivious to everything going on in Sophie's mind... or so she thought. Even now, as she watched her father dying, she still didn't know how much Ross was involved. She buried her face in her hands and tried to stifle the overwhelming urge to scream and cry.

A few minutes later, one of the machines started to beep more urgently. They both looked up from their catatonic state as doctors and nurses rushed in. The beeping became more urgent. One of the doctors checked the machine as it beeped faster and faster. Sophie implored them to do something but they just stood there.

"Why aren't you doing anything?"

"I'm sorry, Miss Parker, but your father has a DNR notice."

"What?

"A DNR notice. Do not resuscitate."

"But… but… I don't agree. I want you to save him."

"We can't go against his wishes."

He flatlined.

Sophie looked at every person in the room, utterly aghast at how they could just stand there and watch her father die. Ross stood up and tried to comfort Sophie but she moved away from him.

"No, no, no, no. This can't be happening."

Sophie ran out of the ward. The opportunity to confront her father had gone.

*

Edward sat in his office, staring at his computer screen. He wasn't engaging with what was on it, his mind full of competing stresses. He called for his uncle to come in as he passed the office.

"I dunno whether I can wait for something to happen. I don't trust Sophie Parker to do the right thing and I'm still worried that Peter knows about Genesis."

His uncle sat down. "I have to say, I'm not sure offering to buy PEMS was a good move. It's just gonna make her more suspicious of your motives. As for Genesis, Peter does not have the skillset to hack into that system and, without Sophie Parker's help, he won't have a clue what to do next. Let him rot in that hotel room."

Edward's mind was racing. He had told himself he

was back in control of the situation, but Sophie and Peter were loose ends, and he didn't like loose ends.

"I agree that Peter doesn't have the right stuff, but that doesn't mean he couldn't buy it in. These hackers are only interested in money and the thrill of the chase. I need the team managing Genesis to monitor it for cyber-attacks."

"Okay, I can get them to up their surveillance, but I really don't think we need to worry."

Edward fixed his uncle with a mildly disapproving look, a look that had his father all over it. "Please don't defy me on this. I can never repay you for saving us when that bitch murdered my father, but now I'm the one entrusted with protecting his legacy. I won't leave anything to chance."

His uncle stood up. "That's fine. I'll get them right on it."

He watched as his uncle left the room, seemingly unfazed by the passive-aggressive stance that he had just taken with him. As Edward tried to remotivate himself to deal with the ever-increasing workload, his phone beeped. It was a text from Jeremy Hogan.

He smiled at what he was reading. "Well, well. Now this is a development. Bill Parker is dead."

He sat for a few minutes reading the text over and over, his mind spinning with the opportunities this now presented. Eventually, he buzzed his PA. "Gemma, can you send some flowers and a letter of condolence to Ross and Sophie Parker. Their father has just died. Oh, and set up a meeting with them both. I have a lot to talk to them about."

*

Halle and Todd were in the bar across the road from the Goldwin Productions office. So much had happened in the day that Halle was too wired to go home. She was on her second gin and tonic, and Todd was making good progress through a bottle of red wine.

"This is all getting a bit real now. I've got my meeting with John in five days' time. Are we gonna have this thing cracked by then? I would love to go in there with the evidence we need to use every piece of footage we have."

"Well, we still need a lot of things to go right. I'm going to try and get my cyber mates to help me tonight to do a co-ordinated attack on that Genesis site. I don't think you are going to be able to lord it over John without the evidence I'm sure they're hiding in that programme."

Halle smiled at Todd. "You'll sort it for me. I know you will. You're my superhero."

The comment increased the sexual tension that they were both trying to ignore. The sexual tension that was cranked up as they consumed more alcohol. Halle checked herself and quickly changed the subject.

"Poor Sophie. I can't believe this is happening just when we've got her back onside."

Todd took a swig of wine. "The best thing we can do for Sophie, is to crack this conspiracy wide open. The memories of her father will be forever tainted until she knows for sure what he has done. I'm sure she'll come back to us when she's ready."

Halle was consumed. Why was it that everything Todd did or said melted her heart? She leant in. Her mouth hovered near his. She went for it. The kiss was fast and passionate.

She pulled away, averting her gaze. "I'm sorry. I shouldn't have done that. Not now."

Todd grabbed her face, tilting it up so their eyes locked. "I ain't complaining."

Halle pulled away, downing the rest of her drink. "No. Come on. There is a time and a place for this and now is not that time. We have to concentrate on getting all our ducks in a row. If you can progress that Genesis thing tonight and Terence can get something from the Pickford site, we will be on our way."

Todd smiled. "Okay, boss lady. Let's do it."

"There's just one more thing."

"What?"

"I want to confront Edward Allcock. I want to goad him into admitting his part in this scam. He sounds like such an arrogant prick. I have a feeling he might just let something slip."

"That's bold."

"I know. It won't be easy, but it might just be the final piece in delivering our kick-ass TV show and getting justice for all those poor children."

64

Todd was back in his technology cave. He had messaged all his mates on Proton about a co-ordinated attack on the Genesis site. As ever, Krypto was at his side.

SNAPDEVIL: How's it looking, Krypto?
KRYPTO: Good, mate. We have seven of us ready to roll as soon as you say the word

Todd sent the group message out. The game was on.

They started their co-ordinated attack, all throwing lines of code at the first layer of encryption. Twenty minutes passed.

SNAPDEVIL: Any progress, Krypto?
KRYPTO: Not yet. I'm monitoring all seven of us but no progress yet
SNAPDEVIL: Bloody hell, Krypto, I ain't letting this thing beat us
KRYPTO: Patience, my young padawan

Another hour passed.

KRYPTO: It's working, Snap. We've just got past the first
layer and the hack is holding

Thirty minutes more.

SNAPDEVIL: Shit, Krypto. I'm in the network. What
about you?
KRYPTO: Yeah, but still some App security to crack

Twenty minutes more.

SNAPDEVIL: Fucking hell. We're in. We've got to the
folder structure
KRYPTO: Look at all these files. Showtime!

*

Edward sat in his normal place, watching as sad punters
lined his pockets by consuming overpriced drinks and
paying for barely adequate lap dances. His uncle was, as
ever, by his side. They didn't speak. They just revelled in
the atmosphere.

Edward's phone started to flash. He picked it up,
concern immediately evident on his face. He got up and
walked into his office to get away from the noise. His
uncle closely followed.

As Edward listened, his mood grew darker and the
rage built. "Kill it. Kill it now!"

He dropped the phone on the desk. "What's happened,
Edward?"

For a moment he was so mad, he couldn't speak. He

bunched his fists up. "Fucking hell. I was right. Peter has found someone to hack into Genesis. We are experiencing a co-ordinated cyber-attack from multiple sources and they have managed to get past all the security. Jesus fucking wept."

"You've told them to kill the programme?"

The volume rose. "Of course, I fucking have! We can't let this happen."

*

Todd started to frantically open files in the folders. Krypto was doing the same. The documents were gold dust. Details of bank transactions. Photos of men in compromising positions with other men, women and, sickeningly, children. Correspondence threatening exposure.

SNAPDEVIL: My God, Krypto, are you getting all this?
KRYPTO: Sure am, dude. I guess what you were looking for
SNAPDEVIL: No shit, Sherlock!

Document after document. The evidence piling up.

Todd's screen glitched. He stared at the screen. Gobsmacked. Every file that they had been staring at was gone in a second. Completely gone. From everything to nothing.

SNAPDEVIL: What the fuck just happened?
KRYPTO: Jesus, mate. They detected us. They've killed the programme

SNAPDEVIL: No, no, no. This can't be happening. Did you grab anything before it went?

KRYPTO: No, sorry, dude. I was too busy looking at it

SNAPDEVIL: Me too. FUCK!!!!

65

Halle had slept remarkably well, despite the nervous energy that was constantly coursing through her body. She walked into the offices just after eight. Todd was at his desk as normal but he had his head in his hands. She moved towards his desk.

"Todd? Are you okay?"

He looked up. His face was not its usual bright, happy expression. In fact, Halle was sure she could see tears in his eyes. "My God. What's up?"

Todd lowered his head in shame. "I've failed you. We got into Genesis last night. The evidence was all there, but… it's gone. All gone."

"Eh, what do you mean?"

"They detected our attack. They killed the programme."

"I don't understand. What happened?"

Todd blew out a breath. Halle had never seen him so emotional.

"We got in. Seven of us did a co-ordinated attack on the Genesis site and it finally worked. We got past the encryption layers that had been causing me so much problem when I was trying to hack it on my own. We got through to the file structure. There were hundreds of files containing the evidence we were looking for. Details of financial transactions, threatening emails and the answer as to how the Allcocks were persuading these council officials to look the other way."

"What? Come on. Don't tease me."

"It seems they exploited dirty secrets in some of the council officials' private lives and threatened to expose them if they didn't issue the permits. There were graphic pictures of them romping with men, women and in one case abusing a child. It was horrible."

"That's amazing."

"But it's not. We didn't get a single file. My mate and I were so seduced by seeing what was in each file that we didn't grab copies of them in time. Every file was deleted in front of our eyes. As I said, they somehow detected our attack and applied some sort of instant 'kill' programme."

They both stopped, trying to rationalise the implications of what Todd was saying. Halle's brain was spinning, so she did what she always did in these circumstances. She asked questions.

"I don't understand. Why would they kill the programme like that? Surely they need the evidence in those files to keep blackmailing all these people."

"I don't know. Maybe the 'kill' programme was designed to remove the immediate threat and restore it someplace else. Either way, we have lost the thread."

Halle tapped her phone against her chin, absent-mindedly. "The thing is, you did find something. We know they are blackmailing officials and possibly paying them off to keep quiet. We may not have the actual evidence but we can surely use this as leverage."

"But how?"

"As I said last night, I think it's time to confront the Allcocks. This is exactly the type of thing I want to use when I speak to them. I want to see their reaction when I tell them we know all about their scam. I need to talk to Rod about setting up some secret filming so we can capture this in all its glory."

She grabbed Todd's hands. "You did good. Don't sweat it that we don't have the actual evidence. If my plan works, we'll get them. Trust me."

Todd cheered up as they made themselves a coffee. As they walked back into Halle's office, their concentration was broken by a lady from the post room, holding a large bunch of flowers. "Here you go, Miss Jacobs. These are for you."

Halle took the bouquet and read the card, her smile broadening as she realised who it was from.

Todd looked at her with a mixture of curiosity and a little hint of jealousy. "Something I should know?"

Halle smiled at him. "They're from my parents."

"Oh. What's the occasion?"

Halle didn't answer. Todd's brain cogs started to whirr and then the realisation hit him.

"Bollocks. It's your birthday. How did I not know that?"

Halle laughed. "It's not important, especially with all this going on."

Todd jumped up. "Of course it's important. Right, here's what we are going to do. You are going to come round mine tonight. We'll order some takeaway, get some wine, you can watch whatever DVD you want, we can have ice cream, we can…"

Todd hadn't noticed the change in Halle's expression. As he was rambling on about her birthday, the brain worm had suddenly resolved itself. That piece of information that was stuck in her brain had come out. Her birthday.

She jumped up, stopping Todd in his tracks. She grabbed the site map. "Look. Here. I can't believe I didn't see it before. This house that had the higher pollution levels is right next door to the community hall. Don't you remember me remarking that it was opened on my birthday? The 30th of November in 2008 or somewhere around that time. I remember it said it on that plaque."

"I'm not sure I'm following."

"Don't you see? The community hall and children's playground were built more recently. If there is something wrong with the way that ALMS and PEMS made these sites safe, isn't it feasible that digging into the earth to build a new structure could have released any residual pollution. My God, we need that site scan now. I think we may have found ground zero."

66

Edward and Andrew flew into the foyer of the Savoy Hotel. The attack on Genesis was the final straw. As far as they were concerned, Peter had betrayed the family and, more specifically, their father's legacy, one too many times.

An immaculately presented receptionist greeted them warmly, unflustered by the aggressive nature of their approach. Edward took the lead. "I want to see Peter Allcock. Immediately."

The receptionist eyed him suspiciously. "Who?"

"Peter Allcock. He's staying with you. He's my brother."

"Do you have any ID?"

Edward produced his driving licence, the faint hint of a 'foreign' accent from the receptionist raising his heckles further.

She examined it and tapped away at the screen. "I'm afraid I'm not able to help you. Our guests expect absolute privacy and discretion. If your brother is here, we are not able to contact him on your behalf. Why don't you call him yourself?"

Edward was just about containing his rage. "I…"

"Can I help you, sir?"

They turned to see another immaculately presented person, flanked by a mean-looking security guard.

Edward eyed them with contempt. "I am trying to explain to this… woman… that I need to speak to my brother Peter Allcock. He has been staying with you."

"I'm the Head Concierge and this is my Head of Security. As my colleague has explained to you, we will not facilitate such a request. Our guests expect us to maintain their privacy and their security, regardless of whether you happen to be family. Please can you leave, unless you are planning to pay for using one or more of our facilities?"

Edward and Andrew made a move forward. The security guard placed a large hand on Edward's shoulder. "Sir. You have been asked to leave."

Edward looked at the hand and slowly raised his head. Andrew instinctively set himself in fight position. Edward was a brawler when he needed to be, and this was just the sort of situation that would have him coming out swinging.

There was a tense stand-off. Edward started twitching. It was about to go off.

The Head Concierge removed the security guard's arm and got in Edward's face. "I would highly recommend you don't do what I think you are planning to do. And, anyway, let me be clear. If there was someone called Peter Allcock staying here, I can tell you with absolute certainty that he is no longer here. He checked out this morning."

Edward and Andrew stood outside the hotel. Fuming.

"Where has that bastard gone, Andrew? Get everyone onto it. Find him and kill him."

67

Halle and Todd drove into the Pickford estate, pushing the speed limit. There was no time to lose. They contacted Terence about their theory and, as they drove in, they spotted the drones, already in the process of scanning the site. *We can't wait,* Halle had been saying, over and over. They needed to stop the children playing on the site and shut down the community centre.

They stopped next to the park. Halle's heart sank. Despite the chilly conditions, there were still loads of children playing on the climbing frames, spinning on the roundabout and squealing as they rode down the slide.

They got out. As they walked towards the park, they noticed the parents reacting to their presence. Hushed words and pointing. Halle's heart was flipping over and over but she had to do this. She had to stop these children being exposed for a second longer.

They walked inside the playground, striding purposively towards the small group of parents. None of them were the parents that were helping them. She spoke before they could react.

"You need to get your children out of this playground

now. We have reason to believe that this and the community centre are the source of the pollution. We are scanning the site as we speak."

The shove from the woman closest to Halle was unexpected and she stumbled back as Todd made a vain attempt to break her fall. As Halle sat there in an unceremonious heap, the vitriol poured out.

"You people. Haven't you got the message yet that we don't want you here? We don't want you preying on our grief. We don't want your outlandish theories. We want you to leave us alone, so we can get on with helping our children recover from this awful disease."

With Todd's help, Halle got back to her feet and brushed herself down. Her patience had been well and truly tested. The stress of the past few weeks poured out. "What is wrong with you all? It's bad enough that you are a bunch of ignorant racists but it's even worse that you can't see past your ignorance and bigotry to see what I'm saying is real. Your children are playing on land that, at this precise minute, could be contaminated and is almost certainly the cause of their cancer. This minute. Look. Where they are standing. The equipment they are playing on could all be contaminated. I'm not trying to exploit your grief. I'm trying to save your children from further exposure. We need to contact the council and get this shut down. Can't you see that?"

There was mild murmuring from the group. The woman that had shoved Halle was close to tears. The tension was broken by a familiar voice. "Get out! You heard what they said. Get out and leave us alone."

It was Jen Wyatt. Halle turned to face the hatred, the

face of this estate, all twisted and enraged. They stared each other down.

Eventually, Halle grabbed at Todd's sleeve and walked away, shaking her head. They got back in the car as the angry mob watched for them to leave.

"My God. You see what I mean. These people. They're beyond help."

Todd did his usual. Stroked Halle's arm. A great comfort. "Are you okay? Not much of a birthday so far."

Halle smiled. "Come on. I want to go and see if Mrs Gupta is in and tell her about this development. At least she can keep the families that are on our side away from that area."

The chat with Mrs Gupta had been emotional but she was at least grateful for the warnings. She agreed to let the other families know. As they drove back to the office, Halle's brain was full of stuff she needed to get out.

"Get back onto Terence and find out when we can get that report. If it says what I think it will, we need to inform the council and get those sites shut down. Make sure flowers have been sent to Sophie and tell her we are ready to speak again whenever she is. Get Rod and Clayton to come and see me about our visit to the Allcocks and phone their offices to set up the meeting. We're in the final stretch, Todd, and I don't care about Genesis. We're gonna have enough to bury these bastards."

Todd smiled. "Yes, boss lady. Consider it done."

*

Victoria Allcock sat in the warden's office. He spoke before she had a chance to say anything.

303

"Are you okay now, Mrs Allcock? The doctors were really worried about you. Seems like you had some sort of mental breakdown."

"I'm fine. I just had a shock, but now I want you to do something for me."

"Well, I can try, provided it's within the rules."

Victoria shook her head at the pomposity of the warden. "I want you to post this letter and get me my box of personal effects. I've invited someone to come and see me and I need that box when she visits. If you do both these things for me, I will tell the parole board what they want to hear and get out of your hair."

The warden looked on with mild curiosity. Victoria was irritated by his smug, arrogant expression, typical of the men that had blighted her life. She had to hold it together if she was ever going to get her revenge. Thirty years of injustice, burning inside her. She was relieved at the next thing he said.

"I can do that for you. I'll get back onto the parole board and set up your next review."

68

Todd poured Halle a glass of wine as they waited for the takeaway pizzas to arrive. She was exhausted after a mind-blowing day. The attitude of the parents on the Pickford estate still astounded her. Had her approach to this investigation been so bad that it justified their hatred for her and everything to do with the TV show? Marjit Gupta and the other families in their camp didn't think so, but the majority still did.

Todd had been his usual brilliant self when they got back to the office. The report from Terence was being sorted and she had a meeting set up with Clayton and Rod about the Allcock visit. A request had been made for a meeting with the Allcocks but nothing had come back yet. They had also received a nice text from Sophie thanking them for the flowers but confirming they would not be seeing her for a while as she sorted out her father's funeral. Halle was still restless, despite all the good progress, but they had done all they could for one day.

A few minutes later, Todd came back into the living room with a small gift bag.

"Here you are, beautiful. I know it's not been much of a birthday so far but here's something that I hope might cheer you up."

Halle allowed herself a smile in a difficult day. Todd was right. She needed to forget about the case for one evening. There was nothing else she could do tonight.

She grabbed the bag excitedly, removing the pile of decorative shredded paper that was hiding what was inside. "Oh my word. Thank you." Somehow, he had managed to get to the shops and buy her a pair of gold drop earrings and her favourite film on DVD, *Breakfast at Tiffany's*.

She leant forward and grabbed his neck, kissing him. Passionately. Urgently.

He moved closer as they entangled themselves in a fuller, closer embrace. The sexual tension was rising. Halle pulled away and looked deep into Todd's eyes. The lust was overwhelming her. She kissed him again. Hands started to wander. The kissing became more frantic.

The doorbell rang.

They both stopped. Breathless. They looked at each other and started to laugh.

"Okay, seems like we'll have to pick this up later. Pizza time."

*

Peter had driven all the way down to the south coast. He sat in his car, right next to the cliff edge. The wind was howling off the English Channel. He had to get out of the hotel. It had served its purpose but without Sophie he was lost. His brothers had won again. He had no leverage and no one in his camp. He tried to contact Sophie but her phone went to voicemail and her PA trotted out the standard response about her being unavailable. His thoughts turned to his mother. *What is going on with her and that reporter? Why doesn't she want to see me?*

He tried to form shapes in the darkness, but as the wind buffeted the car, he felt more and more trapped. Darkness consuming him in more ways than one. Indiscriminate faces of children started to form. What was this? The children from that estate? He started to cry. He had lost everything and now the awful legacy of his family was haunting his every waking hour.

He looked down at the handbrake through tear-stained eyes. It would be so easy to release it and urge the car forward. Over the cliff. All the pain gone in an instant.

*

It was late as Victoria Allcock lay on her bed. It was twenty minutes to lights out. Her daydreaming was disturbed by one of the screws.

"Here you go. A present from the warden."

She grabbed the box and placed it down on the bed. She pulled the lid off. It was still there. The one thing in the world that would help her exact her revenge.

69

Halle and Todd were back in the office bright and early, despite the lively birthday celebrations. They had a great night; drinking wine, eating pizza, watching the film and... yes, they had gone there. Halle had crossed the line that she had artificially set herself, trying to maintain the sanctity of the whole boss/staff thing. She couldn't resist him any longer. The sex had been full of passion and urgency, doing more to calm Halle's tension than anything else that evening. The awkwardness of their previous encounter at Todd's place was gone. They were in a new place.

She couldn't help pulling a playful, beaming smile as Todd brought in her coffee, and he responded with the cheeky smirk that had done so much to attract her to him. Their mutual appreciation society was broken by Clayton and Rod arriving for their meeting.

Halle shook herself out of her dewy-eyed state. "Guys, thanks for coming. I need your help once again. We are so close to ripping this case wide open."

Clayton and Rod nodded their heads, engaged by Halle's obvious enthusiasm.

"We have, or are in, the process of getting good evidence

that shows that ALMS and PEMS have been running a scam for nearly forty years with the brownfield sites they bought and developed. They have been developing robust solutions to deal with the pollutants on each site but actually implementing much-inferior remediation plans to save money. They have been blackmailing or paying off council officials to 'look the other way' when it comes to the final inspections that allow them to issue the development permits. We think the Pickford estate was one of their sites. The more recent construction of the community centre and children's playground has somehow disturbed their shoddy work, releasing loads of residual pollution."

Clayton reacted first. "Wow, so you think that's why all those poor kiddies have got cancer?"

"Yes. I'd put money on it."

"What do you need from us?"

"I want to confront the Allcocks. I want to meet with them to see how they react to the evidence we have and, Rod, I want you to secretly film the meeting."

Rod smiled, an excited smile that triggered his inner nerd. "Oh wow, my favourite type of filming. All covert and tiny cameras. Very *James Bond*."

Halle laughed. "Thanks, you two. I think this might just be the footage we need to deliver a sensational TV programme and get justice for those poor kids."

"If you can prove the criminality, I can't see the bosses having a problem with using all the footage we have," Rod replied.

"I agree. John has been very hard on this one and I have to nail this, or my fledgling investigative reporter career will be over before it's started."

Clayton and Rod stood up. As they began to leave, Clayton turned around. "We'll be ready as soon as you need us, Halle. Those kids deserve our help, even if some of their parents don't."

Clayton's comments tweaked at Halle's conscience. The kids were the story here and she had to deliver a watertight case that both her bosses and ultimately the police would run with. The racism aspect was awful, and she was still determined to have it front and centre in the final TV edit. She had five days before she was due to meet John again. She needed every duck in every row.

*

Edward, Andrew and their Uncle James were deep into their morning meeting. Edward was scanning through the correspondence folder that his PA had put together for the meeting.

"I guess you know by now that old man Parker is dead."

There were nods from them both.

"I've asked Gemma to set up a meeting with Ross and Sophie as a matter of urgency. I want to exploit their grief and up the pressure on Sophie to accept my offer."

His uncle did his usual. Questioning Edward's motives. "Do you really think they'll agree to meet you when they'll be focusing on sorting out their father's funeral?"

Edward gave his uncle his default expression. The one that disapproved of his question but tried to remain respectful, given all that he had done for him. "I'm not going to let it lie. This is the perfect opportunity to get our little problem sorted when they are at their weakest."

His uncle smirked. "Oh, you are your father's son, Edward."

Satisfied that he had ridden his uncle's challenge, Edward continued to go through the file.

"What on earth is this?"

They looked at him, expectantly.

"Er... we have an email from a TV company called Goldwin Productions. They are working on a story centred around the Pickford housing estate in East London and want to meet with us to discuss their investigation."

His uncle reacted first. "Investigation?"

"Yes, that's what it says, but what the bloody hell has that got to do with us?"

His uncle's face was etched with concern. "That estate is one of the last ones your father worked on. We sold it in the late '80s. I have to say, I'm a little concerned that they seem to be investigating that site."

"Why? What are you worried about?"

"I'm not sure, but we don't need bloody reporters sniffing around any of our sites. You know the risks we face if people dig too deep... if you excuse the pun."

"What do you think, Andrew?"

"Get 'em in. Surely, it's better to find out what they think they have found rather than play a guessing game."

Edward nodded. "I think you're right. I want you all at the meeting, including Philip and Stephen. Whatever these bastards think they've found, we will put up a united Allcock front."

Andrew laughed. "Well, almost a united front."

Edward grimaced at the reminder. "Have our guys tracked him down yet?"

"No. He's not back at his flat and he hasn't used his credit cards for over a week now."

"Okay, keep at it. I'm not having another loose cannon wandering about."

*

Halle spent the rest of the morning reviewing the footage library. The stuff they had was good. She had to find a way to make sure they could use it all. As she rewatched the emotional interview with Marjit Gupta, Todd brought in the post.

Halle's attention was immediately drawn to a handwritten envelope. The writing was beautiful, bold and expressive. She opened it and an equally beautifully written letter was inside.

> *Dear Miss Jacobs,*
> *I am sorry that we couldn't meet the other day. I wasn't feeling well but I'm better now.*
> *I want to tell someone my story and I know you are the right person to hear it. Please do try and come and see me again.*
> *Warmest regards*
> *Victoria Allcock*

Halle read it a few times. Short and to the point. She allowed herself a little excited jig. If Victoria Allcock could add something to this story, it might just be the icing on the cake.

70

Sophie Parker sat in her living room with Ross, poring over the depressing task of coffin choices, flowers and the order of service.

Every second with Ross was torture. Here they were, arranging the funeral of a man she felt she never really knew. A seemingly loving father who, all the while, was lining his pockets by... she could hardly say the words in her head... breaking the law. A weak man, no doubt influenced by Edward Allcock Snr. The worst of it was, she couldn't tell Ross what she had found, because she couldn't shake the horrific feeling that he was carrying on what his father had started.

As she continued the depressing task, functioning on autopilot, the offer from Edward Allcock Jnr to buy PEMS was still sharply in focus. She was certain it was a shameless act to cover up the conspiracy but, in her weaker moments, she was tempted to accept the offer and just walk away.

As she flicked through the catalogue of flower options, her phone beeped. It was a text from her PA at PEMS.

"What is it?"

Sophie shook her head. "Jesus. Edward Allcock has

313

been hassling Jane to set up a meeting with us both. Says he wants to discuss the implications of Dad's death. Talk about a lack of sensitivity."

"Oh, I dunno. Maybe it's just what we need. There is only so much depressing funeral stuff you can do in one day. Tell her to set it up."

And there it was. Once again. Ross thinking that the world revolved around him. Their father's legacy grounded in his psyche, condoning every action by an Allcock man. She was now certain she had been right to keep her own counsel on her conspiracy theories. Ross' behaviour confirmed her suspicions. He was as dirty as the rest of them; otherwise, he would not have agreed to this meeting at such a traumatic time. A chill went down her spine.

*

Lunch had been and gone. Halle contacted the prison to see when she could visit Victoria Allcock and they promised to get back to her. As she idly scrolled through her emails, trying to work out what to do next, Todd came bounding in, breathless with excitement.

"Terence is on the way over here now with the land scan at Pickford. Says he wants to explain it face to face. Seems like he might just have the evidence we've been looking for!"

It was only half an hour before Terence was ensconced in the meeting room, but to Halle and Todd it seemed like an eternity. The kind of waiting you had to endure as a kid when you woke at 4 am on Christmas morning and

314

couldn't work out why your parents weren't up yet.

Terence loaded the visuals onto the large TV screen at the end of the room. He had a mischievous smile over his face as the main image came up. Halle couldn't hold it in any longer.

"What are we seeing here? Have we got them?"

Terence paused for dramatic effect.

"Oh yes. I think we absolutely have them. Let me explain. The line across the middle of this 2D image shows the ground level. The darker layer below the earth is the clay barrier and the layer below that is the original sub-layer, the one that should have been cleaned of as many pollutants as possible. The first and most damning conclusion we can draw from this is that the clay layer is only two feet thick. It should be a minimum of four feet."

Halle was gobsmacked. "Holy shit!"

"There's more. You will also notice that the clay barrier in this image is an unbroken installation."

"Why is that a problem?"

"Because the clay layer should have impermeable barriers installed at about ten-foot intervals. They simply aren't there."

"What does that mean?"

"It means that the risk of residual pollution permeating the clay barrier either through water erosion or normal wear and tear is massively increased. The impermeable barriers are designed to contain movement of residual pollution as a result of degradation of the clay installation."

"So, this is proof that they didn't implement the remediation plans they submitted to the council."

"Exactly, and there is still more.

"If we change to the 3D image of the whole site, you can see the footprint of the clay barrier. You can see that they have once again circled the perimeter of the whole site with a clay barrier. Again, this should be an impermeable barrier, which in this case should be a minimum depth of six feet the whole way round. This is nowhere close to being right. It's an unbelievably risky and irresponsible approach to pollution management."

"We know that their motivation has been about the money. I assume this would have saved them hundreds of thousands of pounds?"

"Yes, it would, and explains why the quotes from PEMS seemed so low for this type of work. I couldn't believe it when you mentioned the normal cost of these projects. We would be charging twice or three times what PEMS are quoting to do this type of work properly."

"Which just leaves the prize question. Can we prove the building of the playground and the community hall is to blame for the children getting cancer?"

"I'm pretty sure we can. I've sent my guys over there this afternoon to take soil samples for testing. If we look at this image, which focuses on that specific area, you can see a clear breach in the clay layer. The patch in the middle of the picture, which is lighter than the surrounding area, shows normal top soil rather than the darker shade, which is the clay layer. It looks as though the breach extends from underneath the community hall and into the playground. My guess is something disturbed that layer when the foundations for the centre were being constructed."

They all sat in silence for a minute, trying to take in the enormity of what Terence had discovered.

Halle adjusted her position. "Wow, this is absolutely amazing. I can't tell you how grateful I am for this. You may just have saved our TV show from being a damp squib. If those soil tests confirm it, we have them. We have what we need to nail these bastards and get some justice for those poor kids."

"You're very welcome."

"Would you be prepared to do a piece to camera explaining all this? It would be such a key part of the TV show to prove our investigation holds water."

"Of course. We can do it whenever you're ready."

Halle drifted off in her own thoughts for a second and Todd nudged her back to reality. "You okay?"

"Oh, sorry. I'm just thinking. I wonder whether the evidence at Pickford will be enough to nail these bastards. Do you think we could do a scan on a more recent site? I'd like to get a more up-to-date ALMS project that proves the same approach has been taken by the Allcock boys. I don't want them to have any get-outs because this site was developed and sold before they took over."

Terence's eyes lit up. "Yeah, happy to do that if you can find me a site."

Halle turned back to Todd. "Can we find a more recent site?"

"Easily. We have a comprehensive list of the sites they've bought and sold over the last five years. I'll get the details to Terence ASAP."

Halle tried to calm her nerves. The revelations from Terence and the realisation that she had a cracking story sent adrenalin coursing through her body. Todd interrupted her excitable mood.

"What are we going to do about shutting down the playground and community centre? If these tests come back positive, we should notify the council and get it all shut down so those poor kids don't have any more exposure."

Halle rubbed her chin. "What can we do? You saw how those idiotic people reacted when we went there yesterday. They are so ignorant that they would rather risk their kids' health further than listen to reason. We've done all we can."

"Are you sure?"

Halle was surprised at his apparent disapproval but let it ride. "We also have to protect the TV show, Todd. Now we look like we have a case, I'm sure the bosses would like to get this story in the can and broadcast before we give out our secrets."

Todd grimaced. "Okay, boss lady. Now you are talking like a real investigative reporter."

Terence packed up his things and left, promising to get the soil results over to them as soon as he had them. Halle and Todd walked back to their offices.

"Chase up that meeting with the Allcocks. I am so ready for them now. Bastards."

71

It was late afternoon as Edward sat with his PA, going through the outcomes of their earlier meeting.

"Have we heard from Sophie and Ross Parker?"

"Yes, we've just had a note back. They can see you at their offices tomorrow at two."

"Excellent. Clear anything else I have tomorrow afternoon. This is a priority."

"Okay, done."

"We've decided to grant the request for a meeting with those TV people. I want everyone there, except Peter of course, and make sure the boardroom is set up to record the meeting."

"Okay, sir, shall I set that up for the day after next?"

"Yes. I want to see the Parkers first before finding out what these TV people are after."

"Is there anything else, sir?"

Edward was about to answer when his mobile started ringing. "Hello. Edward Allcock speaking."

Edward's face dropped as he listened to what the caller was saying, confirming bits of information with a pinched 'yes' at various points in the call. As he finished the call, his face was a mix of emotions. It started with shock and ended with a curious smile.

"What is it, sir? What's happened?"

"You'd better get all the family in here immediately. That was the police. They've found Peter's burnt-out car at the bottom of a cliff on the south coast. There are the remains of a body inside. They think he's committed suicide."

*

It was after 6 pm and Halle was still in the office. She had let Todd go home. Alone. The previous evening had been amazing but self-doubt had begun to creep back in. She was his boss, after all, and whilst her lust for Todd had finally weakened her resolve, she felt it was somehow wrong to have exploited the situation. He didn't seem offended when she told him she needed an early night. The day had been full of excitement and astonishing revelations. She was genuinely exhausted.

She knew she should go home but she kept checking her emails, hoping that Terence would send the results of the soil tests. As she refreshed the screen for the umpteenth time, she was disappointed to see nothing from Terence. She was just about to shut her laptop down when two emails pinged in at the same time. Her heart leapt.

The first one was from a Gemma Whitehead, PA to Edward Allcock Jnr. Halle mused to herself, based on what Sophie had told them about Edward's approach to recruitment. *I can imagine what she's like. Pearly white and everything on show.*

She opened the email. He had granted them a meeting. It was in two days' time at 3 pm at the ALMS offices. She quickly sent the details on to Todd, Rod and Clayton. The butterflies started again.

Just as she thought the day couldn't get any better, she opened up the second email. It was from the prison. She had been granted a visiting slot to see Victoria Allcock in three days' time.

Halle stared at the emails. If Terence delivered in the next thirty-six hours, she would have what she needed to confront the Allcocks, backed up by hard evidence. Then, she would hear Victoria Allcock's story, which she was sure would put the gloss on her TV show.

She couldn't shake the feeling of utter excitement. John had been hard on her and she was going to enjoy walking into his office at the end of the week, giving him everything he needed to make a kick-arse TV show. Those ducks were getting in a row.

72

Halle had taken a while to bring herself down the previous evening, but she had eventually cleared the adrenalin and slept soundly for seven hours straight. As they went through their morning coffee- making ritual, Todd seemed unfazed by her apparent rejection of another evening of rampant sex.

"Sorry about last night. I was so wired after yesterday. I just needed to be alone and sleep."

Todd kissed her gently on the forehead. "It's fine, my beautiful one."

"What did you do?"

"I sent Terence details of a couple more ALMS sites that they sold off in the last few years. Hopefully, he will get onto those straight away."

"Good. Good. Have those soil test results come in?"

"I dunno. I haven't checked my emails yet."

They both walked back into Halle's office, Todd grabbing his laptop on the way.

They sipped their coffees nervously as Todd navigated to his emails. A few seconds later, a goofy smile came across his face.

"We've got them. The soil tests from the playground and the community hall show pollution levels off the scale!"

Sophie Parker's gut was churning. The ham salad sandwich she'd forced down for lunch had not settled well as she sat in the boardroom waiting for Edward Allcock and Ross to arrive. She sipped some water, hoping it would calm her angst, but it just seemed to add to the maelstrom in her stomach.

A few minutes later, the door opened and Ross came in, flanked by Edward. He offered a handshake, which she obliged, reluctantly.

Edward didn't stand on ceremony. "Please accept my condolences for your father's passing. He was a great man. My father talked about him like a brother and I grew fond of him during all our business dealings."

Sophie wanted to grab his neck and smash his face into the boardroom table. "What do you want?"

"I want to help you both in your hour of need."

"Hour of need? What makes you think we are in need of help?"

Edward reverted to his default expression. The smug, arrogant persona that told anyone who was looking that he thought he was in control. A superior being to all those around him, pitying the little people that he was forced to engage with. Sophie noticed a furtive glance at Ross, before Edward spoke again.

"As I said when we last spoke, Miss Parker, I don't believe you are cut out to run PEMS and I am willing to take it off your hands for £20 million. Each."

Sophie shot daggers at Ross. She couldn't hold it in any longer. "Are you part of this, Ross? Part of this animal's plan to cover up what's been going on for the last forty years."

Edward shot an amused look at Ross, who responded to Sophie without an ounce of empathy. "I think Edward's offer is more than fair, Sophie. I never wanted to take over PEMS and you have your own business to look after. I could do a lot with £20 million."

"Holy fuck, Ross. You are part of this. You've let yourself be seduced by the money in the same way that Dad was all those years ago. Played like puppets by the Allcocks. Have you no shame?"

"Look, sis, I have no idea what you are talking about. Our business practices have always been sound and our relationship with ALMS has been the foundation of our business success. I don't know who is feeding you these fantasies, but you need to stop and walk away. Take the £20 million and go back to your advertising business."

Sophie forced back the tears as she stared at Edward and Ross, their expressions firm and unflinching. Her rage was so complete that if she had a baseball bat by her side, she would have picked it up and smashed their heads in. Over and over and over.

Instead, she got up and stormed out, stopping briefly at the door to address them both. "I will never sell my share in PEMS to you. Never."

*

Edward fiddled with the pen in his hand as he let the dust settle from Sophie's abrupt departure.

"You see. This is why our fathers never did business

with bloody women. Too emotional, too pig-headed to see a good deal when it slaps them in the face. Why on earth did your father leave her half the business?"

"I'm sorry. I will try to persuade her to see sense, but I can't guarantee she will come round."

"You need to do this, and soon."

"I'll do my best but what is she going on about? Why is she suggesting that there is something off with our business relationship?"

"Oh, ignore her. She's been listening to my fantasist of a brother, Peter. He's always been a spineless twat and has been winding her up about some stupid theories he has, probably whilst he was shagging her brains out."

"Urgh, please don't talk about my sister like that. I really don't want to know about her sex life."

"Well, whatever, you don't need to worry about him any longer. The police have just found his burnt-out car at the bottom of a cliff. Spineless to the last."

73

Halle and Todd met Terence in the reception area of his offices. He had invited them over to review the scans of one of the newer sites that ALMS and PEMS had worked on. Halle was overwhelmed with the speed with which the case was now moving and couldn't contain herself, giving him a huge hug.

"You are amazing. The work you are doing, and the speed you are doing it at, is just incredible. Not only are we going to make a mind-blowing TV show, but we will put those bastards away for good and get some justice for those poor children."

Terence was not fazed by the hug and led them up to the meeting room. Halle couldn't stop her over-excited ramblings as they walked up the stairs. "Those soil tests on Pickford. Your team are certain that they show high pollution levels?"

"Oh yes, no doubt. The split in the clay barrier on those scans yesterday back these results up. Whilst it's strange that the residual pollution has not really seeped out into the wider estate, those levels are highly concentrated in that area."

As they helped themselves to refreshments, Terence

fiddled with the tech. "My team should be uploading their scans any minute. Treat yourselves to a coffee and a Danish. I should be ready in a few minutes."

Halle savoured the sugar rush and the hit of caffeine as Terence tapped away at the keyboard. A few minutes later, he was ready.

"Right, let me just get these loaded up and we'll see what we have."

Halle and Todd both sat forward, expectant, hopeful that their instincts were right.

The first image came up. A 2D image similar to the one they saw before.

"Okay, guys, looks like we have the same profile here. There's the clay barrier and once again, it is only 2 feet thick. We also have no impermeable barriers."

Halle shot a wide-eyed look at Todd.

"Let's look at the 3D image... yes, once again we have the same type of clay barrier around the perimeter and no impermeable barriers here either."

Halle interjected. "Are there any cracks in the clay barrier?"

Terence rotated the image to look from all sides. "Actually, no. This installation at least still seems to be sound."

There was a brief pause as they took in what they were seeing. Halle broke the silence.

"What do you make of this?"

He pondered for a moment before answering. "You know, on some sick level, I really believe they thought they could get away with this. I think this scan proves that provided the earth is undisturbed, their shoddy approach will just about contain whatever pollutants are still in the ground. It's a high-risk strategy but coupled with corrupt council officials, I can see why they have gambled like this. It's taken nearly thirty years for the Pickford issues to appear, and I think they knew the chances of any trouble were quite low. Whoever decided to build that playground and community hall at Pickford may just have saved more lives from being at risk down the line."

They talked some more, and Halle became more and more determined to land this story. The arrogance of the Allcocks, Bill Parker and Jeremy Hogan was astounding. They finished up by arranging for Rod to visit Terence to do a piece to camera. The footage she needed was almost complete.

*

Sophie was back at home, pacing around. She stopped in the kitchen and poured a glass of wine, spilling some on the marble work surface as she tried to control the involuntary shaking that was consuming her body.

The realisation that Ross was part of this awful situation floored her. She didn't want to believe it. She had been struggling to process the realisation that her father was not who she thought he was and now Ross was added to the list. How could she face the funeral? Burying a man who had lied and deceived them all her life and Ross standing at the graveside like some mini-me would-be gangster.

She let out a manic scream and launched the wine glass at the wall. The tears started. She grabbed a blanket and curled up on the sofa. Shaking and crying. Her world in tatters.

74

The day had arrived. The day when Halle would confront the Allcocks and watch them squirm as she laid out the evidence before them. She knew confronting them like this was a risk, but with Clayton's protection, Rod's secret filming and Todd's moral support, she was as confident as she could be.

The morning had dragged on as she tried to distract herself from the hundreds of thoughts and scenarios that were flying through her brain. But now, as they drove into the visitors' car park of the ALMS offices, she was ready.

Before they got out, she did a quick sanity check. Rod was fully operational. A tiny 4k camera with pin-sharp sound and video was discreetly pinned to his jacket. Clayton was exhibiting his usual confident 'don't fuck with me' persona, and Todd just had his usual bright and happy expression plastered all over his face. Halle looked at them each in turn. "Come on, guys. This is it."

They walked into the ALMS reception and announced their arrival. After a five-minute wait, they were greeted by Edward's PA. Halle couldn't help but smile. She had been spot-on. The PA was a long-legged blonde, wearing a skirt that barely covered her arse, a white blouse that was trying to contain ample breasts and a pair of killer heels that shifted everything up, proud and perky.

As they were escorted into the boardroom, they were greeted by five men sat around the semi-circle at the top end of the boardroom table. Four of them looked strikingly similar, flanked by an older man that Halle concluded was their uncle. They sat at the other end of the large table. Full-on confrontation position.

Introductions were made but Halle was distracted by Edward glaring at Clayton the whole while. She was just about to challenge him when he offloaded what was on his mind. "He may be your security detail, Miss Jacobs, but I don't allow people like that in my offices."

Halle looked at Clayton, who looked ready to launch himself at Edward. She placed a restraining hand on his arm. "People like what, Mr Allcock?"

He pursed his lips like he was sucking a lemon. "Non-British people."

Clayton snorted a derisory laugh. The room fell silent. Whilst Halle didn't want Clayton to be abused, she was worried the meeting would be over before it started. A moral crisis. The silent stand-off continued.

Another minute passed. Eventually, Edward looked away from Clayton, shaking his head in mock disgust. "Ask your questions, Miss Jacobs. We are all very busy here."

Halle looked at Clayton, who gave her a reassuring nod. If nothing else, they had got his racist undertones on camera. Halle steeled herself. Showtime.

"Where is Peter Allcock?"

Edward shuffled in his chair. "That's a very insensitive question at this difficult time."

Halle pulled a confused face. "Why?"

"My brother's car has just been found at the bottom of a cliff on the south coast. It seems he committed suicide. He was a very troubled man."

Halle took a sharp intake of breath. She didn't like Peter Allcock but she was shocked to hear he had killed himself. She looked at Todd for reassurance coupled with a 'why didn't we know that' look. He picked up on the vibe and grimaced, apologetically. Her emotions were all over the place, tears welling up as she tried to process the bombshell that Edward had just thrown. As Halle tried to compose herself, she shot a glance at Edward. He was smirking. An arrogant, self-satisfied expression that had power written all over it. That was all she needed. She wasn't going to let him win. She righted herself and cracked on.

"Gosh, I'm so sorry to hear that. Please accept my condolences."

Edward nodded in mock appreciation.

"I'd like to ask you about the Pickford housing estate in East London. A site you bought, cleaned up and sold in the late '80s."

"Yes, I believe it was one of the last sites my father worked on before he was brutally murdered by my bitch of a mother. What do you need to know about it?"

"We have solid evidence that residual pollution has been leaking out from a crack in the clay barrier near the children's playground. Pollution that you should have properly dealt with. Instead, you implemented shoddy remediation plans that do not match what you submitted to the council. As a result, twenty children have developed cancer on that site and two have already died."

There it was. The die had been cast. Halle waited for the rage but it didn't come. Edward glanced at his uncle, his face etched with concern.

"I'm really shocked, Miss Jacobs. How terrible. All those poor children. The thing is, all our environmental studies, site clean-ups and remediation plan implementations are done by our sub-contractor, Parker Environmental Management Services. I had no idea they were doing substandard work. Did you, Andrew?"

Andrew put on the same fake concerned face. "I didn't. All the paperwork that our Project Director at PEMS has provided over the years has always been spot-on. They've also been responsible for obtaining our development permits from the council, so I'm surprised there are any anomalies in their work."

Halle was stunned at their front. She pushed on. "We have evidence to suggest that those council officials are corrupt. They are being blackmailed or paid off to look the other way when your requests for development permits are made. Your Project Director, Jeremy Hogan, also has spending habits way above his salary levels, suggesting he is also getting extra income from somewhere."

Edward took back command of the conversation, allowing himself an arrogant smile that told everyone in the room that he was in total control. "Again, Miss Jacobs, I'm shocked at what you are telling me. As Andrew has said, that part of the process is also sub-contracted to PEMS. We assumed that their services were all above board, but you seem to have opened up a can of worms here. I will need to have an urgent look into our business relationship, although you haven't picked the best time to bring this to my attention."

"Why not?"

"I'm afraid that Bill Parker, who ran PEMS for the past forty years, has just passed away. His son and daughter have just taken over and are still trying to get to grips with the business."

Halle was gobsmacked at the bravado; conscious she was not landing any punches. She looked at her team, who all nodded at her to carry on.

"Your faux concern astonishes me, Mr Allcock. Do you really expect me to believe that you knew nothing of the corrupt working practices at PEMS? Your father and Bill Parker have been working together since they set up their businesses forty years ago, and under your uncle's guidance, you have been running this company for nearly thirty years. Now, I know you're not stupid, so I can only assume you are lying to me."

Edward looked at his uncle and brothers with an amused, mocking expression on his face. As he fixed his gaze back on Halle, his mood changed. A hint of anger on his face.

"I granted you this interview, Miss Jacobs, because I was curious as to what you wanted, but all you seem to want to do is disrespect my family and my father's legacy. If PEMS have been running corrupt business practices all this time, I will root them out and deal with them. So, unless you have any proof that ALMS are in any way breaking the law, I suggest you get out of my offices immediately."

"Oh, we have proof."

Halle noticed the first flicker of doubt in Edward's manner, before he recomposed himself.

"Oh really. I'm listening."

"Genesis."

Edward sat forward; his manner more threatening. "Hmm, how curious you should mention that word. We have a programme called Genesis that holds all our highly sensitive commercial information that we absolutely do not want our competitors to get their hands on. It is protected by some of the most sophisticated security money can buy, yet we recently experienced a significant illegal cyber-attack. We had to take the site down to protect our information and I really need to contact the police about it. You wouldn't know anything about that, would you?"

Halle's guts were in turmoil. How had this gone so wrong? She stood up, ushering her team out. "Thank you for your time, Mr Allcock, but I can see we are not going to get anywhere with this conversation."

She tried to ignore the smug, victorious look on the faces of all the Allcock men as they shuffled out of the boardroom.

As they got back in the car, Halle looked at her team.

"What the hell just happened in there?"

75

His laugh started quietly but gradually grew into a booming belly laugh. His brothers and uncle looked on, mildly amused by Edward's persona.

"Well, well, well. So now we know who was helping Peter hack into Genesis, and I can tell from her reaction that they got nothing. Oh, that felt good to piss all over her theories."

As usual, his uncle was the one to dampen Edward's high spirits. "That's as may be, Edward, but we have a problem if there really is pollution leaking at that East London site. If they start sniffing around any of our other developments, they will find the same remediation plans on every site."

"Do you know, it came to me the other night when I gave the instruction to kill the Genesis programme. Dad was clever in his relationship with the Parkers. By contracting the work out to PEMS, he had complete deniability. I checked the contracts we have with PEMS and all the liability for any problems down the line with the work they did for us, sits with them. It's brilliant and I have no idea how Dad got Bill Parker to agree to it. We have no legal exposure."

"I'm not sure that's enough."

"But it is. I set Genesis up because I thought I needed a record of all the transactions and evidence we had to make sure those council officials never wavered from the threats we posed. But Dad didn't work like that. I remember you telling me when I first took on the business that Dad only kept the paperwork long enough to land the deal and to make sure the relevant people were kept quiet. Once the deal was done, he shredded the evidence. I don't need Genesis. I need to do what my dad did. Complete deniability, with Jeremy Hogan as the perfect stool pigeon."

"What if they get to him?"

"He won't betray us. He's in too deep to wriggle out of this. We have him exactly where we need him."

"What should we do then?"

"Nothing. Genesis is gone. If they get the police involved, we will deny any knowledge and put all the heat back on PEMS."

"Won't it look a bit suspicious if they find out you are trying to buy the company?"

"Quite the contrary. I'm a concerned business owner, shocked at the revelations of malpractice by my subcontractor. It's my way of tidying up the corruption, and I will make sure I install new owners so we continue to maintain our buffer of deniability. It's bloody genius."

"Fuck me, Edward. You've got more front than Brighton beach."

*

Halle was back in the office staring out of the window, Todd sitting across the desk from her.

"How could I have been so stupid, so naïve? He played me like a puppet. I was so sure we had him but he's just knocked down every piece of evidence we had. Without Genesis, we can't prove anything."

There was no response from Todd and as she turned back to look at him, his head was bowed. She leapt up and grabbed his face. "Oh God, I'm sorry. I didn't mean it like that. You did an amazing job to hack into that site. We were just unlucky."

He gave her a pained smile. "We just need to regroup. The evidence that Terence gave us is solid. We just need to somehow link this back to ALMS."

"But how, Todd? They have somehow deflected all this onto PEMS, which puts poor Sophie right in the mix. I told her she would be okay if she helped us, but now, I'm not so sure. What a mess."

Todd brightened up. "Look, the best I can do is go home, get in my technology hub and work with my cyber mate to find some sort of digital evidence that we can use against Edward Allcock. The trails will be there, somewhere. It's not going to be easy, because without Genesis we have no leads. We're good at what we do but with nowhere to start we might struggle to find anything."

Halle grimaced. "You're my hero. Do what you can. I see John in a couple of days' time. I can't go in there like this."

"At least we have his racist outburst on tape."

"Oh, as good as that is, I have to accept that John is not going to champion racism as the main story here. It has to be about the kids. My only hope, apart from you, is that I get something from my visit with Victoria Allcock."

*

It was late afternoon and Sophie Parker was sprawled on the sofa, still in her dressing gown. She had hardly moved from that spot. Paralysed by the situation she was in.

She picked up her phone. There were a few missed calls from Ross and several a few days earlier from Peter Allcock. She bit her nails as she reflected on whether she had been too hard on him. She still had Halle and Todd on her side but her initial connection with Peter had been good. It was emotional, not transactional like the relationship she had with Halle and Todd. A mutual bonding over this horrific situation, an empathy only they could understand.

She had a few text messages, opening up the most recent one from Ross.

Sis, please call me. I don't know what's going on with you and all these fantasies about our relationship with ALMS. Edward is giving us a way out of this hell and we should take it. I'm also sorry to tell you that Peter Allcock is dead. He's committed suicide.

Sophie dropped the phone. Her heart started to pound. What the hell was going on?

76

As Halle drove into the prison car park, her mood was dark. Todd had spent most of the previous day working with his cyber mate, trying to find a digital trail that would implicate Edward Allcock and his corrupt family in this tragedy. They had found nothing. Edward Allcock was a ghost. A proper Mr Big. Somehow, he had made sure that no trail led back to him. Halle knew he was guilty, but she had underestimated his ability to shield himself from all the crap.

She had two options. She either had to persuade John that they were still hot on the trail of the story and just needed more time, or hope that Victoria Allcock could give her something new to focus on.

She got out of the car, pulling her jacket around her as the harsh winter wind bit at her face.

Fifteen minutes later, she was ensconced in a featureless room. Bare walls, a ropey old table and two uncomfortable chairs, placed either side. It was better than being in the large visitors' room with all the noise and chatter of desperate people trying to maximise the time with their loved ones, but the starkness still unsettled Halle.

After what seemed like an eternity, the door opened and Victoria Allcock was escorted into the room, carrying a small box.

Halle smiled at her, hoping that this time she would stay upright. Victoria's expression was different this time. The look of fear had gone, replaced by something kinder. A look of… *love?*

The prison guard left them to it, standing outside the door, ready for action but respecting their privacy.

The two women looked at each other, both taking in the shape of their faces, the life experiences etched in the lines on their foreheads. There was silence.

Halle started to feel uncomfortable and broke the reverence, thrusting her hand forward in greeting.

"I'm Halle Jacobs. It's really great to meet you finally."

Victoria smiled and nodded. "Yes. I'm sorry about the last time you were here. You gave me a bit of a shock."

Halle looked pensive. "Why? I didn't mean to frighten you."

"You didn't frighten me. It was something else. Something that we can discuss in a bit, but tell me first about your investigation. Peter said you are working on a TV show."

The mention of Peter's name interrupted Halle's thought process and she briefly agonised at the realisation that Victoria didn't know he was dead. The selfish, focused investigative reporter kicked in. Halle knew she should tell her but there was too much riding on the conversation, and she had a feeling Victoria was about to say something that would unlock the case. She just couldn't risk upsetting her again.

Halle was conscious that Victoria was staring at her and quickly shook herself out of her malaise. "I was given a story to investigate about a high number of children contracting cancer on the Pickford housing estate in East London. It was a site that ALMS and PEMS worked on, possibly one of the last your husband did before…"

"I killed him. It's all right, Halle. I don't need you to tiptoe around that. I've had thirty years to dwell on that moment, and I ain't bothered what people think of me."

"Yeah, sure. No problem. Anyhow, based on our investigations to date, we've found that PEMS appear to have implemented substandard remediation plans to deal with the pollution on the various sites they cleared up for ALMS. They've implemented different plans to the ones they gave the council and seem to have paid off or bribed council officials to 'look the other way' when it comes to issuing the permits. The problem at Pickford is that the clay barrier was breached when a playground and community hall were built more recently. The soil tests around the playground show pollution has leaked out and levels are off the scale in that area. It seems certain that this has caused the cancers. Sophie Parker has been helping us from the PEMS end, but when I confronted your sons about it, they claimed they knew nothing. They are hanging PEMS out to dry, and poor Sophie could be in real trouble now that her father has passed away."

Victoria raised her eyebrows. "Bill Parker's dead?"

"Yes, it's just happened. The problem is, I know Edward Jnr and the rest of the Allcock men are in the thick of this, carrying on their father's horrific legacy, but we can't find any evidence to nail them. We managed to hack into a programme called Genesis, where we think they were holding all the evidence that would have implicated them. The problem was, they detected our hack and deleted everything before we could grab it. I underestimated just how evil and manipulative Edward is. If I can't find something to implicate him and the rest of your delightful family, I really fear that Sophie will be sitting where you are."

"What about Jeremy Hogan?"

"Oh yeah. You know about him?"

"Yes. Jeremy was always mentioned when my husband was talking with Bill. Is he still around?"

"He is, and again, we have evidence to link him to this scam, but I have a feeling that Edward has set him up to take the fall along with Sophie."

There was a brief pause as Victoria took it all in, nodding in apparent recognition of what Halle was saying. Halle held her breath. Victoria seemed to know something about what had been going on. Was she going to help her?

Just as Halle thought she was going to burst with the tension of waiting for Victoria to say something, she reached for the box. Halle watched with curious excitement. She pulled out a key on a piece of string. Halle stared at Victoria, wide-eyed with expectation. "What's that?"

Victoria smiled. "You know, I never thought this day would come. I never thought that there would be anyone in my corner that would enable me to reveal what I have been sitting on all these years. I was convicted of murder with barely a whimper of defence from my useless male barristers. I'm certain this key will give you access to what you are looking for. I was going to use it as part of my defence, but I could see how the wind was blowing and I decided to sit on what I had. I just didn't realise that it would be thirty years before I was able to use it."

Halle was speechless. "What… I mean… God… what are you trying to tell me…?"

Victoria laughed. "This key opens a safety deposit box. Inside, you will find photocopies of paperwork that should prove my husband was pulling the strings around what you have found. I didn't know what it all meant at the time but there is all sorts of stuff in there, including some disgusting photos, which I assume link to the blackmail you mentioned. I always knew he was corrupt, but I didn't think he could stoop so low as to endanger the lives of those poor kids. I'm just sorry that my sons seem to have carried on his legacy."

"How did you get these documents?"

Victoria gave a disapproving snort. "Huh. My husband thought he was the 'dog's bollocks', treating me like some slave, kowtowing to his every need and every command. He thought I was stupid but he underestimated my resolve. He was so arrogant that he left the documents in a cabinet in his office. He told me never to go in there and assumed I would comply, like the downtrodden creature he thought he had moulded me into. I knew he was up to something and started copying all the documents, hiding them in my shopping bags and taking them to my safety deposit box when I went to buy food. He used to periodically shred the documents, assuming that was covering his tracks. I'm so glad I murdered the bastard. Take the key, Halle, and use it to nail my broken family."

Halle's head was spinning with the implications of what Victoria was saying, but as she tried to reconcile the enormity of this development, the realisation hit her.

"This is so amazing, but the evidence you have will only implicate your husband and probably Bill Parker and Jeremy Hogan. It won't prove that Edward Jnr has carried on with his legacy."

"I don't know. It has to be enough. They can't keep getting away with this."

Halle sighed. "We've got evidence that council officials are still being paid off and a scan of a more recent site that shows the same substandard plans have been implemented. I just hope it's enough."

As they both took a moment to take in all that had been said, Halle was a little unnerved at how Victoria kept staring at her. She had to deal with the elephant in the room.

"Okay, time to spill. You need to tell me the real reason you acted so odd when we first met."

Victoria bowed her head, suddenly unable to look Halle in the eye.

"Victoria? Are you okay?"

She eventually looked up, tears forming. "You had a birthday recently."

Halle was taken aback. "Er... yes, I did, but how would you know that?"

Victoria's faced crumpled and the tears started to flow. Halle grabbed her hands and fixed her with a firm but supportive expression. "Come on. Tell me. I'm sure whatever it is, it can't be all that bad."

Victoria exhaled deeply. "I wouldn't be so sure."

There was a brief silence, Halle giving her the time she needed. Eventually, Victoria spoke.

"I was pregnant when I was incarcerated in this place. I had her whilst I was in here."

"Her?"

"Yes, after five boys, I finally fell pregnant with a beautiful baby girl. But, of course, I couldn't keep her. Not in here. I gave her up for adoption and insisted she was never told that I was her mother. I was heartbroken that something so beautiful could come out of so much abuse."

There was something in the pit of Halle's stomach that was telling her she knew where this was going. She had to ask the next question.

"What has this got to do with me? Why did you faint when you saw me the other day?"

There was an agonising pause as Victoria struggled with her conscience. She leant forward and stroked Halle's cheek.

"When I saw you, Halle, it was like looking in a mirror." She grabbed a crumpled picture out of the box and thrust it at Halle. "This is a picture of me with my baby, when I was about the age you are now. Look. Can't you see the resemblance?"

"Eh? I don't understand."

"The baby I'm holding in that picture is you. You're my daughter, Halle. You're an Allcock."

77

Halle sat in her car outside the prison, paralysed by what she had just been told. How could she be an Allcock? How could her parents have lied to her like that, even if Victoria had insisted she was never to be told? Her emotions were all over the place. She didn't know whether to cry, to scream, to laugh. Everything she had known suddenly thrown up in the air, a betrayal of the life she thought she knew and worst of all, her real father was apparently Edward Allcock Snr.

Victoria had told her to look in the safety deposit box. In there she would find more pictures and her original birth certificate. Born on the 30th of November 1989 in this place. Halle turned the car on. She needed Todd now, more than ever, but she had to know. She had to open that safety deposit box and see it in black and white. She couldn't believe Victoria would lie about something like this but she had to be sure.

She set the satnav to direct her to the bank where the safety deposit box was held. She found some on street parking and fed the meter. Her legs were wobbly as she started to walk towards the bank but she made it to the lobby. The bank teller eyed the key and typed in a code that was on the back of the fob.

"Okay, Mrs Allcock. Please follow me."

The mention of the Allcock name triggered another stress response, as Halle suddenly flushed hot. She was surprised the bank teller had assumed she was Victoria Allcock, without asking for any ID, but she was grateful for small mercies. Sweat was forming on her forehead and she discreetly wiped it away, worried that the physiological reactions would give her away.

The teller didn't seem to notice, unlocking her box and carrying it into one of the private viewing rooms. "Okay. Take as much time as you need. Just press on this buzzer when you are done and I will come back down."

Halle gave her a faint 'thank you'. Her mouth was dry, nausea was rising and she could barely speak. The long metal box sat in front of her on the table. She sat for a minute, staring at it, knowing that lifting that lid could change her life forever.

Her hands were shaking as she opened it. The first thing she saw was a picture. She stared at it. Halle assumed it was another picture of Victoria holding the baby. She examined it closely. Victoria was right. The likeness to Halle was astonishing. She placed her finger on the picture of the baby. Was she really looking at a picture of herself, just after she was born?

She placed the picture on the table and picked up a brown envelope. She slid out the document that was inside. It was a birth certificate. As she went to unfold it, she thought her heart was going to burst out of her chest. The sweat was once again forming on her forehead and her vision was blurring. She put the certificate down and gripped the table. She exhaled deeply, trying to get oxygen in her body to stop herself fainting. After a few minutes, she felt better. Her head was cooler and her heart stopped racing. She picked the certificate back up and unfolded it.

Halle Victoria Allcock, born 30th November 1989, father: Edward Andrew Allcock, mother: Victoria Lucy Allcock…

The next thing she found confirmed it. A copy of the adoption certificate signed by Victoria and her parents, Janet and Gareth Jacobs. The box asking if the child should ever be told about her birth parents was annotated with a clear *No*.

Halle took a while to process it all. Her parents had been so wonderful , bringing her up and not wanting for anything, but she still felt betrayed. The adoption certificate confirmed Victoria's wishes but Halle felt cheated. She would have wanted the choice. To have known the truth, to decide whether Victoria Allcock was someone she wanted in her life. Given the circumstances, Halle would have understood. She fought back tears. How could she go and see John in this state, with all these revelations flying around in her head?

As she agonised over what to do next, Halle's eye was drawn to the large envelope that was still in the box. She exhaled deeply and picked it out of the box. It was thick with paperwork. She pulled the wad of papers out and started to look at them, one by one.

Her eyes grew wider at every document. Incriminating photos, blackmail letters from Edward Allcock Snr to various council officials, bank statements confirming payments out of the Bill Parker Holding Account to various other banks, and correspondence between Edward, Bill and Jeremy confirming the revised approach to remediation plans. It was gold dust.

78

Todd was at home in his technology hub. Stressed. He and Krypto had spent much of the previous day trying to find something that would implicate the Allcock boys in this conspiracy but they had found nothing. They had nowhere to start and were floundering around trying to find the proverbial needle in a haystack. Every digital trail about Edward Allcock Jnr was clean.

As Todd pondered his uncharacteristic failure to find what he needed in the deep, dark spaces of the internet, he realised this was not luck. Edward Allcock was clever, a proper criminal mastermind. He had made sure that no trail got near him.

Todd blew out his cheeks. What the hell could he do now? Genesis was still on his mind. If Edward didn't want any trails back to him, why had he hidden all his secrets in one programme? There was no doubt the security was as good as anything Todd had previously encountered but, at the end of the day, his cyber mates had cracked it. The fact he had introduced a failsafe by killing the programme the instant a cyber-attack was detected was the only thing that Todd could reconcile. Edward had taken a calculated gamble in using Genesis but was confident enough to destroy it at the merest hint of exposure. Todd couldn't help thinking that it was still out there somewhere, removed and restored somewhere they wouldn't find it.

Whatever Todd's opinions were of Edward Allcock, the fact remained that they had nothing. Neither he nor Krypto had managed to grab any evidence from Genesis, and Edward's arrogance when they all met had told Todd that he was super-confident he had protected the ALMS name by using PEMS as his buffer zone. Todd loved watching *Dallas* and he couldn't help feeling that Edward was a modern-day *J.R. Ewing*.

He stood up and screamed loudly. No one was there to hear it, but it made him feel better. He grabbed a Coke from the fridge, savouring the sugar hit as he agonised over what to do next. He couldn't help feeling that he had let Halle down. His self-persecution was interrupted by a knock at the door. Standing there, shivering in the cold and rain was Halle, clutching a bag. Tears were streaming down her face.

Todd bundled her indoors, helping her off with her coat and sitting her in the lounge by the wood burner. She was distraught, gripping onto Todd for dear life. He eventually managed to release her grip.

"What is it, Halle? What's happened?"

The story came pouring out, in between bouts of snot and tears. Todd listened. Shocked and dumbfounded. After the shocking personal revelations, Halle eventually showed Todd the documents implicating Edward Allcock Snr. They were… brilliant. As Halle ran out of steam, Todd shook his head. He didn't think it was possible to love her any more, in that moment when she needed him most.

"What do I do? How can I confront my parents about this? How can I see John in this state? Everything is just… falling apart."

They cuddled on the sofa and Halle lay her head on Todd's shoulder. In an instant, the mental exhaustion had won. She was asleep in seconds.

Todd felt the rhythmic rise and fall of her breaths against his body. He had to help her. He had to find a way to make this all better. As his thoughts turned back to Edward Allcock and the certainty that he was as corrupt as his father, backed up by the reams of evidence that lay in front of him, Todd thought about PEMS.

How could Bill Parker be so naïve, allowing himself to be set up like that? A stool pigeon for the Allcocks. The problem was that he was no longer around to suffer the consequences. Halle was right. Despite Sophie Parker's willingness to expose this conspiracy, she was now in the hot seat. PEMS were in deep shit and Sophie was in it up to her ears.

The digital world that had been Todd's bread and butter as a brilliant researcher had let him down. There was only one choice. He had to go old school. There was only one other option. One person who could help them crack this case, and he needed Sophie Parker's help to convince them to get on the right side of the law. They had to get at Jeremy Hogan.

79

Todd left Halle sleeping in. Coaxing her into bed the previous evening, he had agreed that he would call the office and say she was off sick. She desperately needed some headspace to process everything that had happened, and they agreed that she had to speak to her parents.

He hadn't told her what he was up to. If everything went to plan, he could get her what she needed for her meeting with John the following day. They were so close to a fully-fledged story, but they had to turn to Jeremy Hogan if they had any chance of getting real justice.

Todd found Sophie Parker's address and drove into the pretty close where she lived. The winter sun was thawing the last of the frost, giving the air a clean, fresh smell. He pressed the doorbell. There was no answer. He was sure she was home, as her office had said she had not been in for several days. He pressed it again. This time, he heard movement.

The door opened and Sophie Parker stood in the doorway, looking less than glamorous. Her hair was wild and unbrushed, her eyes were dark and sunken, her skin was blotchy and she was still in her nightclothes and dressing gown.

"Oh, it's you. What do you want?"

Todd tried not to react to her dishevelled state. "Er... can I come in? We've had some major progress on the investigation but I desperately need your help."

She shrugged and ushered him in. "Do you want a coffee or something?"

"Yeah, I guess so. That would be nice."

Todd watched as Sophie went into the kitchen, her movements laboured and mechanical. He had seen this demeanour before. Last night with Halle. Had something bad happened to Sophie as well?

As she brought the coffee in and sat at the other end of the sofa, he went for it. "Are you okay? You seem out of sorts."

She didn't speak for a moment, just shaking her head and staring off into the distance.

"Sophie?"

She turned to look at Todd. "It's all gone wrong. Ross is part of this. He's in Edward's pocket and wants to sell him our business. I'm about to bury a man that I no longer know and Peter Allcock has killed himself, for which I must take some of the blame. So, no, Todd, I'm not okay."

Todd sipped his coffee. He desperately needed Sophie's help but he feared what he was about to tell her would send her over the edge. He agonised for a minute as she went back to staring into the distance.

"Look, I'm really sorry you're having such a bad time and what I'm about to tell you will probably not help, but I think I can make this right for everyone involved."

Initially, there was no response from Sophie. Todd wasn't sure she had even heard what he said. Just as he was about to repeat himself, she turned to look at him. "Okay, I'm gonna trust you. Give me time to have a shower and put some clothes on and we can talk."

Sophie returned to the living room half an hour later looking much more human. After a refill of their coffees, Todd laid it all out. The revelations about how her father and Jeremy Hogan had been working with Edward Allcock Snr on the remediation plan scam, the realisation that the Allcocks, young and old, were using PEMS as their stool pigeon, the revelations about Halle's parentage and the determination by Victoria Allcock to get revenge.

Sophie listened intently, fighting back tears as the story grew more horrifying with every sentence. "I just can't believe this, Todd. I came to accept that my father and Jeremy Hogan were somehow implicated in this horrific situation, but I never thought that the Allcocks would use our family to cover their own arses. I can't believe Dad was so naïve, and now he's left me exposed."

"I'm sorry, but you had to know the full truth. If you help me, I'm certain we can sort this out."

"But how? Edward is an evil man. He won't let this lie."

"I know, which is why we need to cut off his insurance policy. We need to convince Jeremy Hogan that he is in the wrong camp. That he's being played like a fiddle."

They discussed what to do next. Despite everything that was going on, Sophie was sure that Jeremy Hogan would come and see her if she impressed the urgency. After all, she was still the boss.

The call was made and Jeremy agreed to visit Sophie at home, just after lunch. Todd and Sophie took the time to look through the evidence that Victoria had left for them. Every page seemed to strengthen Sophie's resolve, and after a quick sandwich, they were ready for Jeremy Hogan.

He arrived bang on time. Sophie invited him in but he checked himself as he saw Todd sitting there. He flashed a look at Sophie, his suspicions immediately raised. "Who's this?" he growled accusingly.

"Please sit down, Jeremy."

He complied reluctantly. Sophie sat down and looked him straight in the eye. "We have a very serious situation, Jeremy, and I want you to listen carefully to what we have to say. This is Todd Barkley. He is a researcher from a TV company that is working on a story about lots of children contracting cancer on the Pickford housing estate in East London. A site that we and ALMS worked on in the late '80s. A site which is now leaking pollution because we didn't do our jobs properly."

They both waited for the reaction. Fight or flight time. Jeremy went for fight, laughing mockingly as he started to speak. "Are you mad, Miss Parker? What on earth makes you think that we did anything wrong on that site? Our work has always passed the safety inspections. Your father would be ashamed at the way you are talking to me. Forty years, I've worked for him. How dare you summon me like some naughty child and accuse me of overseeing shoddy work."

Todd and Sophie looked at each other. They were not surprised at the reaction. Jeremy was so deep in this conspiracy; he was not going to just roll over. They did the only thing they could do. They started laying out pieces of paper from the evidence that Victoria had given them.

He watched curiously as they laid out several sheets of paper. He was trying not to look at them, but a subtle change in his body language told them he was working out what he was seeing. He went for bravado. "Is there some relevance to you placing all these bits of paper in front of me?"

Todd spoke for the first time. "You're being set up to take the fall, Jeremy. These documents implicate Edward Allcock Snr, Bill Parker and you in the remediation plan scam that you have been running for forty years, including bribing council officials. A scam that Edward Allcock Jnr carried on with and which, we know, you are being paid big bonuses to deliver. The problem is, Jeremy, my boss and I confronted the Allcocks about all the evidence we have. They claimed they know nothing about it and it struck us that they are using PEMS as their fall guys. We can't find a single thing that links Edward Allcock Jnr and his brothers to this scam. Their father set you up, and Edward Jnr has been savvy enough to make sure they have continued to be protected. If we take this case to the police as it stands, Jeremy, they have complete deniability and you are going to jail."

The whole while Todd had been speaking, Jeremy's eyes were darting between Todd, Sophie and the paperwork in front of him. The mental turmoil was evident. He didn't respond. He just rubbed his face, periodically picking up bits of paper and scanning the content. Todd went for broke.

"The added problem, Jeremy, is that now Bill Parker is dead, Sophie is also in the firing line. PEMS will be destroyed and if you don't help us, the Allcocks will take over the company and let you rot in prison. Is your wife's new BMW really that important, or your next flash holiday? Can you really live with the guilt of your part in those poor kids getting cancer and explaining to your grandchildren what you've done?"

Jeremy bolted for the door but Sophie was quick to react and blocked his way. He glared at her, a mixture of rage and fear etched over his face. "Get out of my way, Miss Parker. I can't help you."

He went to move past her but she placed a firm hand on his shoulder. He looked at her hand and then up to her face. "I don't want to hurt you. Please take your hand off me and let me by."

"I won't do that. You have to help us nail the Allcocks."

Jeremy's shoulders slumped, some of the fight evidently gone. He shook his head and looked at Sophie. "He won't let this lie. If I help you, I'm as good as dead. I have no choice."

"You do have a choice. I have to believe that, in your heart, you and Dad are good people. You've let yourselves be corrupted for forty years by greed, but it has to stop. I have to believe that you didn't really understand the implications of what you were doing and never realised that Edward Allcock would hang us out to dry. I have to believe this or I don't know if I can be at Dad's funeral or get through another day."

The speech was deep and impassioned, but Sophie didn't know if it had been enough. Jeremy's head had dropped, averting his gaze from Sophie's pleading expression.

There were a few tense minutes as Jeremy didn't

respond. Sophie looked at Todd, who shook his head, a non-verbal sign not to say any more. Jeremy needed to wallow in his guilt. It worked.

Jeremy spoke, his voice faltering. "What do you need me to do?"

80

Todd was in the office the next day at his usual time of 8 am. Halle wasn't there and she hadn't contacted him the previous evening. She had left his flat at some point whilst he was at Sophie's and wasn't there when he returned. She wasn't answering her phone.

His guts were churning. Jeremy Hogan had come through. He was coming in that morning to do a piece to camera and was going to bring the evidence that was needed to implicate Edward Allcock Jnr and his brothers. He was going to give them access to all the details of the Bill Parker holding account and evidence of correspondence with Edward. Jeremy had accepted that it may not be enough to keep him out of prison but, like Sophie, they hoped it would be enough for them to be granted some clemency. Assuming he lived that long. Todd had no doubt that if Edward found out about Jeremy's betrayal, the fear of reprisals that had been keeping Jeremy in line would be very real. Big-boy gangster stuff. Alive and well. Todd shivered at the thought.

Todd tried to shake it off. Halle's meeting with John was at 2 pm and he only had a few hours to find and brief her. The case was done. The TV show could be produced and there was sufficient public interest and criminal evidence to use all the footage, without the permission of the people involved. Todd mused that Halle may even be able to hook in the racism angle. Maybe it was time that people like Jen Wyatt were charged with hate crimes. He contemplated how the Allcocks also had hate and intolerance on their rap sheet but, in the end, they had to get them for their larger crimes. They had to be put in prison for their part in all those poor children getting cancer.

As Todd continued to play all the future scenarios in his head, his daydreaming was broken by a familiar voice.

"Are you getting me that coffee, or what?"

It was Halle, looking strong and determined. They hugged. Todd cupped her face.

"Are you okay?"

She kissed him and pulled away. "I'm fine, Todd. I spent hours talking it through with my parents. It was all very emotional but I understand that they only did what Victoria asked them to do, and they have been such wonderful parents. The best thing I can do for everyone is to land this case and put those bastards in jail."

Todd smiled. "You'd better sit down then. I've been busy. I've secured the last bit of evidence we need. I went to see Sophie Parker yesterday and we have convinced Jeremy Hogan to betray the Allcocks. He's coming in this morning to do a piece to camera and give us the evidence we need."

Halle was wide-eyed with excitement and kissed Todd over and over. "Oh my God. That's amazing. You really are my superhero."

"I know, but we have a lot to discuss before you meet John at two. Let's get you that coffee and get our heads down."

*

Halle was ready. This was her moment. She had nailed the case and all she had to do was convince John. His greeting was a little cold but she brushed off his brusqueness and launched in. They spent almost an hour going through the developments of the last two weeks, reviewing the most recent footage, including Jeremy Hogan's 'confession', which Rod had bust a gut to get ready for the meeting. John's mood lightened as the minutes ticked by, and he showed genuine empathy when Halle told him about the incredible personal revelations that neither of them could have possibly envisaged when they first sat in his office on her first day as an investigative reporter. He had even softened his line on the racism angle and conceded that an anti-racist message could form part of the TV narrative.

As their discussion drew to a close, he smiled at Halle. "Wow, this is incredible. I'll admit I had almost written you off, Miss Jacobs, but you have well and truly pulled this off. The only sticking point is that we are now obliged to notify the police of our findings. We can't sit on this or the owners could be charged with obstructing the course of justice. I'm sure you'd agree that we need to get the polluted site shut down and stop the Allcocks putting anybody else's life in danger."

"Of course, sir. That has to be our priority but what about the timing of the TV show?"

"Yes, these situations are always tricky because we don't want the story to break before we have been able to broadcast it. So, Miss Jacobs, I think you have just landed yourself a Tragic Britain special. I will speak to the board about approaching Channel 4 to get this on the schedule as soon as possible as well as liaising with the police about keeping this under the radar. It would be great to get their co-operation so we can film the arrests as part of our footage. I'd also like you to do a piece with Mrs Gupta when the council shut the playground down. That would be a nice bittersweet end to this story, depending on how the kid is."

Halle thought she was going to burst with excitement. "Amazing, sir. Thank you."

"Oh, and one more thing. I want you to do the introduction on the TV show. I want you to be the face of this investigation and I will give you some editorial latitude. Come up with an introduction piece and get it filmed so I can review it. I want that anti-racism message in there too."

"Really? That's incredible. Thank you."

"You're very welcome. You've done a great job. Now I need to stop production on everything else we are doing on this series and focus on getting your show in the can. I want this on the TV before Christmas."

Halle left his office in a daze, the grin on her face growing with every step she took back to her office. As she turned the corner towards her office, there was a small group of people hovering. Todd, Rod, Clayton, Sophie and a grey-haired man that she had only seen on grainy CCTV pictures. Jeremy Hogan.

363

As she neared them, they all turned to look at her. The massive smile on her face told them all they needed to know. "We've done it!"

81

The hearse trundled up the short drive that led to the crematorium. Edward, his uncle and the three remaining brothers followed in the black stretch limousine. The mood in the car was sombre and respectful, despite the difficult history they had with Peter.

As the cars pulled around to the entrance to the chapel, Edward eyed the small crowd that had gathered. A number of staff from PEMS were there, including Jeremy, Sophie and Ross. They all got out of the car and walked to the front of the small gathering, exchanging the usual inane pleasantries that frame these types of occasion.

As Edward scanned the faces, his attention was drawn through a gap in the throng to a woman standing back from the crowd. For a second, his mind couldn't process what he was seeing. The woman was much older than the last time he had seen her but, when his brain began to process it, he realised who it was. His mother.

He moved quickly through the crowd to confront his mother, anger consuming him as he made no attempt to apologise to the guests that were unceremoniously shoved out of the way. She was stood with a prison guard and the reporter that Edward had so expertly shoved back in her box.

He addressed his first tirade at the prison officer. "What the hell are you doing letting this murdering bitch out of prison? She's not welcome here."

By the time Edward had delivered his opening salvo, his uncle and three brothers had joined him. They stared at their mother, their faces etched with thirty years of pain and anger. Edward looked back and forth between the guard and his mother as no one spoke. She scanned their faces, not flinching at the presence of so many men that looked just like the man she had killed. Eventually, she spoke.

"I am perfectly entitled to be released from prison to pay my last respects to the only son that had any faith in me. The only one of you who understood that your father was a violent bully who had no respect for women and knew that I was wrongly convicted for murder. It is to my eternal shame that I allowed your minds to be poisoned by that man and I'm mortified that thirty years later, all I see is clones of your father, with no personality and no independent thought." She quickly turned to James before anyone could respond. "And as for you, James, you are as complicit in this situation as anyone. I suppose I should be grateful that you looked after my sons, but I will never forgive you for brainwashing them into carrying on their father's horrific legacy."

The speech was full of passion and hurt but the crowd gasped in horror as Edward's response to his mother's tirade was to raise his arm, ready to strike. The prison guard moved swiftly to block the blow as Victoria sneered at Edward. "Wow, I think you've just shown everyone that the apple doesn't fall far from the tree."

Edward stared at the prison guard. "Get your hands off me and get this bitch out of my sight."

Victoria took a step forward, her face inches away from Edward's. "I ain't scared of you, Edward. I've had thirty years to wallow in the injustice of what your father did, and I'm not going to allow anyone to pull me down any longer. I'm going to be out soon and things are going to change. You and this little bunch of mini-mes have had your time. Me and your sister are going to take you down."

There was silence. *Your sister.* The boys looked at each other, confusion etched on their faces. Victoria smiled at their discomfort and made a point of moving back to Halle and putting her arm around her waist.

The three brothers looked at Edward, desperately seeking an explanation, but he had nothing. He just stared at his mother and Halle, a million thoughts raging through his brain.

82

TWO DAYS LATER

Edward called the monthly board meeting to order. The mood was tense. They had somehow got through Peter's funeral but ever since the revelation that they had a sister, Edward and his brothers had talked about little else.

"Uncle, what's the latest on our so-called sister? Is this for real?"

"I'm sorry to say this, but it seems kosher. Your mother was pregnant with her when she went into prison. She was born inside and your mother immediately put her up for adoption. It seems that Miss Jacobs didn't know she was adopted until she went to see your mother in prison. It's an incredible twist of fate that she was working on a case that led her back to her real family."

Edward shook his head. "This can't be happening. Where do we stand legally with the business? Does she have any claim?"

"Well, preliminary discussions with our lawyers suggest that she has little claim because your father's will left all his assets to us. The only possible risk is Peter's death. There is arguably a place on the board to fill his shareholding. We don't know yet whether Peter left a will."

Edward stood up and refilled his coffee. He stared back at his uncle and brothers. "We deal with this in the same way we deal with every other obstacle. We eliminate it. There is no way our father would have endorsed a woman being on the board of directors, and this bastard offspring is not about to change that. Am I clear?"

"Yes, Edward," they chorused.

Edward sat back down. "Right, let's get back to business. Firstly, the acquisition of PEMS. Ross is very much on our side but Sophie is still being difficult. It's Bill funeral tomorrow, so I will hit them again straight after. I'm determined to sort our little prob—"

The sentence wasn't finished, as there was commotion at the boardroom door. Edward's PA was shouting at the intruders but they were not to be stopped. As they all looked round, they were confronted with six police officers and someone holding a TV camera. The lead officer scanned the room. "Good, you are all here. My name is Inspector Chan Li. Edward Allcock Jnr, James Allcock, Andrew Allcock, Philip Allcock, Stephen Allcock, I'm arresting you…"

The words were being said but Edward was not hearing them. The rage consumed him and he leapt out of his chair, screaming in the officer's face. "How dare you come in here uninvited and film me like some sideshow. You'll be sorry you ever laid eyes on me. I'll destroy you."

The inspector was not fazed by the outburst and finished reading them their rights. The other officers grabbed an Allcock each and cuffed them. As they were led out, Edward screamed at his PA to get their lawyers.

Rod got it all on tape and quietly exited as the police took them away.

As Sophie Parker and Jeremy Hogan were 'helping police with their enquiries', a number of council offices in London were also being disrupted by a co-ordinated police operation to arrest the council officials who had been implicated in the conspiracy.

*

On the same morning, Halle was at the Pickford housing estate with one of Rod's team, filming the council and environment agency staff shutting down the playground and community hall. People in yellow Hazmat suits were seen, with all sorts of technical paraphernalia assessing the pollution levels. Halle did a brief piece to camera with Mrs Gupta and was delighted to find that Sunil had been responding well to treatment.

Halle was aware that a small crowd of other residents had gathered, watching the spectacle. Their mood was hard to judge from a distance but Halle could see Jen Wyatt in the middle of the mob, holding court. Halle smiled to herself. *You'll get what's coming to you,* she thought to herself.

As she finished off and walked back to Mrs Gupta's house, her phone started to beep with text messages. Todd and Rod giving her live updates on what was happening elsewhere.

She smiled. It had been an eventful day.

83

BROADCAST DAY

Halle cuddled up on the sofa with Todd, nervously waiting for the TV show to start. It had a 10 pm slot on Channel 4. John had pulled it off.

The theme music to the programme started and Halle gripped Todd with nervous excitement. As the moody shots of the Pickford housing estate, which framed the introduction, faded away, the footage moved to Halle. She squealed as she saw her face on camera, and Todd hugged her even tighter.

Ladies and Gentlemen. Welcome to this special episode of Tragic Britain. *My name is Halle Jacobs...*

There had been much soul-searching, but everyone agreed that the Allcock name was tainted. Halle would remain a Jacobs.

...and I am an investigative reporter for Goldwin Productions. The story you are about to watch uncovers a forty-year conspiracy, motivated by horrific greed and a complete disregard for human life...

Todd nudged Halle. "You're good."

...where a number of innocent children have developed cancer as a direct result of these criminal

actions. You will see the harrowing accounts of the parents affected by this tragedy, but I'm sorry to say this is not where the story ends. I assumed I would be engaging with a community brought together by this tragedy but instead I was confronted with an estate consumed with racial intolerance, unable or unwilling to see past their prejudices to support each other in their hour of need. We want to make clear that Goldwin Productions support the message that there is no place for racism in our society. As a result, all the footage you will see today has been passed to the police, and we very much hope the perpetrators are charged with hate crimes...

Halle looked at Todd, a satisfactory smile over her face. "That's good."

...We also tell the story of Victoria Allcock and her thirty-year incarceration for a crime she should never have been convicted of. How her sons carried on the Allcock legacy set in motion by their father, and how they had little regard for who they hurt in the process. You will again see the scourge of racial intolerance and misogyny which crafted the lives of her boys...

Halle squeezed Todd a little tighter. She had nailed it.

...And finally, you will see how this sensational story ended up having a very personal impact on me. One that will change my life forever. Please enjoy this special episode of Tragic Britain: The Sins of the Father.

Halle's face faded off the screen, replaced with more moody shots of the estate. The narrative moved to the first meeting with Jen Wyatt, her face blurred out. John got the board to agree that they could broadcast all the footage in the public interest, with the face-blurring an insurance policy against any repercussions. They watched the rest of the programme, growing prouder by the second as the story was told in all its glory. The editorial team had done an amazing job, getting all the content shoehorned into an hour's show. It was compelling.

As the credits rolled, Halle looked at Todd. "We did good, my lovely nerd."

He smiled. "Ain't that the truth."

84

SIX MONTHS LATER

Victoria sat at the head of the boardroom table revelling in the space. Her thirty-year confinement in a cell hardly big enough to swing a cat had been awful, and she took a moment to appreciate the scale of the room. After the full extent of the Allcock criminal activity had been revealed, her parole was ushered through quickly, without her needing to show remorse. She had stuck to her principles and won the battle.

She smiled at the other two people sat around the table. Halle and Sophie. "Ladies, thank you so much for being here on this historic day. I think we are all in agreement that it's time to move forward. The dissolvement of ALMS and PEMS as companies is now complete and all the assets moved over to our fledgling company, New Horizons Ltd, whose primary aim will be to fund research into childhood cancer."

Halle and Sophie nodded in agreement.

"I think we are also agreed that we will make contributions to various charities supporting hate and racial intolerance, as well as women's charities supporting victims of domestic abuse."

"Agreed," they chorused.

"Good. I will therefore talk to my lawyers about formally establishing us as joint directors, and I very much look forward to working with you on these important projects. I will also be reverting to my maiden name of Simpson. We need to consign the Allcock name to history."

The three women stood up and embraced. As they refilled their coffee cups, Halle asked the question that was on everyone's mind. "Victoria, what is the latest on the boys' trial?"

Victoria grunted. "They've got a bank of lawyers pleading their case, but I spoke to the prosecution counsel yesterday and he is confident they will all go down for several years."

Halle turned to Sophie. "What about you, Ross and Jeremy?"

"The police accepted the fact that I helped expose the scam and I wasn't charged with anything. Ross is still under investigation. I have appointed our lawyers to help Jeremy. There is no doubt his willingness to assist the prosecution case will go in his favour, but he was still complicit in this for so long. They think he may still get a reduced sentence or, at best, a suspended sentence."

"That's good. I spoke to Terence yesterday and his firm has been appointed to work through all the sites with inadequate remediation plans and make them safe. That'll keep them in business for a very long while. He also said that Pickford has been made safe. I just hope that community can repair itself and realise they need each other."

As the ladies took a moment to appreciate all they

had achieved, the door to the boardroom opened. Their assistant brought in a tray with a bottle of champagne and three glasses.

Victoria smiled. "Excellent. I thought it was time for a little celebration. Here's to us and a brighter future."

They all clinked glasses. It was indeed a future that was brighter.

*

He sat on a sun lounger overlooking the sea at the Hotel Plaza on the Cayman Islands. If there was one thing he was grateful to Edward Jnr for, it was the fact he had squirrelled away some of the Allcocks' ill-gotten gains to individual numbered bank accounts in the Caymans, away from the clutches of the British authorities. He had moved his money into another account as soon as he reached the islands, just in case the Allcock lawyers were busy liquidating their assets.

He felt guilty about the poor down-and-out he had persuaded to take his place in his car that had gone over the cliff. He had plied him with so much alcohol that he was sure the man was not aware of what was going on. It had been a risk, but he had done everything to convince the authorities that the charred remains were his, including thrusting his wallet and phone inside the man's pockets.

He had nearly done it. He had nearly ended his worthless life, but sitting there in the dark, he'd realised this was the only option. To start a new life away from everything and everybody he used to know. To try to make something of the time he had left. A voice broke his concentration.

"Can I get you anything, Mr Jenkins?"

He smiled. "Yes, please, Pablo. Can you get me a piña colada? Oh, and stop calling me Mr Jenkins. It's Peter."

Acknowledgements

As always, my first thank you must go to my alpha readers, Jacky Wade, Hannah Wade, Anthony Cooper and Karen Warner, who review my draft manuscripts without complaint and always give me good feedback.

A thank you to my family and friends for their constant encouragement and wise counsel. Particular thanks to Thomas Wade for his continued management of my website and to Tony Guntrip, a friend and fellow author, for his wise words and eye for detail.

My gratitude also goes out to the Book Guild for their continued support in getting this book published and marketed.

A big shout out also to the local independent book shops in Oxfordshire who have been supporting me by stocking my books in their stores, putting the bigger chains to shame who consistently ignore requests to support local authors.

Finally, massive thanks to my growing band of readers in the UK and US, for taking the time to read and enjoy my books. It really does make all the difference.

Also by Colin Wade

www.colinwade.co.uk

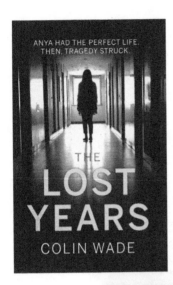

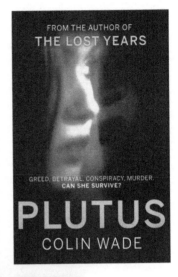